At the Top of the Stairs

By Gregory T. Glading

Table of Contents

PART I

Chapter 1

October 17, 2003

Staff Sergeant Bobby Sand waited single file on the Pope Air Force Base tarmac with his unit, the 878th Combat Engineer Battalion (USAR). The rear hatch of the C-17 Globe Master III military aircraft opened like a crocodile's jaw, intensifying the tenor of the unit. Once the ramp touched the pavement, an airman waved to the soldiers. The commander of the 878th Battalion (BN), Colonel Azshalt, pointed to the open hatch, "All aboard, troops!"

SSG Sand glanced back. He looked for her among his unit's friends and relatives. He had to crane his head and raise his eyes to glimpse the back of Adele Beauchamp and her slightly below shoulder-length ash blonde hair, white blouse, and tight jeans. A plump woman moved in front of her, blocking his view. His parents stood before the group. They beamed and waved to him. He wistfully smiled and waved his hand once on spotting them. He turned toward the aircraft and marched on board. The 878th soldiers filed to the aircraft's front and took their mesh seats in sequence, facing center. The airman conducted a safety briefing before the aircraft began taxiing.

SSG Sands closed his eyes as the C-17's four F117-PW-100 turbofan engines came to life. He wanted time to stand still. *'Only minutes ago…'* He pinched his eyes shut and pursed his lips as the aircraft lifted off. *He had his arms wrapped around the small of her back and rubbed her with his pelvis. She leaned into him, arched her back, and wrapped her hands around his neck. He gazed into her hazel eyes. 'You know I love you, Adele.' He kissed her lips. 'I always will.' He inhaled deeply through his nose to recall the tingle of their tongues, the taste of her mouth, and her skin's texture and aroma. A tear formed in his eye, blurring his vision. He smiled at her. 'You know I wanted to get married the moment I got my activation orders. But I will be home on leave before you know it.' He braced her shoulders. 'We can marry then, you know.'*

'Don't worry about it, Bobby. As soon as your deployment ends, we'll have plenty of time to make wedding plans.' She kissed his lips. 'Till then, stay alive for me, okay?'

Flashing lights and a buzzer broke his reverie. The airman shouted the go-ahead to move about the aircraft.

"Hey, Sandman," SFC Garth Mathews was two years Bobby's senior, but he looked five years older. He stood three inches taller than Bobby's six feet one, and he weighed twenty pounds more. He cuffed Bobby's shoulder, "Is that a frickin' tear I see? What the hey? Adele will be waiting for you until you get back." He grinned. "And I'll be your best man. If she doesn't wait for you, I'll buy you some beers and lap dances at the Pussy Cat Lounge."

"Oh, come on, Matty. When are you going to grow up?"

"The last time I grew up, I lost half my assets. That ain't happening at the Pussy Cat Lounge."

"They'll pick your pocket just the same." SSG Sand smirked.

"Yeah, but not half of all I own." SFC Mathews raised his hands. "Hey, what do you think? The Yankees win the World Series in a four-game sweep? I mean, the Marlins? What the hell is that all about? They weren't even supposed to be any good."

"It's destiny. They won the pennant in '97 because of the worst-umpired game in history. This year, their glass Cinderella slippers were about to shatter until a fan interfered with the second out of the eighth inning." He snapped his fingers. "Go figure. It's as if the Marlins snuck a fourth outfielder into the stands or had a football defensive back cover Moises Alou." Bobby laughed. "The next day, the Fish beat the Cubs for the National League pennant. I think they're Destiny's Darlings. So, I got the Marlins upsetting the Yankees. I just hope the Clemson Tigers get the same breaks."

"You know I'm a Gamecocks man, but you make a good point, Sandman, except the Yankees' Aaron Boone winning the pennant on a tenth inning, walk-off home run says Destiny's Darlings to me."

"Just like I think it's destiny that Junior will win the Daytona 500."

"I hope to get my leave to catch the big race." SFC Mathews grinned. "As much as Junior winning for his father makes a great story, I got Tony Stewart crossing the finish line first."

"Well, they're both driving Chevys. So, at least we agree on something."

"Another thing we can agree on is that we control destiny, Sandman. We're about to make history and change the world."

"Yeah, maybe we'll catch Saddam Hussein? Too bad we're going to Iraq with the Army. If we were going as Wild West cowboys, we could turn him in for a bounty."

"Dead or alive works for me." SFC Mathews grabbed an overhead strap as the aircraft hit turbulence. "And what if we find Saddam's weapons of mass destruction? We'll be in American history textbooks. More importantly, we got a year to keep our unit alive."

"So much for W saying, 'Mission accomplished.'"

"Why complain? He left you with plenty to tell Adele and your future kids."

***

Bobby Sands settled back into his seat. He closed his eyes and tried to doze above the noise of the aircraft's engines and soldiers' banter…*SSG Sands imbibed the aroma of his steak and the sound of its sizzle. Yet nothing overrode her perfume and voice.*

'Are you sure you can afford this?' Adele sipped her Opus One, Napa Valley wine.

'It's just for you, Adele.'

'Just for me.' Adele chuckled, 'You're the steak lover.'

Bobby beamed. 'Hall's Chophouse is the best in Charleston.' He held up his Budweiser bottle. 'Besides, I'm a beer drinker. The fancy wine is just for you.' He tapped his bottle on her goblet. 'Nothing is too good for you,'

'Okay, how about flying me to Philadelphia and taking me to Le Bec Fin or New York City and Sardi's? Just for me.'

Bobby laughed, 'Now that I can't afford.'

A soldier shook his knee. Specialist Wayne O'Connor held up a military issue Meal Ready to Eat (MRE) pouch. "Hey, Sarge Sandman, I got a Buffalo Style Chicken Chunks." He pointed to SSG Sand's MRE. "I'll trade you for your Spaghetti with Meat Sauce."

Bobby nodded. SPC O'Connor handed him his MRE and grabbed Bobby's. Bobby settled back in his seat and closed his eyes…He now walked hand in hand with Adele on Folly Beach, South Carolina.

'I truly enjoyed my steak dinner. Thank you, Bobby.'

'It tasted great, but you were the sizzle.'

'What am I going to do with you?' She faced him, touched his nose with her fingertip, and pecked his lips.

Hey, Adele, look at how the moon glows on the ocean. It looks like the moon poured melted butter on the water.' Bobby grinned. *'Just like you melt my heart.'*

'Melted butter? You make me think of popcorn.' Adele chuckled. *'Not because I'm hungry.'* She laughed. *'But because you're so corny. Again, what am I going to do with you?'*

'I have a suggestion. Adele, how about marrying me?'

Adele laughed. You should be a comedian rather than a surveyor, aspiring civil engineer, and weekend warrior.'

He turned and held both of her hands and gazed into her eyes.

'Oh, my God! You're serious.'

He reached into his pocket, pulled out a tiny box, and opened it. Moonlight shimmered on the ring's stone.

She stared back, mouth agape.

He placed a diamond ring on her finger and kissed the rock. He nodded his head and smiled broad as a boulevard. 'Well?'

'Yes. Yes. I will.' She wrapped her arms around him and gazed at the diamond as they kissed. The warm Atlantic Ocean washed over their ankles.

Turbulence jarred him from his dream. He jerked his head back and forth. Adele's image flashed in his mind. He forced himself to return to Adele…*He saw her ex-boyfriend, Spike McClenahan, dressed in a leather vest that showed off an array of tattoos, some occult, some gang-related, and others of death metal rock bands. 'Adele broke up with you.'* Bobby *prodded at him. 'Face it and hit the road.'*

'You're going to hit the road.' Spike *brandished his fist. 'With your body after I hit you with this.'*

'Go for it, asshole.'

Spike swung first. His punch glanced off the side of Bobby's face. Bobby countered with a right cross to the jaw. Spike staggered backward and rubbed his jaw. He glowered at Bobby and charged, tackling him. They rolled on the street, grappling and punching each other with short jabs.'

'Stop it! Stop it!' Adele screamed and covered her face with her hands.

Bobby rolled on top and hit Spike with a solid right. He held his vest with his left hand and cocked his right fist. 'You want more? I can give you more.' Bobby stood up. 'There's your car.' He pointed to his 1970 Chevelle SS. It boasted an oversized 632 big block V8 engine bursting through the hood. 'Now get lost.'

'This isn't over!' Spike wiped blood from his lips and his nose. 'I'll be back, and I won't be alone.' He pointed at Adele. 'Yeah, so your Bobbilee was an all-county wrestler for Bayhaven High School. Big deal. Mr. Lameness is in over his head. I know you'll get bored real fast. You always said I was a challenge.' Spike pointed. 'He's already housebroken. So, come on, baby, what do you say? For old time's sake.' Spike boarded his car and revved the engine. He nodded to Adele.

'Keep on driving.' Bobby lurched toward the Chevelle.

'I'll be back, Adele.' Spike pointed at Bobby. 'As for you, it's just a matter of time.' He peeled out, spraying pebbles and leaving a black tire track. The odor of burning rubber steeped the air.

Erica Beauchamp burst from the family home. 'What went on here?'

'I had to teach Spike a lesson in respect.' Bobby licked a blood droplet from his lip.

'Adele,' Erica grabbed her younger sister's arm. Standing an inch taller, she glared at her with a furrowed brow. 'What

was he doing here in the first place? You know he's nothing but trouble. You thought being his girlfriend would change him. How did that work out? He's trouble, and he'll always be trouble. I don't want to see him here again.'

'It's still our mother's house, not yours. Come on, Erica. I know you're my big sister…but it's only by two years,' Adele prodded, 'but you gotta back off.'

'What have you done to help our mother since Father died?' Erica put her hands on her hips. 'You've done little to care for her. Spike is not welcome here. End of discussion. Besides, you're much happier with Bobby, and you're staying out of trouble. Let's keep it that way.'

'You gotta admit, guys.' Adele grinned. 'He does drive one hell of a car.'

'He built it on stolen parts and put it together in his chop shop.' Erica tensed her lips and shook her head. 'That's not counting the money he makes selling dope.'

'It won't be long, Adele.' Bobby gritted his teeth. 'It won't be long until he's washing the warden's car in the state prison. If you stayed with him, you'd be pressing laundry in the Women's Prison.'

'Oh, you're the white knight who rescued the damsel in distress.' She prodded at Bobby. 'I already have an overbearing big sister.' I want a boyfriend, not a big brother.'

'Come on. Let's go inside.' Erica nodded toward the house.

'We need a beer and whiskey, not more of your lemonade.' Adele curled her lip.

'We'll compromise.' Erica chuckled. 'I'll pour us a glass of hard lemonade.'

***

A soldier dropped his metal helmet, startling SSG Sand. He stood and paced about the aircraft. Adrenaline surged through his veins. *"No, no,"* He muttered to himself. *'No way she goes back to Spike.'* Bobby gritted his teeth. *'I'll come home and kill him first.'*

"Hey, hey, Sandman." Garth Mathews grabbed Bobby's arm. "Have you gone off your rocker? What's with this talking to yourself and skulking about like a madman?"

"It's nothing," Bobby shook his head. "Nothing at all. Just a bit nervous. Someone dropped their helmet right by me. It startled me."

"It's alright, buddy. We're all on edge. How much combat training did we get out of a weekend a month? Now we're diving into the deep end. But, just like the Yankees and Gamecocks, we got destiny on our side.

"I was thinking Marlins and Tigers." Bobby laughed.

"That's the spirit," Garth cuffed Bobby's arm. "Maybe after the deployment finishes and we're fishing on the Cooper River, you may even catch more bass than me."

"Who shot the four-point buck in Francis Marion Forest last season?" Bobby smirked. "Now we got a year-long hunting season ahead."

***

The plane began to descend. Red lights illuminated. The bulbs were faint. For the soldiers aboard the flight, the lights blazed like a quasar. Colonel Azshalt stood at the front of the aircraft. "We've just flown into a combat zone. We're officially at war. Put on your full battle rattle. It's game time."

***

The soldiers of the 878th marched single file down the aircraft's rear hatch. They held their M16 rifles locked and loaded at port arms. Their "full battle rattle" consisted of a steel helmet, eye protection, and a Kevlar vest with composite plates. SSG Sand looked ahead, '*I feel like we're the first men on Mars rather than a rotation in Iraq.*' The soldiers slogged through mud as they marched toward a large Aircraft hangar. Bobby heard the soldier in front of him mutter, "Ain't this place supposed to be dry desert?"

The unit stood in formation inside the hangar. "Attention!" Sergeant Major Rothrock shouted. He saluted Colonel Azshalt.

The commanding officer returned the salute and stood before the unit. "At ease." Colonel Azshalt had served twenty years of active duty, including Gulf War I. He elected to stay in the Army as an active reservist rather than retire. He stood just under six feet tall and had a lean build. Silver tipped his black hair. He cut his gray-flecked sideburns at precisely the Army's maximum length. His posture announced pride in his military rank and status. He was also happy to get a break from his civilian office job with Bayshore Industries. He also favored the sound of gunfire and artillery over his wife's voice. "Congratulations. Your boots are on the ground. You're at Camp Anaconda in Balad, Iraq. We're approximately 80 clicks from Baghdad. Your orders say one year, but your boots will remain on the ground until the mission is complete. We will spend the night here, in place. Tomorrow at daylight, the 326th Transportation Brigade will take us to our Forward Operating Base near Sadr City in Baghdad. Barring IED or sniper action, it's about an hour and a half convoy. We will begin our deployment in support of the Third Infantry Division. Our mission is to secure and maintain Route Predator and its feeder routes, connecting Baghdad with the southern FOBs.

Your job is no longer eating donuts and drinking coffee on weekends. I hope we all come back alive. If not, you will die for your country and a just cause. You are dismissed. Any questions are to be addressed through your chain of command."

SSG Sand walked about the hangar amidst the grumblings of his fellow soldiers. He spotted a twenty-year-old Airman with a pimpled face. "Hey, where can I take a shit in this place?"

"In here? Welcome to Iraq." The Airman laughed. "Ain't nothin' in here. You must use the porta-potties outside."

SSG Sand walked outside and spotted six green porta-potties in a line. He stepped inside the first one and almost hurled at the sight and smell. "Do they ever empty or even clean these fucking things?" *'My God, a year of this? If I had a choice, I'd drop trou on the runway.'*

A deafening boom. The concussion caused the porta-potty and SSG Sand to topple. The opposition forces had welcomed Bobby Sand to their country.

Chapter 2

"Good morning," Erica Beauchamp opened the window shades. The Sun shone through the window. "It's a beautiful morning." She took her mother, Monica Beauchamp's, frail hand. "Fall is in the air."

"I love that we get four seasons here." Monica smiled, "Just not Buffalo's four seasons."

"That's the spirit, Mom."

"I don't have many more of these mornings to enjoy, so I'd better cherish each one."

"Don't talk like that. We're going to have many more seasons of beautiful mornings together. This one is about to get even better; I made scrambled eggs spiced with chives and country link sausage." Erica smiled. "Shall I bring it up to you with a glass of orange juice? Freshly squeezed."

"I'm a stroke survivor, not a stroke surrenderer." Monica chuckled. "But you can help me out of this bed." Monica managed to sit up on her own.

Erica wrapped her arm around Monica and helped her stand. She seemed even lighter than the day before. Monica put her arm around Erica's shoulder and leaned on her as they walked down the hall to the kitchen of their modest three-bedroom, ranch-style home in the Charleston, South Carolina, suburb of Bayhaven. Erica helped Monica sit at the kitchen table. Her hand jittered as she raised a forkful of scrambled eggs toward her mouth. Erica moved behind her. "No, no, please, Erica, let me do this." Monica smiled after swallowing her forkful of eggs. "Thank you so much. They're delicious."

"You haven't even tasted my country sausages yet." Erica chuckled.

"Where would I be without you?" Monica reached out and touched her daughter's hand. "Six feet under." She laughed. "Which is a lot better than a convalescent home. But maybe I should consider climbing to the top of the stairs and joining your father. After all, you're still young, Erica. I feel horrible about you having to put your education on hold on account of me."

"It's okay, Mom. I'm only one course short of my BA. I have plenty of time."

"But will you have time for law school afterward? I'm holding you up. And you're prettier than ever. I know something wonderful awaits me at the top of the stairs. You have your life to live right here and now. Let me go and be with God while you still have time to get married and have children."

"You stop that, mother." Erica massaged the top of Monica's shoulders. "You made me who I am, and now my life is fulfilled by making yours better."

"At least take some time for yourself. Go to the beauty parlor." Monica steepled her hands. "I've loved your auburn hair since before you could walk."

"You give me my inner beauty. Don't worry. I'm always open to marriage and family." Erica smiled at her mother. "Grandchildren are always a possibility. You stay alive for that day." She leaned over and tapped her hand. "And just for you, I'll try to find time to get my hair styled just the way you like it."

"No, no, Erica," Monica waved her hand. "Your job as a paralegal at the William Crane law firm is demanding enough. Taking care of me is robbing you of what you deserve. Moreover, keeping your sister out of trouble is also a full-time job. Too bad she won't give you a break around the house."

"We'll worry about me later. Besides, Adele has changed since meeting Bobby." Erica poured a glass of orange juice. "I hope married life will further settle her down."

"Married life? You keep an eye on your sister, so it happens. With Bobby gone for a year, I hope you can keep her on the straight and narrow. "Oops," Monica spilled her orange juice. "I'm sorry."

"Don't worry. Mom. It's nothing." Erica grabbed a towel and wiped up the spill. She wrung the towel in the kitchen sink, returned to the table, and poured Monica another glass of orange juice.

Adele trudged into the kitchen and rubbed her eyes. "Hey, thanks for saving some of that for me." She pointed at the empty orange juice pitcher.

"Early bird gets the worm." Erica chuckled. "Don't worry. I'll squeeze you a glass." She took an orange from a bowl on the kitchen counter. "It's almost nine o'clock." Erica sliced an orange in half. "Aren't you late for work?" She twisted the orange half on a plastic reamer.

"I'm taking another day off. Besides, Bobby is their best surveyor. Now that we're engaged and he's off in Iraq, they wouldn't dare fire me."

"That's not the point."

"What is the point?" Adele shrugged. "Besides, I missed three days of gym going up to Fort Bragg to see Bobby off." She patted her abdomen, bare beneath her white, tied-in-the-front blouse. "I want to keep this flat and looking good for his return." Adele sat at the table. Erica held three sausage links in salad tongs. Adele waved her off. "Good thing the county is paying Bobby while he's on deployment. Combined with what the Army is paying, we're going to have a dream wedding. First, I'd better work on my tan. There won't be many more days like this. Pretty soon it will be coat weather." Adele smiled. "I sure smell something good to take to the gym with me."

"It's French roast coffee with a touch of chicory." Erica got up and poured Adele a cup.

"Thanks, sis." Adele poured the coffee from the ceramic cup into a travel mug. She secured it with a lid. "You're the best." Adele pecked Erica's cheek.

"Why don't you stick around? Keep your mother and me company. Bobby may call."

"If he calls, you take it, sis." Adele stood, held her travel mug of coffee, and grabbed her gym bag. "Tell him I love 'em. See you later." She walked out the door, leaving it cracked open.

Erica walked over, watched her sister depart, and closed the door. She turned and made eye contact with her mother. They shook their heads.

Chapter 3

The Sadr City district in northeastern Baghdad had an estimated two million denizens crammed into an area of less than 30 square kilometers. The district is notorious for its poverty and poor sanitation. Forward Operating Base (FOB) Camp War Eagle, known to the soldiers stationed there as the "Dirty Bird," sat on its eastern edge. An Easterly wind blew in Sadr City's sewage stench. A westerly wind shrouded the FOB in dust. Opposition forces mortared the camp several times a day, regardless of wind direction. Camp War Eagle was rumored to be a converted Iraqi prison camp. The living conditions for the soldiers were better than most, as they sheltered in buildings rather than tents. Ablution was outdoor porta-potties. Poor electrical wiring rendered showering an electrocution risk.

SSG Sand was the fourth platoon squad leader of Company A, 878th Combat Engineer Battalion. Standing with his unit in formation, he jutted his square jaw as their company commander, Captain Bernard "Barny" Duckworth, called them to attention. "At ease." A West Point graduate, Captain Duckworth made up for his youthful appearance with military bearing. "You all know your assignments. We will convoy to Deadman's Gulch, approximately two hours south along Route Predator, just outside the town of Hillah. The initial combat operation damaged the existing bridge to the point where it could no longer handle heavy tactical vehicles. The demolition team will remove the existing bridge with 250 pounds of C4 explosives. After we bulldoze away the debris, we'll replace it with a M104 Wolverine heavy assault bridge. We have an Abrams M1A2 SEP Tank with Leguan bridge-laying gear in place of a turret. An M9 ACE bulldozer is loaded on a M1000 semi-trailer pulled by a M11070 Heavy Equipment Transporter. A five-ton M925 cargo truck will carry our supplies and equipment. We will escort them with armed Humvees. You will drive your assigned vehicles and conduct your assigned duties. We must all beware of potential Improvised Explosive Devices. Route Predator is IED Heaven, or better said, IED Hell. Watch for discarded boxes and roadkill. The insurgents use them to hide IEDs. Okay, soldiers, let's get this show on the road. I want to be back for dinner. It's steak night at the Dirty Bird Café. Moreover, there's a good chance that the phone lines will be up. Get the job done right the first time. You'll want to call home before the system goes down again. You're dismissed."

***

The convoy left the FOB, soon rambling down Route Predator through the sprawl of Baghdad. SSG Sand drove the Humvee; SFC Mathews rode next to him. SPC O'Connor sat on a strap between the front and rear seats, his head popped through the roof gun turret with a mounted M240 machine gun locked and loaded. SGT Fuller and SSG Garcia sat in the rear seats. They had their locked and loaded M16 assault rifles pointed out of the windows.

"Does this place have a city center?" SSG Sand steered the Humvee around a bend. "Baghdad's population almost matches New York City's and has more people than LA, Chicago, and Houston. Yet I don't see any buildings higher than three or four stories."

"Welcome to paradise." SFC Mathews chuckled.

"Good thing the traffic is getting out of our way."

"The Tangos have two choices, Sandman. Get out of the way or get totaled." SFC Mathews chuckled. "It seems they're smarter than they look."

"Yeah, Tangos. I like that. T for Target. T for Terrorist. And T for Trash. This place sure has the third T in abundance." SGT Fuller put his thumb on the fire selector, switching his weapon from safe to semiautomatic. "I heard some of the Tangos don't even eat with a fork. And we're supposed to civilize them? Look at this road. Trash and roadkill everywhere. God knows, Tango can hide an IED anywhere."

"Civilization runs on oil." SSG Sand replied. "And Iraq has it in abundance."

"I think you just passed an IED." SSG Carlos Garcia covered his eyes. "I saw a box next to a dead dog."

"Shut up, Garcia." SGT Chuck Fuller poked Carlos in the ribs. "We got a whole year of this ahead. We're already sick of your whimpering."

***

"Dead Man's Gulch?" SSG Sand walked over to the dry arroyo. "It looks and smells more like Dead Dog, Cat, and Rat Gulch. How can this sluice off floodwater and Tigres River overflow? It's bone dry and filled with garbage. Where does it all go if it ever does rain?"

"Who cares where this shithole of a country's garbage goes?" Chuck Fuller put his hands on his hips. "Trust me. It flows in the same direction as shit, downhill."

"Trust me? Is that what you said to Inez before you left? We have to trust each other. We're a team and we're in this mess together." SFC Mathews pointed to a concrete slab bridge with chunks of concrete missing and exposed steel rebar. "We must finish what a cruise missile started. Let's blast this thing out of our way."

SSG Sand, SFC Mathews, SPC O'Connor, SGT Fuller, and SSG Garcia unloaded small crates of C4 plastic explosives from the five-ton M925 cargo truck. After removing the steel straps from the wooden boxes, they opened them up and removed blocks of C4 and detonation equipment. SGT Fuller shoved blasting caps into bricks of C4 plastic explosives. SSG Sand and SGT Fuller worked together on taping the explosives to the abutments on the North side of the bridge. "I heard you got married right before the deployment."

"Yeah, I've been with Inez for fourteen years, but this is the first time I could be killed at any moment. She's not eligible for *Servicemembers' Group Life Insurance* unless we're married. It's five hundred thousand big ones, should the enemy have good aim. The Army also pays a married man more."

"You must trust her."

"Just like we have to trust each other, we must trust the ladies we left behind. We have enough to worry about here and now than what may or may not be happening 5,000 miles away." Chuck laughed. "Besides, it was Specialist O'Connor who mixed powdered Gatorade with our canteen water. If we drop dead as a result, he don't get shit. We all know how much you love and miss Adele. I hope you don't mind me saying this, but some of the guys in our unit talked about how hot she is. I know you wanted to seal the deal before you left, and not many men with a pair of eyes would blame you, but it's good you know that she ain't in it for the money."

"Thanks, Chuck. I appreciate that. Yeah, it's a pleasant thought. No gold digger would date a county surveyor, wanna be civil engineer, and weekend NCO." Bobby pressed the edge of 100 MPH tape, securing a block of C4 to the concrete. "It looks like we got this."

"Carlos and Garth are waving to us." Chuck pointed to the other side. "Time to walk across this thing and meet them in the middle."

"You get to climb under this thing and place the final explosives. After all, Inez gets 500 grand if you fall."

"How about you take honors?" Chuck laughed. "After all, you're single."

"We'll sort it out when we get there."

SFC Garth Mathews met them in the middle of the bridge. "Okay, one of us has to climb under this thing and deploy the final explosives. Whoever takes honors gets to push the plunger. Kaboom!"

***

Twenty minutes later, the company took cover while ensuring their ear protection was intact.

"Fire in the hole! Fire in the hole!" SGT Fuller depressed the plunger. A boom, louder and more concussive than Thor hitting it with his mightiest bolt, shook the ground. A thick cloud of concrete dust accompanied the downpour of concrete and steel. Once the dust and debris had settled, ten soldiers from the second platoon accompanied the M9 ACE military bulldozer on foot.

"Damn," SSG Sands applied his ear protection. "That bulldozer is louder than the frickin' explosion."

"It sounds like the rubble is making one last protest. After all, it survived having a bomb dropped on it." SFC Mathews chuckled. "Remember the movie line, '*I love the smell of napalm in the morning*'? I wish I could say the same about concrete dust, rubble, and trash at lunchtime. I got a chili and rice MRE." Garth held up his plastic-sealed packet. "I get to stink us out on the way back."

The next noise sounded like a stomping brontosaurus. The Abrams M1 A2 SEP tank with Leguan bridge-laying gear instead of a turret trundled to the edge of the gulch. Like a giant jackknife, the M104 Wolverine Heavy Assault bridge opened. It rumbled and growled like a guard dog, interspaced with metallic clanking and grinding. The hydraulic arms added to the orchestration with hissing and whining, finally spanning the gulch with a thud and a dust cloud.

The company assembled next to the completed bridge's entrance. They applied a strip of duct tape across the entrance as a makeshift ribbon. They cheered as Captain Duckworth and Sergeant Major Rothrock drove their Humvee through the strip of tape, taking honors as the first to drive across the new bridge. First Sergeant Martinez hammered a sign planted on a ragged-edged piece of discarded plywood nailed onto a splintery post. Painted on the sign was "Ravenel Bridge East." The company cheered before they started loading their equipment into the tactical vehicles. Like a bolt of blue, they heard rifle report and a snapping noise overhead. A bullet hit the side of the Wolverine tactical bridge with a spark and clank. The piece of hot metal bounced off SSG Sand's body armor. "Get Down!" Tingling nerves and adrenaline fought each other for a split second. Adrenaline won. The company returned fire. Bobby looked to his right. SSG Garcia had dropped his weapon and covered his head with his arms. SGT Fuller furrowed his brow, scowled, and gritted his teeth. He ran into the open, brandishing his weapon. He clicked his M16 to automatic and opened fire. Two seconds later, he ejected its thirty-round magazine and locked and loaded another. He sprayed the area with bullets for another two seconds. An eerie silence shrouded the area. The next fraught ten minutes passed like a slow freight train at a level crossing.

SFC Mathews stood first. "Damn, Fuller, when Sandman told you to 'get down,' he meant take cover, not get up and dance."

"Yeah, well, the only good insurgent is a dead insurgent." SGT Fuller grinned. "I just gave them a lesson in respect, American style."

"You don't want to return in a metal, flag-draped box, do you?"

"Matty, it's like the great general said, 'The object of war is not to die for your country but to make the other dumb son of a bitch die for his." SGT Fuller raised his weapon to port arms. "I may only stand five feet seven, but this makes me feel ten feet tall."

In thirty minutes, the company had loaded the M9 bulldozer onto the M1000 semi-trailer and packed the remaining supplies into the five-ton M925 cargo truck. They returned with the convoy in the same grouping as the initial trip. SSG Garcia pointed his M16 weapon outside the rear window. His gut itched as if infested with flying insects; finger sweat slathered the trigger. SGT Fuller kept finger pressure on the trigger of his M16. He clicked his weapon from safe to semi-automatic each time he spotted a potential target.

***

Adele Beauchamp stepped off the gym's stair climber and wiped sweat from her brow.

"Adele." Claudia Jennings wore leopard-spotted, skintight leotards with a low-cut top. She wore her brown hair in a tight bun. "It's great to see you back."

"I miss Bobby already, but I need to live my life. Besides," She tapped the Stair Climber, "I want to look good for him when he returns."

"He's got his life, and you have yours." Jenny Carter had a pink towel draped over her shoulders, her blonde ponytail extended below the towel. She looked Adele up and down.

"Look good when Bobby returns? Look at you now, girl." She chuckled. "I'm jealous."

"Hey," Claudia put her hand on Adele's shoulder. "Jenny's got a point. We're going downtown to a hip new Mexican restaurant on King Street." She smiled and arched her eyebrows. "Join us for nachos and margaritas."

"You know I shouldn't." Adele leaned on the stair master. "Besides, I want to be home in case Bobby calls.'"

"He hasn't called yet?" Claudia raised her open hands. "Well, what are you waiting for?" Claudia laughed. "Come on. It's only dinner and drinks with the girls."

"Don't worry. We'll keep the guys away from you. But you'd better cover your face with this,' Jenny tossed her towel to Adele. "Make my job easier."

Adele caught the towel and laughed. "Just because some of the Iraqi women choose to wear face coverings doesn't mean I will. I won't cover my face, but I will trust you to keep the wolves away."

"That's my girl." Jenny pecked Adele's cheek. "Shower up. We'll take my car. I'll bring you back after dinner."

***

Claudia slurped the last of her third margarita. "The band is cooking. I love Spanish music. What are we waiting for? Let's all dance."

Claudia, Jenny, and Adele danced with each other in a circle until the band finished their set. When they returned, three fresh margaritas waited for them. "We didn't order those." Adele pointed at the table.

"We did." A tall, thin, athletic man wearing slacks, a button-down shirt with sleeves rolled up to his elbows, and enough hair gel to lubricate an army tank's treads put a hand on Claudia and Adele's shoulders.

"We'll pay your entire bill if you let us join you." A shorter, thinner man in a business suit moved behind Jenny.

"Hey, I think I know you." A third man pointed at Adele. "Aren't you Erica's sister. She works at my law firm. I remember you dropping by one day to pick her up after work."

"I don't remember you."

"Wow! You have a sister." The man with copious hair gel stared at Adele. "If she looks anything like you, invite me to your next family reunion."

"Her sister is plenty pretty. Slightly taller with longer legs but not quite as well endowed." The third man cupped his hands over his chest. "Auburn hair rather than ash blonde. Green eyes rather than hazel. Too bad she's not here. But I'm glad you're here," he pointed at Adele, "and that makes me glad that I'm here. Erica has talked about you." He chuckled. "Don't worry. All good. I'm Henry Sawyers. I'm an attorney at the William Crane Law Firm. But you can call me Hank."

"An attorney?" Adele scowled at him. "You sounded more like a cattle dealer. We're at Rosa's Cantina, not a pet shop. So, if this were a pet shop," The left side of her mouth slightly lifted. "Who would have a higher price tag? Me or Erica?" Her eyes opened wider.

Henry shrugged.

"You're an attorney?" Jenny beamed and steepled her hands. "Her man is only a surveyor." She pointed at Adele. "But she's taken. Why don't you sit here?" Jenny beamed. She nodded to the seat next to her.

The three men sat at Jenny, Claudia, and Adele's table.

***

Bobby Sand locked his arms to his side and tensed his lips while standing in line for his turn with one of the phones.

'*Shut up, man, hurry up and shut up.*' The soldier finished his conversation. '*Finally,*' Bobby exhaled and took three quick steps to the phone and hastily punched in the Beauchamps' number.

"Hello."

"Adele! It's me! Bobby! I don't want to upset you, but I've got to tell you what happened today…"

"Bobby, it's Erica. Adele's not here." Erica fidgeted with the phone cord. "I'm glad to hear you arrived in Iraq safely. I'll make sure to tell her. What happened today?"

"We took enemy fire after deploying a tactical bridge. A bullet missed me by about a yard. It ricocheted off the bridge and hit my body armor."

"Oh my God, Bobby! I'll say a prayer of thanksgiving this Sunday at church."

"Thanks, after all, we are at war."

Erica heard the front door open. "Bobby, great news. Adele just got home. I'll go get her."

A tremendous boom shook the room. The tables rattled and the lights went out. After catching his breath, "Erica? Adele? Can you hear me?" Bobby gritted his teeth and squeezed the phone. He pursed his lips and returned it to the receiver.

Chapter 4

Camp War Eagle "The Dirty Bird."

At 0517 hours, a mortar blast buckled the walls of the 878th BN barracks. SSG Sand leaped from his cot. The boom caused his eardrums to ring like a tuning fork vibrating in F-sharp major. He squeezed his head with his palms over his ears like a vice.

SSG Garcia jumped up and scurried under his cot.

"What the…" SFC Mathews swung his legs over his cot's edge.

SGT Fuller got up and grabbed his alarm clock. "I set this damn thing for 0600 hours. Tango did us a favor. Now that we're up early, we can be first in line for breakfast at the Dirty Bird Café and have time to order an omelet."

"As long as that thing didn't break all their eggs." SSG Sand chuckled.

***

Company A of the 878th Combat Engineer BN stood in formation before their tactical vehicles. Four days of relentless Iraqi sun had darkened the soldiers of all races. The 878th's Executive Officer, Major Douglas Whitehead, quickly returned First Sergeant Martinez's salute before using his right hand to shield the sun from his eyes. He had military-cropped brown hair and wore black plastic glasses with clear lenses. The morning sun glistened off his pallid complexion. "Good morning, soldiers." He paused until the unit replied.

'Good morning, Major' was their tepid response.

"I have good news. Today, Iraq is showing its gratitude for toppling Saddam Hussein." Major Whitehead paused for effect. "They're giving us free use of their sauna. Today's temperature is expected to reach 114 degrees. More good news. There's no threat of rain, so I recommend you take plenty of fluids. Here's some incentive to come back alive. We may have the phone lines up and running tonight. Captain Duckworth will lead the first and second platoons to Balad to repair several concrete barriers outside Camp Anaconda. Sergeant Mathews, as team Falcon is assigned to demolitions, your team will patrol Route Predator from here to Ravenel Bridge East and report all IEDs. Team Black Mamba will accompany you for security. Don't try disarming any IEDs yourselves. Call them in to Company headquarters. The First Armored Division will send an EOD team to dispose of them. You are dismissed."

SSG Sand squinted as he watched Major Whitehead walking away and disappearing into the air-conditioned headquarters building.

***

Team Black Mamba drove in front of Team Falcon, southbound on Route Predator. Team Black Mamba's Corporal DeJean Jackson sat in the roof gun turret with a mounted M240 machine gun. He pointed it at every Iraqi in range.

"Is that all Whitehead got us for security?" SGT Fuller kept his weapon pointed out of the rear window. "One lousy Humvee?"

"How are we supposed to clear the entire route in one day?" SSG Garcia added. "Why can't Whitehead help?"

"He's too busy making more money than us." SFC Mathews looked back. "Besides, he needs the day job. If he tried today's comic act in a theater, they'd hook a cane around his neck and yank him off the stage."

"Yeah, Carlos," Bobby Sand squeezed the steering wheel. "The government invested too much money in his ROTC scholarship to risk him leaving the FOB."

"Hey, what do you see from up there?" SSG Sand glanced up at SPC O'Connor.

"Nothing that Corporal Jackson won't see first. He's locked and loaded, ready to shoot first and ask questions later."

"Good. That will free you up to scan for IEDs."

"Oh my God!" SSG Garcia prodded. "Over there! That dead dog. I see wires."

SFC Mathews and SSG Sand nodded to each other. SFC Mathews radioed Team Black Mamba. SSG Sand pulled the Humvee to the roadside, a safe distance from the dead dog.

SFC Mathews and SSG Garcia disembarked along with four members of Team Black Mamba and stood guard with their weapons at port arms. Corporal Jackson and Specialist O'Connor remained in position. Sergeants Sand and Fuller walked over to the dead dog. Wires protruded from the fetid, rotting animal. Fuller poked it with a stick. "Huh!" He gasped at two sticks that looked like dynamite. "Damn, that fucking thing looks like Tango ordered it from ACME."

"If she blows, we won't just look charcoal coated like Wile E. Coyote and trudge away," SSG Sand looked to SFC Mathews and put his finger over his lips as a signal to cease all radio transmission, "we'll be clear coat like Casper the Friendly Ghost and float away."

"It figures those assholes would use a dead dog to hide an IED." Sgt Fuller again poked the roadkill. "It reminds me of when Dick Dastardly made Muttley dig a hole and put a charge of TNT in it. He pushed the plunger when the *Wacky Racers* drove over it, but nothing happened. While Dastardly was checking it out, Muttley realized the wires weren't attached." SGT Fuller laughed. "He connected the wires and, Kaboom! Dastardly got it." Fuller guffawed.

"Did it kill him?"

"No. He turned burned black like Wile E. Coyote after attempting to blow up Roadrunner backfired. Dastardly extended his arm and pounded Muttley on the head. Muttley still sniggered because Dastardly got his. I like the scenes when Muttley bites Dastardly in the ass. That's what I'd like to do to Whitehead." Fuller mimicked Muttley's signature wheezy snigger.

"If we don't get out of here, Fuller, we'll have to come back as not-so-friendly ghosts if we wanna bite Whitehead in the ass."

They walked back to the Humvee. SSG Sand grabbed a large red traffic cone and placed it next to the IED. After they drove a safe distance away. SFC Mathews radioed headquarters.

As Team Falcon drove off, Sgt Fuller glanced up at SPC O'Connor perched in the roof gun hatch. "You look like Snoopy sitting up there. Fuck Snoopy. He was a daydreaming wanna be warrior. A damn hippy in a flight cap. We're like Muttley. We're not cute, and we've got attitude. Like Muttley, we don't take shit. Especially from the likes of Major Whitehead." Fuller mimicked Muttley's signature grumble, "Sassafrassuh rassa-frassin chickenshit Whitehead." Fuller again looked upward. "You listening, O'Connor? When did Snoopy ever bite Charlie Brown in the ass? Muttley bit Dick Dastardly in the ass, and one day I'll do the same to Douglas Whitehead."

***

Adele Beauchamp sat in her cubicle at the Charleston County Planning and Zoning Department. She shuffled permit applications, zoning requests, and property plats into

29

respective piles. Next, she sorted each completed form in order of its postmark before logging them electronically into her computer. She exhaled and dropped her shoulders after clicking the icon to send them to the Planning Director. *'I hope I got it right. If I didn't, Haisley will call me into his office to point it out as a cover to stare at me and comment on my appearance.'* Adele paused to file her nails with an emery board. She placed the emery board on the desktop, moistened her fingertips, and kneaded her eye shadow before putting the zoning requests, permit applications, and property plats into manila folders and placing them in a filing cabinet. She glanced at her computer, ensuring the electronic downloads got transferred to Malcolm Haisley, the Planning Director. After glancing at the time in the corner of the screen, she fidgeted and twirled the phone cord. The phone rang. She bit her lower lip. "What does Old Man Haisley want this time?" She wedged the receiver between her shoulder and cheek and again filed her nails with the emery board. "Yes, Sir."

"Sir?" A female voice answered. "Since when did I transition?"

Adele laughed. "I thought it was Mr. Haisley. I'm glad it's you, Jenny. What's up?"

"Hey, girl, if you can break out of the slave galley a little early, I'd like you to join me at the gym for the Pilates class. That new instructor is leading the class."

"You know he's queer as a three-dollar bill." Adele chuckled.

"Oh, so what if he's gay? He's a hoot, and he knows Pilates better than any straight guy, or woman of any orientation."

"Let me check on Mr. Haisley and ask if I can leave early."

"Unfasten a couple of blouse buttons first." Jenny laughed, "You know how the dirty old man operates."

"Let me see." Adele put the receiver on her desk and walked to the Planning Director's office. His door was locked. His secretary didn't notice her. Adele slinked back to her cubicle, lifted the receiver, and whispered, "I'll be there in fifteen minutes."

***

"Come on dolls, lift your butts." The Pilates instructor lay on his back with his feet on the floor hip-width apart, arms at his side. "We're going to do a Pelvic Curl. Come on, ladies and tramps, you're not going to convert me by being lazy. Let's see some glutes of glory, lift 'em and squeeze 'em. Come on, my bendy babes, you can do it. Activate."

Adele and Jenny turned to each other and giggled.

"Okay, divas, back to the palace and your wicked stepmothers. That's all for today."

Adele wiped sweat from her face with a towel, "I'd never let a straight guy talk to me like that. After all, I put that Henry Sawyers guy in his place the other night."

"He's my date for tonight."

Adele blanched, "I'm sorry, Jenny."

Jenny's eyes reached the top of Adele's head. Today, she wore her blond hair in a bun. She held Adele's shoulders. "Don't worry about it, girl. He's a successful attorney. That gives him some leeway."

"Does he know where you work?"

"Why should he care? I'm only a waitress at the Pussy Cat Lounge, not a dancer." Jenny chuckled. "Besides, I've seen him there, and he later realized who I am. Seeing how much money he spends on the dancers, it doesn't surprise me that he made those sexist remarks about you and your sister.

Don't worry. I've dealt with his kind and put them in their place every time. And, as I said, it's easier to tolerate his type when they're rich and successful attorneys." Jenny dropped her eyes to Adele's chest. "You've got something hours gym and diet will never achieve. Why don't you join me and work at the club? They're always looking for waitstaff. The tips are great, you keep your clothes on, and the customers can't touch you."

I don't know if Bobby would approve, but the way dirty old man Haisley undresses me with his eyes, how much worse can it be? Anyway, we are getting a pay raise."

"How much?"

"Four and a half percent. About fifty cents an hour."

"When you want to make some real money, you know I can open that door." Jenny laughed. "Anyway, it's my first date with the lawyer. We're going to Rascal's tonight. It's a hip new place on King Street."

"Yeah, I saw it from the outside the other night when we went to Rosa's Cantina."

"You also saw that the joint was jumping. They have a beach music band tonight." Jenny held both of Adele's hands. "Remember the shorter guy in the custom suit? He's Michael Evans."

"So?"

"So?" Jenny squeezed Adele's hands. "I'm sure everyone in the Planning and Development department has heard of Evans and Carlton construction?"

"Yes. I've processed some of their applications."

Well, I'll have you know he's a partner. He'll be there with Claudia. That leaves that good-looking tall guy."

"He was stylishly dressed." Adele chuckled. "But that hair gel was something out of the fifties."

"Well, he's from California. His father bought out the copper smelting plant off Clements Ferry Road. He's Trevor Brocton. He's well-connected and has political ambitions."

"Stop it, Jenny. Yes, he's tall, cute, and rich. But," Adele held up her left hand, showing off her engagement ring.

"Hey, no one is suggesting you cheat." Jenny let her blonde hair down and shook her head. "Just come along. Okay?"

"All right." Adele sighed. "But I'm driving myself. Just let Mr. Hair Gel know that I'm coming along just as a friend."

"Meet us there at eight. After dating an asshole like Spike McClenahan, it will do you good to go out with some wealth and class."

"Don't bring Spike up. It's over. Thank God. I'm Bobby's fiancé now."

"I'm sorry if I touched a raw nerve." Jenny pecked Adele's cheek. "I'll make it up to you tonight."

***

"Look at the faces of the Iraqis." Carlos Garcia kept his gaze and weapon aimed out the rear window. "They hate us. I don't understand it. We removed a tyrant; we're building schools; we're building soccer fields; we make food drops…But they don't appreciate a damn thing."

"Who the fuck cares, Carlos." SGT Fuller scowled at SSG Garcia. "We're not the fucking Peace Corps. We're the United States Army. Our job is to kill people and break things."

"You got me thinking, Fuller." Bobby Sand inched his head back while keeping his eye on the road. "These team names. They're too generic. Team Black Mamba? Team Falcon? Team Hornet? Team Sea Hawk? Unpleasant animals and aggressive but unintelligent birds. How about we rename ourselves Team Muttley?"

"Hey, Sandman." Garth Mathews lowered his weapon. "I like that. Like Fuller said, we ain't cute and we got attitude."

"And we got a rebellious streak." SGT Fuller added. "Whitehead gave us the name Team Falcon. I don't want nothing from that REMF - Rear Echelon Mother Fucker. And that's assuming his mother would have him."

"Team Muttley, it is." SFC Mathews raised his thumb. "Hey, step on it, Sandman. I want to get to the phones before the line is too long."

"I already got pedal to the metal. Just like Junior when he wins the upcoming Daytona 500 ahead of Tony Stewart. Hey, I haven't heard Adele's voice since arriving in this shithole. If I could make this thing go faster, I would. I wish I had magical power and could make this slow-ass Humvee sprout wings. Fortunately, Team Black Mamba has the same idea."

***

Erica Beauchamp finished work early and got home before four O'clock. She wore business attire of navy-blue slacks, a collared blouse, and a matching jacket. "Mother, how are you keeping?"

"Better now that you're here." Monica sat up in her easy chair. "Don't worry about me. I had my soap operas to keep me company."

"You should invite some friends over when I'm at work."

"No one wants to see a dying old lady."

"What did we talk about this morning?" Erica folded her arms. "You know, about that dying stuff. You're going to be with us for a long time." Erica poured her mother a cup of tea.

"I hope not too much longer." Monica sipped her tea. "After all, you need to get a life. Sticking around too long may prevent my future grandchildren's birth."

"Stop it, mother." Erica chuckled. "I first need to make sure you stay alive to meet your future grandchildren."

"I'm hoping your sister will give me a grandchild with Bobby. Where is Adele, anyway?"

"Adele's a big girl. She can take care of herself. As soon as I change out of my work clothes, I'll cook us spaghetti and meat sauce."

***

Erica had set three places at the dining room table. She placed a pot of spaghetti and a bowl of meat sauce on the table. "Well, look who just arrived and just in time for dinner? Adele, have a seat. I cooked us spaghetti and meat sauce."

"Hey there, sis. Hey there, Mom. Thanks anyway, but I'm meeting the girls at a trendy new restaurant on King Street called Rascals."

"Shouldn't you spend some time with your family and save money for your future family?"

"It's okay, mother, Bobby's double dipping with his deployment. Besides, Jenny promised to pick up the check. Hey, Erica, do you work with an attorney named Henry Sawyers?"

"Did you say *work* with? He's employed at the law firm as an attorney." Erica laughed. "I'd hardly call what he does there work. He only has a job because he's Mr. Crane's nephew. Otherwise, he'd be living under an overpass."

Adele went to her bedroom and changed into her evening attire. She returned to the dining room. "What do you think?" Adele raised her arms and twirled, showing off her black, form-fitting, backless mid-style with an off-the-shoulder neckline."

"I think those pumps make you look as tall as an NBA basketball player." Erica chuckled.

"Basketball player? Look who's talking," Adele pointed at her sister. "You're the one wearing sneakers."

"Why the fancy dress just to go out with the girls?" Monica asked.

The phone rang.

"I'll get it." Erica walked over to the phone.

***

"Miracles of miracles." Bobby squeezed the phone receiver and held it to his ear. "The phones are working." He hastily dialed the Beauchamps' Number. With each ring, his vision of Adele intensified.

"Hello," Erica answered.

"Adele! Is that you? Is it really you? I've missed you so much! I feel like I've been here a lifetime."

"Bobby! Oh my God! It's Erica. Adele's here. I'll get her." Erica put her hand over the mouthpiece. "Adele! It's Bobby!"

Adele ran over and grabbed the receiver. "Bobby! How are you? I hope you're keeping safe."

"Adele! You're all I think about when I'm not thinking about staying alive. I'm a full-time soldier now, and war is a dangerous business. So much is out of my control. Keep me in prayer. Let it remain in God's hands. We were in a firefight the other day."

"Yes. Erica told me. Thank God you're all right."

"Yes. Thank God. Erica sounds great. How is your mother?"

"Oh, she keeps kicking along."

Monica's eyes opened wide. "Hi there, Bobby. We miss you."

"Did you hear? She misses you. We all miss you. Have you heard anything about getting leave?"

"We just got here, so I'm afraid that's a long way down the road. But I live for that day. I love you so much; I always feel you in my heart."

"I feel the same."

"Adele, I wish you knew how much hearing your voice means to me. I hope the phones are working tomorrow so we can speak again. Unfortunately, right now, it looks like my turn is over. I have some impatient soldiers waiting in line behind me. I love you, Adele."

"I love you more." Adele returned the handset to the base unit.

"Now that you've heard from Bobby, why don't you stay with us? I'm sure Jenny and Claudia will find a way to have fun without you."

"Thanks, sis, but a promise made is a promise kept."

***

Rascal's Bar and Grill featured exposed face brick walls, high ceilings with hanging pendant lighting, and restored wooden floors. Its long, sleek bar featured backlit shelves with flavored vodkas, premium liquors, and imported liqueurs; the beer taps were brushed aluminum.

Jenny and Hank, Claudia and Michael, and Adele and Trevor sat in high-backed chairs upholstered in olive green, faux alligator leather. A pitcher of Mojitos and six glasses were placed on the table. Hank put his arm around Jenny; she rested her head on his shoulder. Trevor grasped Adele's hand. He remained oblivious to her retracting it. He motioned to the waitress. She wore short shorts and a tight-fitting cotton blouse. "We'll have another pitcher of Mojitos." He leaned over and whispered in her ear. "Make it with the 151-proof Bacardi, and your tip will also get more potent."

"The band is coming on in ten minutes." Jenny had threaded her blonde ponytail through the rear cutout of her Clemson Tigers billed cap. They're called the *Shagadelics.* Everyone is talking about them."

"Ahh, our waitress is here." Trevor raised his hands. "And what did you bring us, Alice?"

Alice winked at Trevor as she placed the Mojito pitcher on the table.

Trevor poured Mojitos for the group. He raised his glass. "Just a few nights ago, we were strangers. Now we're friends. Cheers."

Adele sipped her drink, "Woo! This tastes different." She held her glass to her eyes.

"Go ahead, look closer, Adele." Trevor crossed his arms. "It's mint leaves, lime wedges, sugar, club soda, and white rum, same as before. Come on. Finish up. The band is about to play."

"Too bad for you, they're going to perform Carolina Beach Music, not California Beach music." Adele laughed. "I'm afraid the Beach Boys haven't resonated around here since your greasy kid's stuff hairstyle was in vogue. So, as far as dancing with me goes, you're out of luck."

"The Beach Boys? I'm feeling a song from eighty years ago. "'Nothing could be finer than to be in Carolina in the morning.'" Trevor squeezed Adele's hand. "'No one could be sweeter than my sweetie when I meet her in the morning."

"Nice try." Adele allowed him to hold her hand. "But it's nine o'clock in the evening."

"We're just three hours of dancing away from the most perfect Carolina morning." He looked in her eyes and arched his eyebrows.

Adele laughed. "There's no quit in you, is there?"

"Are you kidding? If I were around when Sammy Kahn wrote *Carolina in the Morning,* I wouldn't have any hair to gel," he chuckled, "or any teeth to brush. But I'd lean on my walker and still beg you to dance."

Adele laughed.

The band was on stage, about to begin their set.

Hank and Jenny got up and strolled toward the dance floor. "Come on, you guys." Jenny waved to the dance floor. "Let's get a spot on the dance floor before it gets too crowded."

Trevor gripped Adele's hand and tugged her arm. He winked and motioned toward the dance floor.

Adele pursed her lips. She glanced at Jenny and Claudia. They nodded. Adele let Trevor lead her by the hand to the dance floor.

The band opened with Creedence Clearwater Revival's '*Fortunate Son.*' Trevor held Adele's hand and twirled her. He kept his grip on her hand and rapidly shuffled his feet in a six-count rhythm. Adele casually twisted her hips in synch. Five beats later, he pulled her into him, wrapping his arm around her waist. She smiled and leaned back, letting her hair rain behind her. She kept hold of his hand and twirled under his arm. Eight other dancers stopped and watched them. Adele was too caught up in their dance for the band playing an anti-war song to evoke a thought for Bobby.

After the song, the band leader, wearing a paisley-patterned shirt and a fitted black blazer, addressed their audience. "That was a fast number from CCR. Let's slow it down. Gentlemen, hold your ladies close, our next song is

Philly soul, now Beach music. It's from The Intruders. We're going to do the '*Slow Drag.*'

Trevor wrapped his arms around Adele and pulled her close, not giving her a chance to decline. She felt unnerved. '*He's a couple of inches taller than Bobby but less stocky.*' She gave in and hugged him as they swayed. '*His body fits, though.*' She placed the side of her head on his chest. Trevor held her closer and rubbed his pelvis against hers. "No. No." She muttered. The music cloaked her objection. Detached from reality, three seconds later, she also gyrated her pelvis against his. As the sentimental and sensual, intimate and nostalgic groove continued, he put his hand on her back and pulled her bust into his chest. Adele gritted her teeth before smiling and embracing him tightly. She rubbed her breasts against his pectorals.

***

After the band's set, the six returned to the table. Trevor had ordered another pitcher of Mojitos with 151 proof Bacardi. "You're quite the dancer." Adele tapped her glass to Trevor's, "You got CCR's Southern beat down pat. How does a California transplant pull it off?"

"Easy," Trevor smirked. "CCR are from California, not the Southeast, and you didn't do so bad yourself with that Philly soul number."

Jenny put her arm on Hank's shoulder and leaned into him. "Maybe the vibe is from the dancers and not the music." Jenny smiled with the left side of her mouth and glinted her eyes.

***

"Nothing could be finer than to be in Carolina in the morning." Trever looked at his watch. "Nothing could be sweeter than to be with my sweetie in the morning."

"Jenny, you work a night shift. But Adele and I must get up and work early." Claudia finished her drink. "Besides, the band finished their last set. Let's all pitch in and pay the check."

"I got it." Trevor raised his hand. He stood and walked over to their waitress. He leaned over to whisper into her ear. "The 151 Bacardi did the trick." He put two one-hundred-dollar bills in her hand.

"Huh." She beamed and kissed his cheek.

"Don't get carried away." He laughed. "I invested that money in her." He motioned toward Adele.

Trevor walked behind Adele and put his hands on her shoulders. "Well, my morning sweetie, you had a lot to drink. Why don't you let me drive you home?"

"I'll be all right, Trevor. Besides, I need my car for tomorrow."

"There are some questionable-looking guys in here who also drank too much." Trevor took Adele's hand. "You're the hottest gal here, so don't think they haven't checked you out. At least let me walk you to your car."

Seconds after Adele and Trevor left the premises and the door closed behind them. They couldn't hear the disc jockey. "The band finished their set with a classic Philly soul number. Let's keep the vibe cooking with a number on Phillies Records, Darlene Love, and *Wait Until My Bobby Gets Home.*"

***

Adele allowed Trevor to hold her hand and walk her to her car. They stood in front of her 1992 Hyundai Excel 2-door hatchback. He placed his arms around the back of her neck. Adele was too inebriated to pull away. Trevor looked into her eyes. "I can't recall a better evening or a lovelier lady."

Before Adele knew what was happening, Trevor kissed her lips and darted his tongue into her mouth.

Four seconds later, she pulled away. "No. No. I shouldn't." She blushed and lowered her head to his chest level. She couldn't help but inhale his *Amouage Gold for Men* Cologne. She pressed her nose through his shirt's unbuttoned hem and into his chest. Using her arms around his neck as a brace, she boosted herself onto her toes and kissed his lips. Their tongues mingled. She gazed into his eyes before retreating into her car and driving away. Trevor smiled like a Cheshire cat.

***

Bobby lay on his cot. He covered himself and lay on his side, facing the wall. After Garth, Carlos, and Chuck fell asleep, he gently stroked himself. "Adele. Adele. Adele. I love you, Adele."

Chapter 5

Team Muttley stood in the chow line at the "Dirty Bird Café." Bobby nodded to the civilian cook, hired from India by Halliburton subsidiary Kellogg, Brown, and Root (KBR), "I'll have a ham and cheese omelet."

A mortar blast shook the mess hall with multi-decibel shockwaves. It shook the egg flat from the counter; three dozen eggs cracked open on the floor.

"Better make it scrambled." Bobby chuckled.

Team Muttley shared a table. SFC Mathews sipped a cup of orange juice. "I've got some good news. Major Whitehead isn't coming out for formation."

"Sometimes you've got to hand it to the enemy." SGT Fuller clenched his fists. "I'll take a mortar blasting out my eardrums over listening to that clucking chickenshit in black glasses any day and every day."

"We got word from the Sergeant Major." Bobby Sand sipped his black coffee. "Now that Operation Iron Fury is over, headquarters wants us to pacify the Iraqis by building them a soccer field. The 478th Civil Affairs Battalion has already negotiated and arranged it with the local leadership. They're expecting us today. We're bringing bulldozers to clear the land, and we've got two soccer goals through Haliburton. The 478th has hired Iraqi workers."

"What?" SGT Fuller banged on the table. "Who's the idiot from the 478th that negotiated with the Tangos? Didn't the President say we don't negotiate with terrorists? I trust a Tango for one thing, and one thing only- to shoot us in the back, first chance they get."

"I agree with Fuller." SSG Garcia nervously stirred his scrambled eggs. "Why so soon after Operation Iron Fury? The Marines and the 3rd Infantry Division hit 'em with multiple casualties. They destroyed several blocks of apartments, and we even piled on by blowing up one of their overpasses." Carlos pushed his plate aside. "I bet they're still pissed. Couldn't it wait until things calm down?"

"I guess that's the point." SSG Sand raised his hands. "Part of our job is to pacify the civilians."

"Pacify civilians?" Chuck Fuller furrowed his brow. "I said it before, and I'll say it again. I'm a United States Army soldier, not some Peace Corps hippy. I'm here to kill people and break things. If I build something, it's to further our mission, not make a bunch of sand niggers happy."

A black soldier seated at a nearby table scowled at SGT Fuller.

SSG Sand held his hand in a halt gesture and spoke to the black soldier, "He's talking about the insurgents." He turned back to SGT Fuller, "Come on, Chuck, I know you're gung-ho. The unit appreciates it, but you've got to tone down the rhetoric. I came to fight enemies of my country, not fellow soldiers you piss off."

"All anger aside, I hope building the soccer field works." SFC Mathews tensed his lips. "Sandman is right. It's our job and part of the mission. We are now US Army active-duty soldiers. No backing down. Of course, we can pacify them all we want. Only the Prince of Peace can end the war. Let's all pray." SFC Mathews steepled his hands and closed his eyes. Sand, Fuller, and Garcia followed. "Heavenly Father, in the name of Jesus, be with us as we perform our duties as soldiers. Most of all, protect the loved ones we left behind. Amen."

"Amen." The team replied. SSG Garcia made the Sign of the Cross by touching his forehead, chest, and each shoulder.

SGT Fuller steepled his hands. "And God, show 'em your might. Vengeance is mine, thus sayeth the Lord." Fuller clenched his fists. "Now lead us to avenge 911."

***

Adele Beauchamp sat in her Charleston County Planning and Zoning Department cubicle. She glanced at the clock. Like a heavy barbell, memories of the previous night weighed down her back and neck. She lowered her head and stared at her keyboard. She typed nothing, grimacing as her stomach knotted. After fidgeting with her phone cord, she inhaled deeply and tilted her head back. An image of Bobby walking onto the C-17 Globe Master III military aircraft with his unit haunted her. "I'm sorry, Bobby. It will never happen again." She bit her lower lip.

"Delivery for Miss Beauchamp." A slender man wearing a white suit covered by a white smock interrupted her muse. He handed her a rectangular package longer than his arm and almost as wide as his torso. The package had a clear plastic cover.

"Huh," Adele covered her face with her hands. "They're beautiful!" The deliveryman handed her the package. She tore off the clear plastic cover and buried her nose into the red, yellow, and white roses, pink peonies, and creamy white gardenias. She read the attached card. *'From the Temples of Genetrix and Aeneas to Heaven above, flowers for the true Goddess of Love, my Venus of Charleston, the light of my eternal lamp, Miss Adele Beauchamp. Love, Trevor.'* Adele sniggered at the campy limerick, put the card aside, and buried her face in the flowers.

"That's not all, doll." An even thinner man and shorter man, wearing tight green slacks and a silky, long-sleeved shirt with flowery embroidery, stepped into her cubicle. He had cut his blond hair short on the sides, long in the back,

45

and had a prominent, curved nose. "I designed this myself." He opened a black box and held it by the shoulders. "Voila! Your new dress for this evening."

"Huh," Adele beamed wider than a mare. "Oh my God! It's gorgeous." Adele took the black silk evening gown from the designer and held it up. "And the jeweled bodice!" She put the dress in front of her eyes. "Those purple gemstones are real! They're beyond precious." Adele hugged the dress.

"Real Amethyst, your birthstone. I can see that you're an Aquarius. Independent and intelligent. It's easy to find someone's birthday. I don't know how Trevor got your measurements, but it's a purrrfect fit." The designer cupped his hands over his chest. "It makes you look so, fab-u-lous, and these will make you look even hotter. I didn't design or make them, but I selected them for you on behalf of Trevor." The designer opened a shoe box.

"Oh my God! Oh my God!" Adele held a black Salvatore Ferragamo spiked shoe to her eyes. "Oh my God, I've never seen anything so gorgeous!"

"Size 9?"

"Yes! Yes!"

The designer's cell phone rang. He flipped it open. "You're not going to believe this." He handed her his phone. "It's for you."

Adele held the phone to her ear. "Good morning. Miss Beauchamp. This is Jose Cordova of Prestige Limousine. Our best stretch limo will pick you up at work at four and take you for your dinner date with Trevor at Labrador's House of Seafood and Lobster on Folly Beach."

"I can't afford to eat there."

Jose laughed. "Trevor Brocton will not only pay the check; he will tip the waiter. Will you be ready at four?"

Adele pursed her lips. She got an image of Bobby. A prickly sensation and a sweat bead broke out on her face. Perusing the flowers, dress, and shoes, she smiled. "Yes. Yes. But…"

"But what?"

"My hair, my nails, my makeup. I can't wear such a beautiful gown and spikes and eat at such a fancy restaurant looking like this."

"You don't understand," Jose chuckled. "Mr. Brocton has arranged a pit stop along the way. He made an appointment for you with Mr. DePlume."

"Jude DePlume? He's the most sought-after beautician and hairstylist on the Eastern Seaboard. You need a recommendation, and even then, his waiting list is weeks long."

"Well, Mr. DePlume will see you today at five."

"I'm supposed to be here until five." A vision of Bobby in uniform flashed into her mind. She glanced at the flowers, gown, and shoes, and gritted her teeth. "My boss, Mr. Haisley, is out of the office today, so I'll sneak out a little earlier. Pulling up in a stretch limo will attract too much attention. I'll park at the Walmart on Lee Street. Can you pick me up there?"

***

Company A of the 878th CEBN loaded two M9 ACE bulldozers onto M1000 semi-trailers pulled by M11070 Heavy Equipment Transporters. Other supplies were loaded into a five-ton M925 cargo truck. The unit assigned ten armed Humvees as security escorts. Team Muttley stood in front of their Humvee. "I got some bad news." SFC Mathews addressed the team. "Major Whitehead has disapproved of our renaming ourselves Team Muttley. We're still Team Falcon."

"To hell with him." SSG Garcia shook his fists. "Let's rename Whitehead, Major Dastardly."

"No, Carlos." SGT Fuller held his M16 at port arms. "Dick Dastardly was to the Wacky Racers what Freddie Blassie and Lou Albano were to professional wrestling. They cheat, but they never harm anyone, and they make the show better. Whitehead is like Snidely Whiplash. Trying to murder Nel by tying her to the railroad tracks is sadism from the Ted Bundy, Richard Ramirez playbook." Chuck smirked. "Or Douglas Whitehead's."

"No. Whitehead is more like John Wayne Gacy." SSG Sand laughed. "Whitehead's a clown and a bad one at that."

"You got that right, Sandman." Chuck Fuller guffawed. "Well, I did a Dick Dastardly on Whitehead. The other night, while I was in the computer room," Chuck grinned. "I printed and laminated this." He pulled out a picture from under his body armor. It was of Muttley wearing a red collar. Head bent, Muttley had his paw over his mouth, covering a smirk. Chuck grabbed a roll of duct tape from the Humvee and taped Muttley's picture to the vehicle.

Specialist O'Connor accurately impersonated Muttley's wheezy snigger.

"Good one, Wayne!" Chuck slapped SPC O'Connor on the back. "Can you do Whitehead?"

"Yeah, Wayne, you heard his briefing." SFC Mathews laughed. "Let's hear it."

Twenty-year-old Wayne O'Connor slumped his thin shoulders and bent over slightly, imitating Major Whitehead's posture. He adjusted his round, wire-framed glasses, mimicking how Major Whitehead wears his black plastic glasses. He impersonated Major Whitehead's weak, raspy voice. "I've got a hard day in front of me. Shuffling papers in my office is a dangerous mission, but it takes a man like me to do it. I must endure hardship because sometimes the air conditioning is too cold. The other day, I banged my knee on my desk. It hurt. I asked Colonel Azshalt to put me in for a Purple Heart. You will proudly stand at attention in the 110-degree heat and salute me while I get my award. You have it easy today. You get to sit on your asses while riding in your Humvee along an IED-infested road to the proposed soccer field in Adhamiyah, northwest of Sadr City. Even better, an IED may have you fly there so the potholes won't jolt you. You will get to watch the heavy equipment operators clear a soccer field. Adhamiyah is a Sunni area. The Shiites don't want them to practice soccer. They may get good enough to beat them, so they may try to kill you. Don't worry. If you're killed, we'll wait until steak night to honor our tradition of putting a meal by your empty place at the table."

Bobby, Garth, Chuck, and Carlos laughed so hard they bent over.

"But when we pour beer over your coffin," Specialist O'Connor continued. "It will have to be alcohol free near beer. Army regs still forbid soldiers deployed to Iraq from drinking alcohol."

***

"I don't know how your parents did it." Jude DePlume had one eye on Adele in the beautician chair and another on her mirror reflection. "But I applaud them. Two gorgeous sisters. Who is competing for Miss America and who for Miss USA?"

"How do you know about Erica?"

"The talk I hear from my clients would shock you."

"Who do they say is prettier?"

Mr. DePlume turned Adele in her chair to face the mirror. "Have a good look at yourself now and compare yourself to Erica when I'm done with you. It will be no contest, not just with your older sister, but for all of Charleston." The beautician brushed Adele's hair. "I adore your sister's auburn hair. This ash blonde must go. Let's make you a true blonde."

"I don't want to look like a cheap bottle blonde."

"I said true blonde. You're already ash blonde, we're just going to give you a lighter tint. One that will match your hazel eyes." The beautician put his hands on his hips. "I didn't get my reputation by using cheap stuff. I could work on Broadway or Hollywood if I want. I stay here because it's where I am happy living. Besides, Johnny is from here and would never tolerate moving. Your new boyfriend paid for you to have the best, and that's what you're getting." Mr. DePlume applied moisturizer to Adele's face. "Your hair is not even styled. It hangs loose and is uneven at the back. Here's what I see. You have large, almond-shaped eyes. Their hazel color is perfect for the lighter hair tint. Just the right hue and amount of eyeshadow will enhance the whole package. A flipped-out, slightly below shoulder-length bob," he held a hand mirror so she could see the back of her hair, "would make you look like a Sandro Botticelli figure. You have gracefully arched eyebrows. They're already proportional, and I will have them frame your face with refinement. Making those eyelashes flash like fine feathers will add the la touche finale. I love your straight and finely shaped nose. It adds symmetry to your face. My partner, Johnny, is an artist. He'll tell you that beauty is one with harmony, proportion, and order, and that's cross-cultural. Your upper and lower lips are even. Perfect. I already have the right lipstick shade in mind. Your smooth, tapered chin and gently rounded chin. Wow!" He held his hands in imitation of a picture frame. "You look like the golden age of Hollywood movie star Gene Tierney."

"Who's she?"

"You never saw her movie, *Laura*? The one she made with Dana Andrews? A who's who of singers recorded the theme song. Frank Sinatra. Vic Damone. Jo Stafford. Ella."

"I've heard of Frank Sinatra anyway."

"Well, by the time I get through with you, everyone in the Charleston area will have heard of Adele Beauchamp."

***

"Viola." The beautician raised his hands, "The new Adele Beauchamp. While working on you, I had the mirrors covered. I don't want you to see yourself until you go to the change room and put on your new silk gown and Italian shoes.

Adele emerged from the change room. "Oh my God!" She beamed on seeing her reflection in the uncovered mirrors. "Is it really me?"

"No need to compare yourself with your sister. I can put you up against Gisele Bundchen, Adriana Lima, and Laeticia Casta." Mr. DePlume smiled with a slight curl to the left side of his mouth. "Looks aren't everything. Your new boyfriend invested in this." He sprayed her with Chanel No. 5 perfume. Adele covered her chest after he sprayed it into her cleavage. "Relax, sweetie, they're a gift from God, now let's make them smell and taste ambrosial."

***

The 878th CEBN convoy drove down the center of the road. Traffic from both directions got out of their way.

51

"I'm happy for the traffic jam." SSG Garcia pointed his weapon at the cars as they yielded the right of way. "The insurgents won't blow up their own."

"What the hell are you talking about, Carlos?" SGT Fuller scowled. "You never heard the word, Martyr? These people would love to die with you so they can pull you down to Hell with them. So, you'd better pray you arrive in Adhamiyah in one piece.

"Have you spoken to Adele?" SFC Mathews turned to SSG Sand.

"Only a few times. As you know, the phones seldom work. I think I've spoken more to her sister, Erica."

"I felt sad and lonely not having a wife or girlfriend see me off at Pope Air Force Base. Now I'm glad I'm single and unattached. It's one thing getting stuck in this shithole; it would be another to have to worry about Jodie back home."

"That's okay, Matty. I trust her."

"I hope so. 'W' won't let us leave this shithole until the mission, whatever it is, is accomplished. Donald Rumsfeld said we're nothing more than fungibles. Don't count on any favors from the government."

"Yeah, Matty, imagine dying for the Wolfowitz Doctrine." Bobby grimaced. "It's not worth it in this life or the life to come."

"If we do ever get out of here, I'm going to obey the Jimmy Soul song. 'If you want to be happy for the rest of your life, never make a pretty woman your wife. So, from my personal point of view, take an ugly girl to marry you.' Adele is hot. She was the prettiest gal at our departure. I would not want to leave her behind."

"I don't either." SSG Sand winced. "After staying alive, she's all I think about."

"I'm glad she's with you. I hated it when she was with that dirtbag Spike McClenahan."

SSG Sand bit his lip and clenched the steering wheel.

"I'm sorry I brought him up. It looks like I hit a raw nerve."

"That's okay. I already sorted him out."

"I don't think you have to worry. Major Weston is a high-ranking cop in civilian life. He says McClenahan is already under investigation for dealing dope and stolen auto parts. He says it's just a matter of time before he's in prison on felony charges. I was thinking, Sandman. When we get back, can you help me get a date with her sister, Erica?"

"What happened to marrying an ugly girl?" Bobby guffawed. "You do know that a glamour photographer offered to photograph the sisters together."

"What happened?"

"As you would expect. Goody-goody two-shoes Erica turned him down. Adele did the shoot alone but made far less money than if Erica had joined her. I'll talk to her, but I can't promise anything. Erica is picky and strong-minded. Between caring for her mother and her job at the law firm, she has no time for dates or boyfriends. She even had to give up part-time law school."

"Please try. I promise not to make demands on her time." Garth slapped Bobby's shoulder. "Besides, wouldn't it be cool to be brothers-in-law?"

"Don't worry. I'll talk to her, but she already knows you."

"What does she say?"

"You know, Erica, she's private and doesn't badmouth anyone. Moreover, she's too busy to have a life of her own. She took it hard when her father died and later when her mother suffered a stroke. Anyway, Matty, I'll try. I would rather see you with her than with a Pussycat Lounge stripper.”

“The dancers only take some of my money, not half my money.” SFC Mathews beamed. “Now, a woman like Erica, I could settle down with. She’s someone whom I can trust. Fortunately, my ex and I had no kids, so at least I’m not on the hook for child support. But Erica is the type I’d be happy to make little Matty’s with.” He laughed. “Matty. I could give that name to a boy or a girl. After you get married, have you thought of good names for your children with Adele?”

“I think of everything about Adele. All the time.” Bobby looked ahead. “It looks like we’re here.”

The convoy pulled into an open field splayed with trash and building debris. Apartment buildings, some abandoned and bombed out, others ugly and bare, surrounded the field. “I don’t like the looks of this place.” SSG Garcia disembarked first. “I got a bad feeling. People are gathering around the field. They don’t look happy.”

“You’re right about one thing, Garcia. The Tangos don’t appreciate nothin’ we do for them. So, I believe in shoot first and ask questions later. If a Tango doesn’t like us,” SGT Fuller pulled his weapon’s charging handle, “I got sixteen reasons, and they all begin with an M, why I don’t care.” Fuller switched his weapon from safe to semi. “And none of them are in the Connie Stevens song.”

“What if women and children get killed in the crossfire?” SSG Garcia scanned the area.

“It’s like Donald Rumsfeld said, ‘*collateral damage*’. Besides, it stops little terrorists from growing into big terrorists.” SGT Fuller chambered another round. “I don’t mind a little pre-emptive action.”

Team Muttley and the other 878th CEBN teams surrounded the field as the bulldozers cleared the land. Six

478th soldiers had already unloaded a pair of soccer goal posts from the five-ton truck.

After three hours of work, the 478th and 878th broke for lunch. SPC O'Connor jumped the line and grabbed a chili con carne MRE.

"Hey, O'Connor. What's the big idea? Wait your turn."

"No way, Matty. I'm getting the chili con carne before you do. Gas rises, and I sit up top."

"Thanks for telling me. Now I know what you're willing to trade me."

"Speaking of gas, this damn heater contraption didn't work again." Bobby Sand held up a plastic bag, an eighth full of water, containing an olive-drab foil pouch. "I again have to eat spaghetti and meat sauce cold."

"I'll trade you my Tootsie Roll." Garth Mathews held up his dessert, "for your Skittles."

SSG Sand and SFC Mathews swapped candy.

***

The limousine pulled up under the Labrador's House of Seafood and Lobster's concierge. A young male uniformed valet opened the door. Trevor Brocton, wearing a Dom Bottigliari black shark skin suit with an open collar white silk shirt, extended his hand and helped Adele alight from the limousine. Standing in front of her, he placed a thin, gold chain around her neck. Its amethyst stone dangled a centimeter above her cleavage. Adele blushed and beamed at her gift. Trevor kissed her lips, darting his tongue into her mouth. He pulled back before she could. They walked through the door, holding hands while sauntering into the restaurant. Adele gazed at her reflection in a mirror mounted between two framed vintage maritime maps and grinned. Chandeliers with blown glass, coral-shaped ornaments cast shadows on the contours of her face. The head waiter showed them their table. A murmuring could be heard as heads turned toward Adele. The head waiter pulled the chair for her and bowed as she sat. A pearl linen drape covered their table. A vase of fresh flowers sat between two silver candle stands. She silently moved her lips to say, "Thank you."

"Wine, sir." Another waiter stood by their table with an order pad.

"Chablis Grand Cru will do."

The waiter returned with an elegantly curved bottle in a stainless steel, ice-filled wine bucket and stand. He placed steaming bread rolls and a pinch bowl of garlic butter next to the flowers. The waiter poured Adele and Trevor wine into crystal goblets.

"To us." Trevor raised his glass.

Adele hesitated. She pictured Bobby on the night they got engaged. "Um, you're drinking wine and not Budweiser."

"Do I look like a Budweiser type?" Trevor laughed. "Budweiser bills itself as the King of Beers, although the last time I visited Buckingham Palace, they didn't have a bowling alley." He chuckled. "Chablis Grand Cru is pressed for kings. And in the case of tonight, a queen." Trevor raised his glass. Adele tapped her glass on his. They hooked arms and quaffed.

"I've never tasted anything like this." Adele held her glass to her eyes. "And I've never felt so beautiful." Adele drank the rest of her wine.

"Tonight, you look like a Southern Belle." Trevor refilled her goblet with wine. "Next, we'll make you look like a gorgeous California girl."

'What?" Adele winced. I don't look beautiful enough?"

"You look beautiful enough. Beautiful enough for the heir to a copper smelting plant. My ambitions go well beyond copper smelting. I got an MBA from the University of California, Berkeley's Haas School of Business. It taught me how to help run my father's business. I'm in charge of the business operation. We hire geeks to take care of the geological and technical part of it. We also own forty-eight percent of Picardi Developments. They have dealt with your boss, Malcolm Haisley."

"What do they say about him?" Adele arched her eyebrows.

"What's there to say?" Trevor moved closer to Adele. "He's a typical, boring county official."

"I think he's a dirty old man." Adele laughed.

"My family owns everything, but I'm my own boss." Trevor touched fingertips and steepled his hands. "Copper smelting and real estate development are only for now. In the future, I plan to run for office. I have my sights set on a governorship and higher. Maybe the Senate, even the president of the United States. If it's the Governor of South Carolina, you must look like a Southern Belle. If it's California, we need to elevate you to a California girl. A movie star." Trevor reached out and held her hands.

Adele squeezed his hands while lowering her head and blushing. "I only have an AA from Charleston County Community College. Bobby was studying part-time for a BS in Civil Engineering at the Citadel before getting deployed."

"Playing Army is fun, but civilian politicians have the power to run the military. And that's my goal."

"But you have an MBA and come from a wealthy family." Adele lowered her head. "Don't you look down on me?"

Trevor raised her chin with his finger. He planted a long, wet kiss on her lips.

Adele returned the kiss but ended it first.

"I hope that quenched all doubt," Trevor smirked and lifted his chin. "Your beauty perfects my brains." He folded his hands behind his head.

"But you're so tall and handsome." Adele's glazed eyes met Trevor's dry eyes. "You can get any woman on Earth."

"But I only want one special gal." He grinned. "Oh, will you look at what the waiter brought us?" Trevor beamed.

The waiter put a platter of raw half-shell oysters on the table.

"Bon Appétit." Trevor held up his wine glass for Adele to tap. "The wine perfects the fresh oysters."

***

"The oysters were delicious, as is the wine." Adele finished her glass of wine. "And the smells! From the hot bread rolls to the garlic butter to the seafood. It's delightful."

"Ahh…But not as delightful as the perfume on your lovely skin." Trevor grinned. He raised the left side of his lip higher than the right side. "And nothing tastes better than your kiss." Trevor French kissed her. Adele returned his affection. "And talk about tasty, here comes our main course."

Two waiters approached their table. They brought two silver-domed platters. They raised the domes and put the plates before Adele and Trevor. "The Labrador's renowned specialty. Lobster Thermador." Trevor beamed. "The best meal on the Eastern Seaboard."

***

Bobby Sand sat on the ground, resting his back on the team's Humvee. "Cold Spaghetti out of a foil pouch, complete with dust and the smell of raw sewage." Sparks and a metallic rattle ringing from the Humvee interrupted his lunch. A second later, they heard gunfire. "What the fuck!" Multiple rifle reports and bullets rained upon them. They crawled under the Humvee. Bobby spotted a muzzle flash from behind a wall at about 150 meters away. The shooter emerged from his cover and fired an errant shot at him. Bobby got a clear line of fire. He squeezed his M16's trigger. His mind and vision became fuzzy. The bullet seemed to fly in slow motion, almost as if his eyes could follow its path. He saw the shooter clutch his chest before falling over.

SGT Fuller sprang from under the Humvee. His weapon on automatic, he sprayed the area with bullets. "Shit!" He ejected his empty magazine. SSG Garcia lay under the Humvee with his head covered. Chuck reached under and took his ammunition. Fuller locked and loaded and fired at the buildings.

After SGT Fuller ran out of ammo, the area became eerily silent. Fuller stood in the open. The rest of the unit remained under cover. They waited for an interminable ten minutes. The Sergeant Major yelled, "All clear."

Bobby, Garth, and a medic walked over to the fallen Iraqi. Charlie gazed into his eyes. Their eyes met. He saw a flash. It seemed like live wires connected them. The Iraqi's pupils wildly dilated. He met Bobby's eyes with a tear. His jaw chattered along with short gasping breaths. It lasted three seconds before stopping. His breathing ceased, and his eyes went blank.

"Do something!" Bobby grabbed the medic by the arm.

"Don't worry. The Geneva Convention dictates that I help him." The medic dropped to one knee and took the fallen Iraqi's pulse. He looked back at Bobby and shook his head.

***

Adele and Trevor waited under the Labrador House of Seafood's concierge. Adele locked her arms around his neck. "I feel woozy from the wine. I need to hold myself up."

"Only because of the wine, my breathless evening star." He embraced her and kissed her deeply.

The kiss made her head buzz like a whiff of laughing gas. She lowered her arms to his torso and squeezed him.

The limousine pulled up to them. The valet opened the rear door. Adele boarded the Limousine. Trevor bent down and raised her chin with his finger. "I just can't say, good night. We enjoyed such a lovely evening. I surely won't make you ride alone. I will ride with you to your car."

"You can't do that."

"Of course, I can. Besides, the limo is paid for until noon tomorrow. The driver can bring me back." Before Adele could answer, Trevor entered the car and slid beside her. The valet closed the door. Trevor signaled to the driver. As soon as the limousine moved, he closed the hatch separating them from the chauffeur. He took her right hand and pulled her closer. He kissed her. She returned his kiss with slight hesitation. He continued kissing her. She now vigorously kissed him. His kisses moved to her neck. She tilted her head back and moaned. He pressed his nose into her cleavage and imbibed the delectable mix of flesh, perspiration, and Chanel No. 5 perfume. With skilled timing, he kissed the top of her breasts, pulled aside her dress, and sucked her right nipple. Although he lacked the talent and education to design fashion, he did consult with the couturier on the type and location of the fasteners. Adele closed her eyes and hummed "Mmm" as he sucked on her nipple, not realizing that he was disrobing her.

***

Bobby skipped dinner. Besides having no appetite, he wanted to be first in line to use the phone. "Thank God," He looked upwards on hearing a dial tone, "They work." He punched in the country and area codes before the Beauchamps' home phone number. "Hello." The connection was fuzzy, but as well as could be expected.

He breathed a sigh of relief on hearing the female voice. "Thank God! Adele. Something terrible happened today. I don't know how to tell you about it, but thank God I can at least try to talk to you about it."

"Bobby! Wow! It's you! I'm sorry. It's not Adele. It's Erica."

"Where's Adele? I really must talk with her."

"She went to dinner with some friends. Probably Jenny and Claudia."

"Oh, no." SSG Sand clenched his teeth. "I really need to talk to her. I must talk to someone."

"I'm her sister. Talk to me. I'll make sure to convey everything to her."

"Erica," Bobby inhaled deeply, "I don't know how to tell you...I killed a man today."

"Oh my God! What happened, Bobby?"

"We were building the Iraqis a soccer field...we were on lunch break...First, I saw a spark and heard a pinging noise. A second later, gunfire...We took cover...I spotted one of the snipers...I got him in my sight...I didn't hesitate to pull the trigger...I saw him clutch his chest and drop."

"It's okay, Bobby. I'm here. I'm listening. Please. Talk to me."

"After the fight, we went to him. Erica, he was still alive. He looked at me with eyes stranger than you could ever imagine. I felt a spiritual connection."

"Did you feel his wrath or anger?"

"No. It was more like he wanted me to know he had a soul like mine. That just because we're at war and we're supposed to be enemies, we're both human beings of equal value to God, even if our religions are different. SGT Fuller says, 'kill them all. Let God sort out the rest.' That's not the God I believe in, Erica." Bobby bit his lower lip. "I'm not a murderer."

"Bobby, I could never in a million years experience what you're going through. Forget the laws of war. It was self-defense by any definition. He tried to kill you first. Jesus already died for all of mankind. You're not obligated to die for a stranger trying to kill you."

"Erica, I confess, I have no idea why we're here. Oil? Isreal? Halliburton and corporate profiteering? I want to be a civil engineer, Erica, not a hitman."

"As a civilian, I'm not crazy about the war either. I know they're lying about weapons of mass destruction, and how is a country five thousand miles away without a navy or an air force a threat? But you're a professional, Bobby. The Army is paying your tuition at the Citadel as part of your enlistment benefit. You knew what the job entailed, and you knew this could happen."

"I know, I know, Erica. But I never thought it would actually happen."

"Bobby, remember in Luke 3:14 when John the Baptist told the soldiers, *'Don't extort money and don't accuse people falsely, and be content with your pay.'* He never tells them to abandon their profession. Later, Jesus commends the Centurion's faith and heals his servant. He never tells him to lay down his arms and leave his profession. Only God can beat the swords into plowshares and spears into pruning hooks. You're a professional, Bobby. You're not a cold-blooded killer by any definition."

"I'm a professional. I just don't want to be a professional by Big Joey Massino's definition."

"Bobby. You're not a hitman. You are a United States Army Soldier. What happened today was not for profit, nor was it driven by revenge or intimidation. You did not act lawlessly. You are sworn to uphold the US Constitution and are bound by the laws of the Geneva Convention. The God of the Old or New Testaments does not prohibit your profession. The scriptures guide your conduct as a soldier, and you didn't violate any of them."

"Erica, I can't thank you enough." Bobby wiped a tear from his eye. "I have much to deal with. They can yell peace, peace, all they want. But there is no peace here, and I'm not coming home anytime soon. Yet your words are my first step to finding inner peace. Please tell Adele I love her and I miss her. I hope we can soon marry and have a child to replace the life that I took."

"Bobby, you're making me cry. Of course, I'll give word to Adele. I'll be happiest the day of my life when I can call you 'Brother-in-Law.'"

***

Team Muttley sat silently on their cots. The five of them lay with their portable DVD players.

"I can say one good thing about the Tangos." Sergeant Fuller put a DVD into his portable player. "They're crooks and sell us pirated first-run movies."

"You sure don't sound too guilty about buying one for five bucks." Bobby Sand sat at the end of his cot.

"Five bucks?" Fuller guffawed. "You have much to learn. That's what they ask. Why give a sucker an even break? I tell 'em three, take it or leave it."

"But doesn't buying a pirated movie also make you a crook?"

"Listen, Mr. Goody Two-Shoes. Think of it as Hollywood supporting the troops by donating first-run movies." Fuller pointed at Bobby's DVD. "What do you got there?"

"It's the twenty greatest horror movies." Bobby held it up to him. "I got it out of the five-dollar bin at Walmart. I need something scarier than what happened today to free my thoughts. I'm going to watch Barbara Steele in *Black Sunday.*"

"Barbara Steele?" Staff Sergeant Garcia reached into his footlocker. "The British actress? She must be in an old folks' home by now. I got me a Jenna Jameson DVD, and she's a whole lot younger than Barbara Steele."

Sergeant First Class Mathews stood. "Well, Jenna Jameson had nothing on Barbara Steele in her day." He pointed at the DVD. "And those things are contraband. I can have you up on an Article 15 for possessing that."

"Do you wanna borrow it?"

"Sure." Sergeant Mathews grinned, took the pornographic DVD from Carlos, and plugged it into his DVD player.

Bobby Sand fell into a restive slumber while watching Barbara Steele's *Black Sunday*. Visions of the bleeding and dying Iraqi haunted him. His thoughts were like carrion birds, dragging him into the edge of sleep again and again.

Chapter 6

Trevor Brocton stood in front of his bathroom mirror. His reflection smirked back. '*Adele. I've caught bigger fish, but none more fun to reel in.*' He breathed through his nose, recalling the Chanel No. 5 perfume scent on her breasts and thought, '*tasty pair,*' before splashing Amouage cologne on his cheeks. He spotted a stray hair and plucked it. He held it to his eyes and smiled. "No gray." After applying L'Oreal Studio gel, Trevor combed and slicked back his hair, adding waves and a slight lift in the front. He brushed his teeth with Lebon Whitening toothpaste, lifted his lips, and examined his teeth like a horse trader. After applying La Mer Lip Balm, he chuckled at a memory of Jenny and Claudia telling him how Adele was taken, and therefore, he had no chance. He recalled Hank talking about working with her stuck-up sister, Erica. Trevor sniggered at recalling Hank telling him he wouldn't have any better luck with Adele than he did with her older sister. 'Stupid ass Lawyer.' He pictured Hank. '*Lazy sod. Your uncle is why Brocton Copper Works and Picardi Developments consult your law firm. How challenging was Jenny? A waitress at a tittie bar. Low-hanging fruit, good buddy. Remember Marilyn Monroe's line to her boyfriend's father from How to Marry a Millionaire?*' Trevor laughed. '*I don't want your son's money. I want your money.' That says it, young Henry. I got Adele on my own.*' A childhood memory of himself as a twelve-year-old made him laugh harder…He sat at the breakfast table with his ten-year-old brother, Edgar, and his nanny, Irma, in the family's San Francisco, *Pacific Heights,* mansion. His 81-year-old grandfather, Thomas Brocton Sr, was frail, even for a man his age. He sat at the head of the table, slack-jawed and staring blankly ahead. Trevor often overheard his parents saying, "*Senile old fart.*" "*Decrepit old bastard,*" and "*Why *can't he hurry up and go?" Most of all,* Trevor detested his grandfather's urine stench. He heard his parents talk about '*Depends.*' He learned enough Spanish to understand their Mexican servants when they complained, "*Odio tenor que limpiar su mierda.*"

"Grandpa, let me get you another glass of orange juice." Trevor stood and grabbed the orange juice pitcher. He stifled laughter as he reached into his pocket and snuck GoLYTELY, a powerful pharmaceutical-grade laxative solution, into his grandfather's glass. Trevor covered his mouth as his grandfather drank it. The next sound was louder than sitting on a whoopee cushion. The revolting stench further confirmed his ploy worked. Irma's ranting made him break out in laughter. "Get to work, bitch." He pointed at his nanny. "There's shit for you to clean." Edgar also guffawed. "Don't laugh too loud, little brother. I put some in your orange juice, too." Trevor laughed so hard he bent over while watching his younger brother hold his butt cheeks together with his hands while he staggered to the bathroom…

…Trevor grabbed his cellphone. "Claude. Is it ready yet…Great…I'll be over in an hour."

***

"What's up with you, Sandman?" SGT Fuller sliced his omelet into bite-sized chunks. "You haven't touched your breakfast."

"It's just that…"

"Oh, I get it." Fuller threw up his hands. "Guilt over killing that terrorist. Last night I stomped on a cockroach. Have I lost my appetite? Look, Sandman, the only good terrorist is a dead one. Madeleine Albright was responsible for killing 500,000 of them, and she said it was worth it."

"There's no way it was 500,000 combatants. Almost all were civilians, women and children."

"Women who give birth to future terrorists. Children who will grow up to be terrorists." SGT Fuller prodded. "And how do you know who is a combatant and who isn't? Those Tango bastards will strap a bomb to a baby to kill us."

"How do you know all of that, Fuller?" SSG Sand raised his open hands.

"I don't. But God does. That's why I say, kill them all. Let him sort out the rest."

"I don't know Chuck, but what about the mother of the man I killed? What if he had a wife? Children?"

"Look," SGT Fuller prodded. "Stop being a pussy. It's his wife or Adele. It's his mother or your mother. It's his kids or your future kids. You made America safer. You're helping to bring democracy," Fuller looked around before shielding his mouth with his hand and mumbling, "to the sand niggers. I know you're not a sissy, so be proud. Besides, I heard Whitehead put you in for a medal."

"Remember what happened to Eddie Slovik for refusing to fight." Garth Mathews folded his arms. "I'm just saying this for your own good. Today's Army won't put you in front of a firing squad, but they will lock you up before hitting you with a Dishonorable Discharge. After that, you're as good as dead. If you go out into the sector and don't fight back, the insurgents will shoot you. Eat up. We've got to clear Route Predator of IEDs today. "

"Matty is correct," SSG Garcia sipped his coffee, "If you won't shoot them, they'll shoot us. I don't want to die because you've become Mr. Nice Guy."

"Carlos has a point," SGT Mathews made a thumbs-up gesture. "Our lives depend on each other. You never had a problem shooting deer, and you always bagged more than I did. You're one of the best shots in the unit."

"Deer are a nuisance," Bobby replied. "They no longer have natural predators. They're overpopulated, run in front of cars, and cause accidents."

"Exactly." Chuck Fuller laughed. "Except that deer do it accidentally. The terrorists do it on purpose. That makes them a bigger nuisance. Rather a fender bender from a deer than getting blown to bits by a terrorist IED."

"Yeah, Sandman," Specialist O'Connor adjusted his glasses. "You're a baseball fan. I am too. Yet you're the only one who made money betting on the Marlins to win the World Series. It's like Leo Durocher said, 'Nice guys finish last.'"

"You are all correct. I am a soldier. I took an oath. I took their money to pay for my civil engineering courses at The Citadel. I know what I must do, and I'll do it. If not for my country, if not for you guys, I'll do it for Adele."

***

Adele ran hot water until her sink nearly overflowed. After soaking a towel in the piping hot water, she washed last night's makeup from her face. She glanced at the reflection of her bloodshot eyes, winced, and looked away. Her queasy gut made her bend over and brace her hands on her knees. "Forgive me, Bobby. Forgive me, God. It's not what I wanted. It's not my fault." She entered her bedroom, donned a bathrobe, and trudged into the living room.

Monica Beauchamp sat in a lounge chair watching a soap opera on TV. "Good morning, Adele." She turned to her younger daughter. "My goodness! Your hair! I've never imagined…It's beautiful. I love it. Who did it for you?"

"Just the usual beauty parlor at the mall." Adele covered her mouth and looked away.

"It's almost ten o'clock. Aren't you going to work today?"

"No." Adele sat on the couch next to her mother's favorite chair. "Mr. Haisley is out of the office. Nothing is going on. They won't miss me."

"You got a solid county job with good benefits, don't lose it."

"I won't, Mom."

Monica folded her hands. "I love having you keep me company, but I don't want you to get in trouble at work."

"I'll be fine." Adele smiled. "By the smell of things, Erica brewed us some coffee. I'm going to get a cup. Shall I pour you some?"

"Yes, please, Adele. Where were you last night? Bobby called. He had a terrible experience in Iraq. He needs you. He loves you, you know."

"I know." Adele turned away from her mother. "I love him too." Adele handed her mother a cup of coffee.

"Thank you, Adele."

Adele looked away from her mother. "You're welcome."

***

After stopping at fashion designer Claude Van Fleet's studio, Trevor Brocton looked at the MapQuest image on his phone. *'This must be it. Modest neighborhood. Modest house. Nothing modest about her sexiness.'*

Adele looked out of their living room window. She spotted a black 2003 Porsche Carrera GT pulling into their driveway. She gasped. Trevor disembarked. He held a white, rectangular box. Adele glanced at her mother, *'Sleeping,'* and snuck out the front door. She closed the door slowly and quietly, taking one last glance to ensure that her mother slept. "Trevor! You can't just up and come here."

"After last night's warmth in the back of the limo, I never expected a cold reception."

"About last night…I didn't want it. I'm engaged."

"You didn't want it?" Trevor chuckled. "You voiced no objections, at least not in words. Your moaning spoke volumes, and we did it twice."

Adele glanced at her reflection on Trevor's polished, ceramic-coated Porsche and smiled. "No, but it was wrong." Her smile faded.

"You're not into religion, so what's the issue?"

"You don't understand," Adele showed him her ring. "I'm engaged."

"If he came back tomorrow, would you be any different?"

"Now I'm the one who doesn't understand." She put her hands on her hips.

"You're not exactly damaged merchandise." He grinned. "If anything, the experience has made you more of a woman. You weren't a virgin before you and Bobby met. Hank and Jenny told me about Spike McClenahan. I had him investigated. They didn't find a lot of refinement in that one. So, what's wrong with you getting some enriching experiences to pass on to Bobby? Besides, I got something for you." Trevor put the package on the hood of his Porsche. He opened it and tossed the top aside. "Viola." He held a full-length silk dress in seafoam tones by its shoulders. It had a plunging neckline and delicate hand-embroidered pearl and crystal detailing around the cuffs and neckline.

"Huh," she covered her face. "It's beautiful. But…"

Trevor reached into the box and placed a wide-brimmed, straw hat on her head and oversized, rose-gold rimmed sunglasses over her eyes.

"What's with the hat and sunglasses?"

"You're going to need them where I am taking you," Trevor smirked and arched his eyebrows. "It's for an experience that you never dreamed possible and an opportunity that will never again come your way. I'm taking you out on the Brocton yacht. It's a seventy-foot Bennetti. The seas are calm today, and the weather's unseasonably warm. Come on." Trevor nodded at his Porsche. "Oh, by the way," Trevor stepped over to his Porsche and took a shoebox from the front seat. "You're going to need a little something for your feet." Trevor opened the shoebox, took out a white leather sandal, and showed it to Adele. "Top of the line Berkenstock."

Adele's jaw chattered; her head twitched. She looked back at her house. "My mother is sleeping."

"No need to wake her up. Everything you'll need is onboard. Besides, your sister will be home soon. She can mind your mother." Trevor opened his Porsche's passenger door.

Adele boarded his car.

***

Team Muttley led Team Black Mamba in a two-vehicle convoy down Route Predator. SSG Bobby Sand had his weapon locked and loaded. He had it pointed out his driver's window. "That's the spirit, Sandman." SGT Chuck Fuller aimed his loaded weapon at the pedestrians on the passenger side. "Kill a few more and you'll forget the one you wasted."

"Does anybody ever clean up these streets?" SSG Carlos Garcia aimed his M16 at vehicles in the oncoming lane. "An

IED can be hidden anywhere." Carlos tucked his rifle stock under his left armpit and pinched his nose. "I'll never get used to the stench of this place."

"All clear from up there?" SFC Garth Mathews looked up at Wayne O'Conner.

"All clear from up here. No IEDs."

"I hope all is clear at home, Sandman." Garth turned to Bobby. "Have you spoken to Adele?"

Bobby clenched the Humvee steering wheel and winced. "No. Every time I call, she's not home. I have spoken to Erica. She says all is well."

"As far as dealing with stress from the war, back in basic training, I used to picture the faces of my drill sergeants on the pop-up targets. Bam. Bam. I never missed. Now put Jody's face on the Tangos so you don't feel so bad about bumping them off."

"If she were seeing someone, Erica would tell me."

"Well, Spike McClenahan would make a great target." SFC Mathews shook his fist. "That hideous long hair and beard; his occult tattoos. No one would feel guilty about exterminating that one."

"Drill Sergeants? Spike McClenahan?" SGT Fuller aimed his weapon at the civilians. "McClenahan's an asshole, I agree. But Inez has never met the creep. The one making our lives miserable is Whitehead. I want his ugly face on a target."

"Come on, guys. McClenahan is in the past. Adele has matured since then. Besides, I kicked his ass and he's too much of a wuss to try me again. Erica also hates his guts. She will not let him come near their home."

"The law may sort him out before you come home on leave. I'm glad to be single and unattached. I don't have to worry about Jody." SFC Mathews cuffed Bobby's shoulder.

"Although, like I've said, Adele's sister Erica… she's someone you would never have to worry about." Garth smiled. "I know she's too busy caring for her mother to see anyone, so, when we get back, help me out there, good buddy."

"Stop!" SPC O'Connor yelled, "I see something! Straight ahead!"

Team Muttley and Team Black Mamba halted. SFC Mathews looked at the object in binoculars. "No question about it. That's an IED."

"Great job, O'Connor." Bobby looked upward. "You may have saved our lives. Okay everyone. We're going to back out of range before calling it in. Our radios may detonate it."

"Yeah." SSG Garcia covered his face. "Thanks."

After backing away from the IED. "As the driver, I get honors." Bobby grasped the handheld mic. "Get ready, everyone. I'm calling this into headquarters so they can alert other convoys and deploy the detonation team. Be aware, when I key the mic, it may make that thing blow sky high. Put in your ear protection and cover your eyes." He pushed the PTT button. They saw a flash and heard a deafening blast. The ground quaked as if a herd of sauropods stomped past; their Humvee rattled like an enraged diamondback. Despite the ear protection, all eight of Team Muttley and Team Black Mamba's soldiers' ears rang like the bells of Notre Dame.

***

Trevor reached out and held Adele's right hand. Her grip was cool and clammy. She carried a tote bag in her left hand as they walked along the docks of Safe Harbor, in Charleston City, South Carolina. A gentle breeze wafted in from the bay. Adele reached up and secured her new hat. She squeezed his hand upon gazing at the executive yachts.

"There she is." Trevor pointed at a seventy-foot boat. "The Copper Dream."

"Huh!" Adele gasped on seeing the sleek hydrodynamic yacht. Its tapered upper deck aesthetically blended with the stem, bow, hull, and main deck. "She's beautiful. Is that yours?"

"Sort of. It belongs to the company. My father has given me use of her and the crew for today, so you can say that she's mine. Look. The crew is greeting us."

Two young men and one young woman wearing blue and white uniforms topped by Sailor caps stood on the dock by the passerelle.

"Welcome aboard. I'm Captain Savagiou." A stout, white haired man waited in the yacht's main aft deck at the end of the retractable, teak passerelle. He tipped his peaked seafarer's cap to them.

"Thank you, Niko." Trevor took Adele's hand and helped her board the seventy-foot Bennetti yacht. "No change of plans."

"Aye, aye, sir. And my respects, madam." He nodded to Adele. "The seas are calmer in your presence." The captain departed for the yacht's bridge. The crew unhitched the yacht from its moorings.

"Come to the upper deck." Trevor led Adele by her hand up a flight of stairs. "It has our master state room. The deck is private from the crew. Here, you can change into your new dress." He led her into the stateroom. "I got you this to wear under your dress." He gave her a skimpy black bikini with gold frills. "It's unseasonably warm today. It will be even nicer once we get to the Gulf Stream. It will be your last chance until next Spring to get some rays and a tan."

Adele beamed while taking the upscale bathing garment.

"Well, aren't you going to change?" Trevor opened his eyes wide enough to raise his brow.

"Right now?" She brushed him off. "Shouldn't you give me some privacy?"

"I've more than just seen you before." He chuckled.

Adele shrugged before undressing. She donned her new two-piece bathing suit and wore her new silk dress over it.

***

Adele lay on top of a padded deck chair. She had taken off her silk dress and sunbathed in her revealing two-piece bathing suit. She raised her arms, lifting her breasts to absorb more of the mid-afternoon, late Fall sun. Trevor strolled over to her. He wore a red, silk bathrobe with a black monogram. He lit up a cannabis filled water pipe, inhaled deeply, and smiled at the Sun's reflection from Adele's body. He blew cannabis smoke in her face, awakening her from her daze.

"Woo," she brushed the smoke away.

He handed her the water pipe.

"No." She shook her right hand and her head.

"Nonsense. It's Super Silver Haze from California. I drive a brand-new Porsche, and now you're on a luxury yacht. Did you think I would smoke cheap stuff?"

"Now that I'm free of Spike and I'm with Bobby, I'm done with that stuff. Besides, it only makes me hack and wheeze."

"I learned more about Mr. McClenahan. He wouldn't know Super Silver Haze from a Swisher Sweet cigar. He wouldn't know a rowboat from a Bennetti Yacht. You went from an over-aged juvenile delinquent to a redneck who swapped his Boy Scout uniform for Army camo." He handed her the pipe. "Try it. Nobody ever OD'd on pot.

Adele glanced at Trevor, then at the water pipe. She inhaled deeply. "You're right, this is smooth."

"Don't stop now."

Adele took another hit. "Wow. Wow. Wowie. My head is spinning. I feel so lightheaded. I feel like I'm floating on air and at one with the waves below and sky above."

"Ahh…A perfect prelude to fine champagne." Trevor pulled a smoky black bottle from an ice jorum and poured champagne into crystal goblets. "So first we drink to a happy landing."

Adele took the glass of champagne from Trevor and perused the bubbles.

"Cheers. Adele. To us." He tapped her glass.

"To us." She tapped back before downing her champagne in one gulp. She lay back on her deck chair. "I think I just arrived in a fantasy land."

"You ain't seen nothin' yet. I had the captain turn the boat. We're facing west. We're beyond the horizon. Do you know what that means?

"No." She felt her brain swirl.

"We're going to enjoy watching the Sun set over the horizon."

"Oh my God! Yes! It's beautiful. I've never experienced anything like this. I remember Bobby describing the moon rise over the ocean as pouring melted butter on the ocean. This sunset is so much more. I see it opening like a treasure chest, spilling its gold on the sea."

"If not for me, you wouldn't be experiencing it. You're an East Coast gal stuck in your hometown. In my yacht, you get to be a California girl." He held her hand and watched the setting sun with her.

"It's breathtaking, Trevor." She turned and smiled at him. "It's absolutely breathtaking. Awesome! Thank you so much, Trevor."

Trevor stood and tilted his head. He curled his lips halfway and half-opened his eyes. He took off his robe.

Adele gasped at his erection. "No. No. Trevor. Not now. I'm still engaged."

Trevor straddled the deck chair, standing over her. He leaned over, pinned her shoulders to the deck lounger, and kissed her deeply. Adele's tongue remained flaccid for three seconds before fluttering with his. He mounted her. Earlier, he had Claude Van Fleet design her bikini with Velcro attachments. Adele didn't hear the Velcro '*Rrrrip*' over his grunts and moans. Trevor had disrobed her without hindrance or resistance. While he kissed her breasts, Adele opened her legs, allowing him to slide between them.

***

Erica walked through the front door of the Beauchamp residence. Monica sat in their living room chair. Her eyes were slit open, mouth slack. "Mother." Erica squeezed her bony shoulder. 'Are you okay?'

Monica opened her eyes fully. "Yes, Erica." She rolled her head. "The usual."

"Isn't Adele here? I see her car."

"I don't know, Erica. I'm sorry. She was still here when I dozed off."

"Did she at least leave a note?" Erica looked around the room. "Evidently not. I guess someone picked her up. You don't remember a car pulling up or someone knocking at the door."

"I'm sorry, Erica, it's just that I…"

"It's okay, Mom. Don't worry about a thing."

"It's not fair to you, Erica. This morning, Adele looked so pretty. She had a new hairdo with a lighter blonde tint. Please, Erica, take some time for yourself and stop spending all your money on me. I want you to look your best, too."

"It's all right, Mother. Always remember, what I do for you is out of love, and it's my pleasure. I would rather look after you than look at a mirror. Are you okay in that chair while I make us dinner?" The phone rang. "I'll get it, Mom. You stay put."

Erica put the phone receiver to her ear. "Bobby! It's you! How are you coping with what we talked about?"

"Coping is the word. I must put up a front for the team. You know Fuller. He's hard-core and gung-ho. He wants to kill them all. Carlos is afraid they all want to kill him. Wayne is too young and naïve to know what's going on. Matty is the most understanding. Still, I feel like a sissy for feeling guilty. They don't understand. I'm the only one to have actually killed someone."

"I can't begin to understand. But I am always here to listen. Why not talk with the chaplain?"

"I'll do that this Friday. Friday is like Sunday here. Erica, I think you can understand that soldiers' lives depend on each other. We still have no idea what the overall mission is. I can tell you right now. It's not to bring freedom to Iraq. We're shutting down newspapers and locking up all dissidents in Abu Ghraib prison. I heard rumors that Abu Ghraib is worse than when Saddam Hussein's henchmen ran it. How is any Iraqi a threat to you or the United States? They're six thousand miles away from the US East Coast. They have no Navy or Air Force. Even if they had the weapons of mass destruction Colin Powell talked about on TV, how are they going to deliver them? UPS? Fed-ex? Our mission is a day-to-day thing. Build something here; knock down something there; patrol for IEDs. Same shit, different day. This place is hideous. And you should get a load of Saddam Hussein's so-called palaces. They're what someone living in a single-wide in Adams Run who hit the Powerball would build. Huge, elaborate, garish, and without a shred of class. Iraq is scorching hot, and it stinks. All I want to think about is Adele. I love her so much. I live to come home to her. The uglier this place gets, the more beautiful she becomes. Can I speak to her?"

"I'm sorry, Bobby. She's not here. I wish she were. She would love to hear your sweet words. Is there any way for her to call you?"

"I'm afraid not. Where is she?"

"I don't know. She's probably working late or hanging out with Jenny and Claudia. I'll tell her you called."

"Tell her I love her. The soldiers behind me in line are getting impatient. I'd better go now. Bye."

Goodbye Bobby. I'll pray for you with Adele and my mother. Remember what the Lord says about two or more gathered in my name."

"Amen." Bobby winced and hung up the phone.

***

Trevor Brocton, wearing his silk red bathrobe, held both of Adele's hands. She was dressed in a pink evening gown. "Have you ever seen the stars so clearly? We're at least twenty miles from the nearest artificial light. Now it's just moonlight, starlight, and you." He turned and kissed her.

Adele returned his kiss. "It's lovely, but I must go to work tomorrow. I already no-called, no-showed today. I can't miss two days in a row unexcused."

"Relax. You can't get a signal from here even if you tried to call in."

"Maybe we should head back to shore," Adele pursed her lips. "I don't want to lose my job."

"We can't very well just head back at this hour. Besides, Dirty Old Man Haisley would never want to lose his eye candy." Trevor put his arms around her waist. "Have I not delivered on my promise of a once-in-a-lifetime experience?"

"Yes," Adele blushed, "You have. I've seen yachts like this before. Never have I entered one, and never did I dream of sailing in one."

"I bet you've dreamed of being with such a handsome captain," Trevor smirked. "But that was as a little girl watching an old Disney flick. Now you're a princess for real, and I'm the prince of your dreams."

"I know, babe, but I do have responsibilities."

"Nonsense, you sit in a cubicle with a boring county job and a dirty old man for a supervisor. A year of your pay couldn't lease a yacht and crew like this for half a day. Did you take any English lit courses in your community college program?"

"No. I studied marketing."

"Well, an English lit course would've introduced you to Oscar Wilde. His book, *A Picture of Dorian Gray,* has Lord Henry saying to Dorian, 'The best way to get rid of temptation is to yield to it. Resist it, and your soul grows sick with longing for the things it has forbidden to itself.'" Trevor led Adele by the hand to their stateroom. "From here, you can see the moon and the stars in bold display. The ocean's breeze is free of all automobile and factory emissions. Feel this." Trevor lifted the corner of the bed's sheet.

Adele rubbed it.

"It's genuine satin. I bet you never slept on satin sheets. It's yet another experience that only I can give you." Trever reached around Adele's neck and unfastened her evening gown. It fell to her feet.

Adele covered her breasts.

Trevor grabbed her wrists and pulled her arms to her side. He next untied the band around his robe and pulled it off his shoulders, letting it drop to the floor. Adele gasped at his erection. Trever pushed her onto the bed and mounted her.

"No. No." Adele squirmed. Three seconds later, she returned his kisses and held him tightly with all four limbs.

***

Bobby lay awake on his cot. The rest of Team Muttley were snoring. Anxiety tightened his nerves like piano wire. He felt atonal vibrations strumming his being. He pictured the man he killed and his plaintive blank stare as if asking, *'Why did you kill me?'* The Staff Sergeant mumbled aloud, "Because you tried to kill me first. We both had a job to do. I happened to be better at mine." Bobby rolled over on his side, *'Adele, Adele, I love you so much. I know you don't love me as much as I love you. Mr. Spock had a point, 'For the Vulcans, the act of mating is not just physical. It is the joining of two lives. One mates…and the other agrees? I feel like I am as far away as Planet Vulcan. When can I talk with you? Yet I trust you, and I know you're waiting for me. I will love you forever as your husband.'* Bobby at last could stroke away his anxiety. He fell into a restive sleep…

…Bobby saw himself walking through the wastes of Sadr City. Rather than a few bombed-out but otherwise functional structures, every building was destroyed. The remains of the apartment blocks, not reduced to rubble, were pointed and sharp, like icy penitentes. Debris splayed the ground. Smoke and fire rose from everywhere. A woman wearing a black niqab approached him. She doffed her head covering. Her skin looked like ashes. Her eye sockets were empty, their

blackness darker than an unlit cave. "Why did you take my son from me? I am going to take your first, unborn son in exchange." She growled and bared long, serrated, triangular teeth.

"No. No. Go away."

She lunged for him.

"In the name of Jesus, depart from me!"

The woman disappeared, yet Bobby remained trapped in his nightmare. Two little boys and one little girl wandered about aimlessly. "Daddy! Daddy! Where are you?" As the children drew nearer, Bobby saw that they were also missing eyes. Black lines were etched in their cheeks. Their clothing was tattered and worn. "Daddy?" The children ran to Bobby. "You're not our daddy! You killed our daddy!" The zombified children attacked him and bit chunks of flesh from his legs. Bobby kicked them away. He tried to scream out loud. His vocal cords remained paralyzed. An adult man appeared. He also had black holes for orbits. His cheeks were ashen and drawn. His shirt was fraught with blood and bullet holes. "Look at the Hell your country made of my city. The Hell you sent me to isn't much worse. Fire and waste. Fire and waste." He extended a shriveled, bony hand. "I don't blame you. I tried to kill you first. I expect a man to shoot back. Too bad for me, you were the better shot. Just like shooting deer, right? I'm not some ignorant savage. I was a man just like you. I was once a child. I saw the Bambi movie. Just like shooting deer, right? Only this time it was a human, and the children lost a father rather than a mother." The zombie stepped closer. "No hard feelings, Sergeant Sand. If you knew what your fiancé was up to, you would shoot yourself. You don't have to kill yourself to end your pain. Take my hand and join me in my netherworld. We'll go together as two warriors."

Just as Bobby was able to muster a scream, a mortar blast rocked their barracks. Garth, Wayne, Chuck, and Carlos sprang awake. SSG Garcia crawled under his bed. SGT Fuller opened the window and aimed his weapon out of it.

"Damn." SFC Mathews looked at his watch. "Three AM. Can't Tango wait until the chow hall is open?"

"That's another reason to kill them all." Chuck Fuller looked through his weapon's sight. "The sooner they're all dead, the sooner we can get a good night's sleep." He looked back at Bobby Sand. "I know you miss Adele. I miss Inez. I'm glad I married her before I left. At least if Tango takes me away from her, she'll be well off. Tango gets you, and Adele stays poor." Chuck grinned. "You got us off to a good start. Now let's kill some more and go home."

Bobby closed his eyes. *'What did he mean by, I'd shoot myself if I knew what my fiancé was up to?'*

***

Adele slept with her head on Trevor's chest.

"Wakey, wakey." Trevor nudged her awake. "Let's go on deck. We have a sunrise to watch." He held her hand and helped her out of bed.

Adele reached for her evening gown.

"Nonsense. Come as you are. It's a bit nippy, but I'll keep you warm. Don't worry, the crew is sound asleep." Trevor led her by the hand to the upper deck, into dawn's early light. "Here she comes."

"Huh…It's beautiful. I've seen sunrises but never like this." She smiled at Trevor. "The ocean, I've never seen a lovelier shade of blue, and the sun. It's a darker shade of gold. Thank you so much, Trevor." She kissed him, pushing her nipples into his chest.

"The crew is going to prepare us a better breakfast than you ever imagined." He looked into her eyes and smiled. "An Alaskan omelet and smoked salmon. Until then, I have the most delicious appetizer imaginable." He braced her shoulders and pushed her down, forcing her onto her knees. Gripping her hair, he pulled her head toward him.

Chapter 7

The Copper Dream's crew had lashed the yacht to its moorings. They extended the passerelle and waited on the dock. Adele wore her black silk dress with hand-embroidered pearl and crystal detailing around the cuffs, her wide-brimmed straw hat, and oversized sunglasses. She walked hand in hand with Trevor. He wore navy blue slacks and a navy blue jacket with oak leaf embroidery on the collar over an open white silk shirt. The crew stood at attention. Captain Savagiou saluted them. Trevor returned his salute.

"Thank you for everything, Captain." Adele and Trevor walked hand in hand on the dock, arriving at the parking lot ten minutes later.

"Well," Trevor took both of Adele's hands and faced her. "This is it. I wish I had the words to express how much I enjoyed my time with you." He embraced her and kissed her.

Adele returned his kiss with ardor. "What happened shouldn't have happened." She kissed him again. "But I'm glad it did."

"After the time we spent together, how can you say it shouldn't have happened?" Trevor smiled, placed his arms around her neck, and gazed into her eyes. "What is meant to be, will be, and we shouldn't try to stop it."

Adele held up her hand and showed him Bobby's engagement ring.

Trevor pulled the ring from her finger, put it in her hand, and squeezed.

Adele put the ring in her handbag.

Trevor walked her over to a waiting taxi. "This is goodbye." Trevor gave the driver a single currency note and told him Adele's home address.

"Aren't you going to drive me?" Adele put her hands on his shoulders and her forearms on his chest. She gazed plaintively into his eyes, "I want you to take me home in your Porsche."

"Hey," he grabbed her wrists and pushed her arms away. "I got a Copper smelting operation to run." He pecked her lips. "I'll give you a call."

***

Monica Beauchamp sat alone in a semi-stupor. A soap opera droned on her TV. Adele crept open the front door and walked on her toes past her mother. Monica snapped awake. "Adele! You're home. Where were you?"

"Nowhere, Mom."

"Nowhere? You were out all night, Adele. And those clothes? You didn't…"

"That was ten years ago, and I was only a teenager. They've expunged it from my record. I learned my lesson. Stop treating me like a child."

"Bobby called again. What do I tell him the next time you miss his call?"

"You let me worry about him." Adele put her hands on her hips. "I'll send him an Email."

"Your ring!" Monica gasped and pointed at her. "You're not wearing your ring."

"It's right here." Adele reached into her purse, pulled out her ring, and showed it to her mother. "I took it off for safekeeping."

"Bobby's a brave, hard-working man serving his country. Every moment, he's in grave danger. He deserves the best, and I know you can give him the best."

"Yes, Mom, we'll start over when he returns. What time is Erica getting off work? I'm starving."

***

Trevor drove his Porsche up to the security gate. He flashed his ID to the guard. "Good afternoon, Mr. Brocton." The guard waved him in.

The Brocton Copper Works offices were a two-story brick building separate from the plant. Trevor strolled in and sat on the receptionist's desk. "Any messages, Miss Moneypenny?"

"No, Mr. Bond." The receptionist chuckled. "Except that your father wants to see you right away."

"What can the old buzzard want this time?" Trevor stood, walked around the desk, and massaged the receptionist's shoulders. "I prefer spending time with a certain bird of paradise."

"Will you ever learn?" The receptionist held his hand. "I'm closer to your father's age than you." She chuckled. "But I accept your charm and flattery. Seriously, your father wants to see you right now. I can tell by his demeanor that he's serious."

***

Trevor flounced into his father's office. Thomas Brocton Jr. sat with his palms down on a battleship-sized, teak desk. Trevor had applied copious hair gel to ensure nary a single follicle strayed. His father's contrasting baldness made his head appear round. He wore half-eye, wire glasses low on his aquiline nose. He glanced at his son before burying his face in a folder. After placing the folder on his desk, he touched his fingertips and steepled his hands. "I hope using the company yacht helped you conquer your latest floozy. I tried to raise an executive. It looks like I got a shiftless

87

Playboy instead. While you were having fun at my expense, we failed to deliver our promised shipment of copper pipes to Picardi Developments. You told me the task was complete. I let you use my yacht as a reward." He prodded. "It's one thing to suffer a fuck-up. It's another thing to tolerate a liar. Even worse, you thought you could pull one over on me. You can't do it thinking with your big head, and you surely can't by using only your little head. Lie to me again, and you'll be homeless, as in living on the streets. I think you know I'm not bluffing."

"I'm sorry, Father." Trevor slumped his shoulders and lowered his head. "It's just that we own forty-eight percent of Picardi Developments. I told you we could short sell their stock and use outsiders to buy up enough shares to give us majority control."

"So," Thomas Brocton Jr. skewed his face, "you can run it?"

"Um," He bit his lips before flicking his tongue over them. "Yes."

"You know as much about the stock market and real estate as you do the dark reaches of a sphincter." His father scowled at him. "Your brother, Edgar, knows about that, seeing how my detectives caught him cruising the Castro District back in San Francisco." He tensed his lips and interlaced his fingers tightly enough to whiten his knuckles. "We don't need to talk about what I did about it. If you weren't the final Brocton, you'd be lucky to get a job stoking the furnace in my plant." He shook his head. "At least, you're good at wooing females. Well, it's high time you settle down with a real lady who can carry on the Brocton line, unlike the common sluts you pick up in bars. In which dive did you find your latest little conquest?"

Trever bobbed his head left and right. "Um…No…We didn't meet at a bar. I met her at Rosa's Cantina on King Street."

"A trendy bar where townie tramps hope to hook up with a rich yuppie. You're more than a yuppie. You're heir to Brocton Enterprises." The senior Brocton lowered his eyes. "For now, anyway." He paused for effect. "It's time you live up to my expectations, and that time is running short." He tilted his head. "You seldom demonstrate common sense. I hope this time you found enough sense to use protection. The last thing we need is for you to knock up some redneck slut. She'll take you to court and claw into the Brocton fortune by making you pay child support for her little hayseed/blue blood hybrid. Moreover, you want me to back your political ambitions. Fathering a bastard with one of your hussies will derail your political career before the engine even leaves the station. And it will scandalize the Brocton name!" He prodded at his son. "Did you use protection?"

"Um…Yes, Father." Trevor covered his mouth for a second and looked away.

The senior Brocton stayed silent, letting his son stew in shame. "I have cleaned up your latest mess. I made sure Picardi Developments received their shipment. You're dismissed. Get back to work." He waved his hand dismissively, shifting his eyes away from Trevor. "You have a lot of catching up to do."

***

The 878th CEBN stood in formation in front of their barracks. "Attention!" First Sergeant Martinez called the unit to attention. "Staff Sergeant Robert Sand. Front and center"

Bobby Sand pivoted an about-face, marched behind the unit, half-pivoted to the left, and marched forward before halting in front of Colonel Azshalt. He saluted. The commander returned his salute.

1SG Martinez read from a briefing. "SSG Robert Sand, on November 7th, 2003, at approximately 1100 hrs, while helping your unit build a soccer field in support of the 478th Civil Affairs Battalion, the 878th Combat Engineer Battalion came under enemy fire. SSG Sand, you rose above and beyond as a soldier. You proved your willingness to sacrifice your life on behalf of your fellow soldiers, your unit, and your country. Out of courage and valor, you gallantly returned enemy fire and eliminated an enemy of freedom, an enemy of your unit, and an enemy of the United States of America. For your uncommon dedication to duty to the United States Army, you are hereby awarded an Army Commendation Medal with a 'V' for valor."

Colonel Azshalt pinned the medal on SSG Sand's chest. SSG Sand saluted his commander. Colonel Azshalt returned his salute.

***

Adele Beauchamp sat in her cubicle at the Charleston County Planning and Zoning Department. Her stomach was a chrysalis of anxiety. She wore a cotton, low-cut blouse. She unfastened the top two buttons and sprayed Chanel Number 5 perfume on her cleavage. Her phone rang. The moment she dreaded had arrived. She put the receiver to her right ear. Before she could speak, she heard Malcolm Haisley's monotonic voice, "Miss Beauchamp. Come see me in my office." The Chrysalis of her gut burst into a swarm of butterflies.

Walking to her office, she wished a chaplain accompanied her. Old Sparky waited behind the next door.

***

Malcolm Haisley adjusted his glasses on his snub nose. Although his eyes were sunken and rheumy with age, they still managed to glint. He was not looking at her forehead.

Adele felt like Atlas relieved of carrying the world on his back. Her crimson fingernails subtly opened her hem another quarter of an inch. The butterflies fluttered out of the office window.

He tapped the greasy follicles covering his bald pate and licked his lips. "Miss Beauchamp, I have no choice but to address your lack of attendance. Last month, I gave you three days off to see your fiancé off to Iraq. It was the least I could do for you and our country. Unfortunately, you took an extra two days off without calling in." For the first time, he made eye contact with Adele.

She fluttered her eyelids and flicked a lock of blonde hair over her shoulder.

"Um…Yes…Miss Beauchamp." The lines around his mouth deepened. "An unexcused no-call no-show is a terminable offense. And you did it two days in a row." A draft blew toward him. He twitched his nose and imbibed Chanel Number Five; the fragrance drew his eyes to the source. His heart's lub dub cadence beat loud enough for Adele to hear. "It's not just that the office needs you." He wiped a sweat bead from his right temple. "We were worried about you. You either didn't answer your phone, or you turned it off."

"I had no signal. Otherwise, I would've called you."

"Where were you?"

Adele pictured last night's sunset. "Um…Uh…I was attending to my mother in the hospital." Adele covered her face and looked away. "Yes…Um…We had no signal. I was too worried about my mother to call you."

"Yes. I know your mother suffered a stroke, and it's demanding to care for her. And how is your sister coping?"

"She wasn't there." Adele furrowed her brow. "I had to fill in for her."

"That doesn't sound like Erica." Malcolm Haisley picked up a pen. "At the very least, I should give you a written reprimand. Taking care of your ailing mother is understandable and excusable. I do need you to sign this. It is only a counseling statement. It won't go in your personnel file. It's just for me to cover myself. All it says is that I spoke to you about your absences."

As Adele bent over to sign the counseling statement, Malcolm stared at her buttocks. His bony arm crept out to pat it. *'No. No. I can't.'* He retracted his empty hand.

Chapter 8

Adele walked through her front door. Erica and Monica were seated at the kitchen table. "I'm glad you could make it home in time for dinner." Erica smiled at her sister. "I made chicken cacciatore."

"It's not Labrador House of Seafood," Adele chuckled. "But it will do."

"When did you ever eat at the Labrador House of Seafood? On our salaries?" Erica laughed. "I'm afraid I'll go broke just smelling their fare from the sidewalk." She glanced at her sister and raised an eyebrow. "I'm thankful for what God has provided. Have a seat, Adele. I kept it warm for you." Erica walked over to the stove.

"You got a letter from Bobby." Monica's arm jittered as she held the letter toward Erica.

"I'll read it after I change." Adele raised her hands.

Erica glared at her sister, took the letter from Monica, and shoved it into Adele's hands.

Adele was taken aback, but upon seeing the seriousness in her sister's expression, she tore open the letter and read it as she walked to her bedroom.

My dearest Adele,

I cherish every rare second of time and solitude that enables me to dream of you and express my love for you in words. The stench of death is thick enough to cut with a knife. Yet with you in my heart, I have never felt so alive. I love you, Adele. I love every thought of you. Each memory of your voice plays like a symphony. Your picture is the silence before the strings. I worship the ground you walk on, for I know that Heaven has blessed your steps. I pray that each step you take brings you closer to my loving arms.

Adele folded the letter, winced, and looked upward. She walked into her bedroom and placed the letter on her vanity table. Her cellphone rang in her purse; she opened her purse and saw that it sat next to her engagement ring. After a deep breath, she grabbed the phone and looked at the screen. *'Trevor.'* Closing her eyes, she looked upward. "Oh God, what should I do?" She squeezed her phone so hard that it vibrated her metacarpal bones. She imagined Bobby driving his 1996 Ford F-150 pickup truck before picturing him fishing in Garth Mathew's bass boat. Her vision shifted to Trevor's 2003 Porsche Carrera GT and his family's yacht. She looked into her open closet and spotted her new clothes. She opened her phone. "Hello, Trevor."

"Well, hello, Adele." He laughed. "I hope you haven't eaten yet. I've hired Takumi Kawasaki, an acclaimed Japanese chef. He's going to cook us dinner before our eyes. Shall I pick you up in about an hour?"

"I don't know Trevor. My sister is home, and my mother is awake. I can't just walk out dressed in the fancy clothes you bought me."

"Come as you are. I've bought you something just for the occasion."

"You bought me another outfit?"

"Yes."

Adele looked at Bobby's letter. She pursed her lips and paced back and forth. "Meet me again at the Lee Street Walmart. Erica and my mother better not see me get into your car." Adele laughed. "Especially not one as fancy as a Porsche."

"It's more than just a Porsche. It's a 2003 Porsche Carrera GT."

Adele grabbed her purse and strolled past Erica and Monica without looking at them. "Sorry, Jenny and Claudia invited me to dinner on King Street. They're picking up the check. How can I say no?" She opened the door slowly and closed it carefully behind her.

"I don't know how to say this." Monica put her elbows on the table and locked her fingers. "I sensed something suspicious in how your sister left. Do you think she's really just meeting Jenny and Claudia, or do you think she's up to something?"

"You never can tell with her." Erica sat next to her mother. "She's always had an independent streak; she's been a free bird for a long time now."

"But she's no longer free. She has Bobby, and he's a good man. Adele is beautiful like you and can attract them. And, in the case of Spike, sometimes like poo attracts flies, but Bobby is a keeper. Is what you call independence a good thing? She lives under my roof, and you cook her meals. She hardly helps at all while you're sacrificing your life for me." Monica closed her eyes and lowered her head. "Maybe it's time for me to check out and ascend to the top of the stairs. You deserve better. Besides, I miss my husband."

"Please don't say that." Erica squeezed Monica's hand. "We've discussed this before. I love caring for you. You have a lot of life left in you. We'll enjoy every moment. I know that's what Dad would want."

"The phone is ringing." Monica lowered her hands. "Can you get it?"

"Hello," Erica wedged the receiver between her ear and shoulder. "Bobby!" She held the receiver in her mother's direction.

"Hi Bobby!" Monica shouted from across the room.

"I'm sorry, Bobby." Erica fidgeted with the phone cord. "Adele is not here. You just missed her. She's meeting Jenny and Claudia."

"Oh, no. It's a seven-hour time difference. I couldn't sleep. We aren't supposed to leave the barracks after dark, but I just had to hear Adele's voice."

"I don't blame you. She sounds as lovely as she looks. Stay safe, Bobby. She misses you as much as you miss her."

"If I try to stay too safe, I'll get court-martialed." Bobby laughed. "We're at war, so it's danger at every turn. But I'll do everything possible to make it less dangerous. I have Adele and our future children to consider."

"Yes. Of course. I know your future mother-in-law," Erica smiled and turned toward Monica, "can't wait to have grandchildren running around the house. How are your parents doing?"

"Other than always worrying about me, they're coping just fine."

"I'll tell you what, Bobby." Erica smiled at her mother. "I'll cook up some food to go, take my mother with me, and pay them a visit."

"You would do that for me?"

"Of course, Bobby. We're about to be family. Oh, I ran into Sergeant Fuller's wife, Inez, at Walmart. She invited us over. How is Chuck doing?"

"He's often on edge and wants to shoot anything that moves. He's gung-ho and mission-oriented to say the least. Send Inez my regards. I hope Adele will join you. Inez is a good influence."

"That goes without saying. I'm sure Adele will be happy to join us."

"I worry more about Adele than I do my own life."

"Worry no more, I'll take care of my sister. You take care of yourself and your unit."

The next sound was a boom. The phone went blank.

"Bobby? Bobby?" Erica winced and hung up the phone.

***

Trevor and Adele zipped along I-26. "Shouldn't you slow down?" Adele glanced at the speedometer. "You're driving faster than 90."

"Are you kidding me? This baby is built to do 205 on the autobahn. I'd go faster, but American highways suck."

"Aren't you worried about speed cops?"

"Why should I?" Trevor smirked. "I'm a Brocton. Our copper smelting plant is a major employer. Even if a cop doesn't recognize the name, we can easily fix the ticket."

Trevor drove off the highway at exit 221, soon reaching Wentworth Street in downtown Charleston. Five minutes later, he turned onto the Wentworth Mansion driveway.

"Trevor," Adele pointed ahead. "That's the Wentworth Mansion. It's the most expensive hotel in town. I thought you were taking me to your home and introducing me to your parents."

"My father is all work and no play. He's a dull boy. My mother is on the dowdy side. I figure the Wentworth Mansion is more your speed." Trevor held Adele's hand. "Besides, I booked us the Grand Mansion Suite."

***

Bobby returned from the phone room and lay awake on his cot. He stuffed plugs into his ears to drown out Chuck, Carlos, Wayne, and Garth's snoring and the roar of helicopter engines and rotors. He glanced at their alarm clock. *It's 0330 hours. Why wasn't Adele home to take my*

97

call? She's never home when I call. The chow hall opens in a couple of hours. Why bother sleeping?' He closed his eyes and pictured Adele. 'I love you, Adele…Don't worry, baby…I'll get my leave soon…Adele…Adele…Wait for me…' Bobby fell into a fitful sleep…

…He strolled into his Charleston apartment's bedroom: the last place he made love to Adele before getting deployed. She stood by his bed, waiting for him. Wearing the same faded blue jeans and tight white blouse, she had the same hairstyle as in their last moments at Pope Air Force base. 'Was it only weeks ago? Adele, Adele, it feels like forever. I love you so much.'

Adele smiled and walked over to him. 'I love you too, Bobby. Forever.'

Bobby closed his eyes and breathed deeply through his nose. He opened his eyes. Adele now wore a black velvet, 17th-century aristocratic, Italian-designed gown. Its bodice was fitted and severe with a high neck. A black veil covered her face. The effect was a combination of wedding and funeral. She now seemed taller and slimmer. She lifted the veil. Her skin was luminous and pale, while her hair, black as Onyx, flowed down her back. Her eyes were huge and expressive, with dark, arched brows that intensified her gaze. Yet long lashes gave her eyes a haunted, doe-like quality. She stepped toward him with ethereal steps; her gown whispered as her movements dragged it on the floor. "You're…You're…Not Adele…Who are you?"

"Adele is with whom you American soldiers call 'Jody.' I was the wife of the man you killed." She prodded. "I am here to mourn my former husband and to marry my new husband."

"I don't know you, and I don't know of what you speak."

"By the rules of warfare dating back for centuries, I am your spoils of victory. I am now your wife." She pointed at him. *"I must obey you. You may take me.'* Her gown fell to her ankles.

Bobby stared. *Her naked body was no longer a source of fear, but desire. It was not gym-honed like Adele or her friend Jenny, but had the allure of a classic Hollywood film siren or pre-Raphaelite painting. Her oval, sharply defined face went from severe to delicate. 'I love Adele's cute celestial nose...but her straight nose is classical, just prominent enough to add character and severity to her beauty. Her arched eyebrows added intensity to her gaze...she's smiling at me with full lips. They're slightly parted. Oh God, forgive me, I want to kiss her.'* She flicked her thick black tresses. She raised long, feminine arms to embrace him.

'No. No. God help me, I can't. I can't.' *"No!"* Bobby prodded. *"You stay away from me!"*

She flounced over and hugged him, rubbing her breasts against his pectorals. His heart paused, and his mind went blank. Out of carnal instinct, he kissed her, scooped her up with an open hand on her soft yet firm buttocks, and cradled her. They continued kissing, their warm breath mingling. He placed her on his bed. He entered her. Her face aged with each stroke until it turned ashen and layered like an abandoned hornet's nest. Worms crawled out of her empty eye sockets. Her lips were gone; her teeth were two-inch daggers, sharp and curved. "No!" He screamed and backfisted her head. It burst into a pile of ashes and dust. Cockroaches and centipedes scuttled from the stump of her neck. "No!" Bobby managed to scream aloud. He sat up on his bed and muttered to himself. "I'm sorry, Adele. I'm Sorry. I'm sorry."

"What the fuck, man?" Carlos sat up in his cot. "What's the big idea of waking us up?"

"What are you complaining about, Garcia?" SGT Fuller got out of bed and secured his weapon. "You have nightmares every night."

"Fuller's right, Carlos." SFC Mathews sat up and swung his legs over the edge of his cot. "You woke us up the other night. So, give it a rest. Besides, the Army includes nightmares in the tour package."

"Thanks, Sandman." Wayne O'Connor stood up. "You did us a favor by waking us early. The Dirty Bird Café is already open. You gave us more time to chow down. After all, today we have to finish what a cruise missile started. Blow up a building."

***

A uniformed bellhop dressed in exaggerated formality like an *Alice in Wonderland* Palace guard unlocked the door. He stood aside and gestured toward the room. "Proudly presenting the Wentworth Mansion's most esteemed room. The Grand Master Suite." The bellhop stood with raised open palm. Trevor and Adele marched past him. Trevor closed the door behind him.

"Oh my God!" Adele covered her mouth. "It's beautiful. I've never seen anything like it. It even has chandeliers and stained glass."

Those are original Italian chandeliers and authentic Tiffany-stained glass. Mother Nature keeps smiling at us. She gave us an unseasonably warm day to take you out on my yacht. Now she has given us a cold day. Perfect for this. Viola!" Trevor lit a floor-to-ceiling marble gas fireplace. "First, you'll need to change for dinner."

"Are we going out?"

"No. We'll eat right here. But not something so vulgar as room service. I promised you a Takumi Kawasaki-cooked meal, and that is what you're getting. First, you must dress appropriately. It's waiting for you on our bed."

Adele walked into the bedroom. *'Our bed?'* She opened a white rectangular box sitting on the bed. "Huh!" She gasped as she pulled the garment from the box. *'It's gorgeous!'* Five minutes later, Adele emerged from the bedroom. She wore a pink silk kimono with a sable fur collar. "I love it, Trevor." She folded her arms across her chest. "I utterly and totally adore it."

They heard a knock on the door. "Come on in."

The bellhop ushered in a Japanese man in his early forties. He wore crisp whites with a black waist apron embroidered with red Japanese lettering. The bellhop pushed a silver cart.

The bellhop held open his palm. Trevor ignored him. After putting his hands on his hips, the bellhop scowled at Trevor before marching from the room.

"Mr. Kawasaki," Trevor bowed. "Welcome. Here is the lovely lady for whom you will prepare dinner." He gestured toward Adele.

Takumi Kawasaki bowed to her. "Okusama ni omenikarete koei desu. Maru de kisetsu no utsoroi o utsushita yona, utsukisa o omochi desu ne. It is an honor to meet you, Madam. You possess a beauty that reflects the changing of the seasons."

Adele blushed, glanced at Trevor, and bowed to the chef.

Chef Kowasaki set up his teppanyaki grill. He cut beef into wafer-thin slices with the speed and precision of a magician. He added prawns and noodles, took two spatulas, and tossed the mix skyward. He caught it midflight, returned it to the teppan, and added a precise measure of soy sauce, garlic butter, sesame oil, and mirin. He flipped and stirred the blend. The chef held up his spatulas like a painter with his brushes, showing off his masterpiece. He bowed to

Adele. She applauded. Takumi Kawasaki added onions. He piled them like a volcano. He swept his hands behind his back and emerged with a silver rod lighter. He ignited the onions. It erupted like a volcano.

"Oogh!" Adele beamed and shook her hands.

The chef adroitly scooped up the flaming meal and placed it on Trevor and Adele's plates. Trevor took the lead and blew out the flames. They applauded as the chef smiled and bowed.

***

After dinner, Trevor changed into a white bathrobe with gold frills on the collar. "The dinner was only the first course. Come." Trevor led her by the hand to a spacious bathroom. A two-person hot tub awaited, steaming and bubbling. Trevor doffed his bathrobe. He placed his hands on Adele's shoulders and kissed her before grasping the kimono and pulling it off her, letting it drop to her ankles. He stepped into the hot tub and took Adele's hand. She stepped into the tub and lay back, resting her head on a vinyl pillow. Trevor mounted her. As they made love, her moans were louder than the roiling water.

***

Team Black Mamba led Team Muttley down Route Predator. SSG Garcia looked up at SPC O'Connor. "You'd better keep a good lookout. We're carrying enough C4 explosive that an IED will blast us to the four winds."

"And speaking of winds," SGT Fuller scowled at SSG Garcia and pinched his nose. "Fart again and we'll wire you to the explosives. You're filing this Humvee with enough methane that Tango won't need an IED to blow us sky high."

"You sure had a doozy of a nightmare last night." SFC Mathews adjusted the SINCGARS (Single Channel Ground and Airborne Radio System). "Was it anything Adele said?"

"No." Bobby tensed his lips. "She wasn't home. I did speak to Erica."

"Did you put in a good word for me?"

"No. Sorry. You didn't come up."

"Hey, Sandman!" SSG Garcia's hands jittered. "Keep your eye on the road. The insurgents are bad enough without you crashing us."

"Yeah, well, Fuller's right about your farting, Garcia. Baghdad's sewage and garbage are bad enough without you conducting chemical, biological warfare against your own team." Bobby quickly glanced back. "And Fuller, Erica has only good reports on Inez. It seems you don't have to worry about Jody."

"Who says I'm worried about Jody? She answers the phone every time I call her, and I make sure it's not always at the same time." Fuller aimed his weapon at a passing Iraqi. "Have you spoken to Adele?"

Bobby grimaced and gripped the steering wheel tight enough to turn his knuckles white.

"All you suckers worrying about Jody," Carlos laughed. "No worries from me. My gal is safely secured in my footlocker. Miss November is my kind of girl."

"You said that last month about Miss October." Garth glanced back at Carlos.

"Yeah, but Miss November is perfect. Miss October had a staple scar."

"Up ahead." SSG Sand pointed with his right forefinger. "That's the building headquarters wants us to turn to rubble, as if it's not already demolished enough."

Teams Muttley and Black Mamba pulled up to what was once a government building, now a cruise missile-blasted shell. The boxy building had its west side blown away. Jagged steel rebar jutted from concrete chunks. SSG Sand climbed out of the Humvee. "First, we have to clear the building of any people."

"You got that right." SSG Garcia stood beside the Humvee. "It looks like sniper heaven to me."

"I'll go in with you, Sandman." SGT Fuller walked over to Bobby. "If an enemy sniper is hiding inside, he'd better come out with his hands up or it's frontier justice, baby." Fuller pointed his weapon at the building.

SSG Sand and SGT Fuller slipped into the building, weapons drawn. Bobby and Chuck crept up to the end of a hallway and paused at an opening to a large chamber. Bobby peered around the edge. Three seconds later, he signaled all clear to SGT Fuller. Four seconds after entering the open space, they heard muffled noises coming from behind a door. SGT Fuller grit his teeth and nodded. He kicked open the door. SSG Sand followed. Two men were sitting around a hookah pipe. "Hayya!" They both leaped to their feet, drew jambiya daggers, and charged them.

SGT Sand, his weapon on semiautomatic, fired one round into the taller man. Before he could acknowledge the thud and blood on his chest, he collapsed on the floor. Lifeless. SGT Fuller had his weapon on burst. He sprayed bullets at the shorter man. Blood pools sprouted from his right arm, left shoulder, right rib cage, and left pelvic area. He lay on the floor muttering, "Law samaht. Law samaht."

Bobby gazed into his eyes. He remembered the first time he shot a deer. The Iraqi's dark eyes had the same glazed, helpless look as the wounded, dying deer.

"Law samaht. Law samaht."

SGT Fuller walked up to him. "Law samaht, my ass. My president says you hate us because of our freedom and prosperity. Here's some American prosperity, thirty-five cents at a time." Sergeant Fuller shot three rounds into his torso at close range.

The impact slid the Iraqi back two feet. He lay lifeless: eyes open, jaw slack.

Bobby Sand looked at Fuller with raised eyebrows, widened eyes, and slightly open mouth. "Why did you do that? You just violated Article Three of the Geneva Convention."

"Are you a soldier or a gawd-damned lawyer? We're fighting for freedom here, while back home, the fucking lawyers are taking away our freedoms. Too bad we can't also shoot all the lawyers. Look, Sandman," Fuller prodded. "You're a hunter. You know that the most dangerous animal is a wounded animal, so what I did was no war crime but a necessary act of self-defense." Fuller pointed his weapon at the dead combatant. "Besides, to quote Darwin, any creature who brings a knife to a gunfight deserves extinction. Moreover, why take medical care from an American soldier for a stupid bastard who tried to kill us?"

Bobby blanched at the dead bodies.

"I must say," Fuller lowered his weapon and slapped Bobby's right arm, "you're a hell of a shot. You finished him with one round. I needed extra bullets to finish the job." Fuller grinned. "Another dead body, another medal. By the time our deployment is over, your uniform is going to look like a fricken Christmas tree. I hope Azshalt gives me my medal and not Whitehead."

"You sound like Muttley begging Dastardly for a medal. Let's tag these stiffs and get out of here. We got a building to blow up."

SFC Mathews, SSG Garcia, and Team Black Mamba's five soldiers met SSG Sand and SGT Fuller at the entrance. "What happened?" SFC Mathews asked.

"Just removing some bio-garbage." SGT Fuller smiled. "We tagged them for the trashmen."

"Yeah, you got a couple of KIA combatants, like Fuller said, we searched and tagged them." SSG Sand nodded. "Come on. We came here to demolish a building. Let's do it."

***

Trevor helped Adele out of the whirlpool tub. He dried her by rubbing her with a Turkish cotton bath towel.

"Mmm…Is it the towel that's so comfortable or the hands behind it? "Mmm…Yes." She moaned as he pressed his body to hers from behind and dried her breasts. Once dry, he helped her into a white bathrobe. He put his arms around her and kissed her.

"I loved making love to you." She pecked his lips. "But I do have to get home. I have work tomorrow. I got in trouble today. I can't count on Old Man Haisley's lust bailing me out forever."

"You're putting that sleazy old bastard and your low-paying job above me and what I can offer?"

"You're spending so much money on me." She pressed her clothed breasts into his pectorals and gazed into his eyes. "I just wish we could spend some of it on my mother's care. I'd love it if you could buy her something. She had a debilitating stroke, you know?"

"Stop worrying. You said your sister has it taken care of." He took her hand and walked her to the platform bed.

"Sometimes I think it's unfair that I'm always leaving Erica alone with our mother."

"Since when is life fair? Your friend Jenny's new boyfriend, Hank Sawyers, works with your sister. He told me she's a stuck-up bitch. Furthermore, he told me that Claudia also doesn't like her. I know. Hank's law firm consults Brocton Copper Works. Moreover, Jenny told Hank that your mother always favored Erica over you. So, let her have first prize. Let me show you part of your grand prize." He lifted the duvet. "Just like the yacht. Satin sheets." In one motion, he pulled the duvet from the bed. Next, he untied the waistband of Adele's bathrobe and pulled it apart. She shimmied her body to remove it. He spread his bathrobe and pressed his pectorals to her naked breasts and his pelvis to hers. He raised her chin with his right forefinger and delicately kissed her lips.

"Oh, Trevor." She could hear her heartbreak. "I think that I'm falling, falling in…"

"Shh…" He put his forefinger over her lips. He kissed her deeply before scooping her up and placing her on the bed. He lay on top of her. "I take it we're spending the night together." Narrowing his eyes, he grinned with the left side of his mouth. "Now for your grand prize."

Adele hugged him and wrapped her legs around him.

***

"Speed it up, Sandman." SSG Garcia jutted his head between the front seats. "The Dirty Bird Café is closing soon."

"Shut your mouth, Garcia," SGT Fuller scowled at him, "I'll tell you what, if we miss dinner at the Dirty Bird Café, we'll give you first choice of MRE."

"And I'll tell you what, Fuller." SSG Garcia elbowed Chuck in the ribs. "In gratitude for your generosity, I'll leave the good MREs to you. I'll take the chili con carne."

"You two fight it out alone. I'll drop you guys off at the Dirty Bird Café and take care of the vehicle. I can't think of food right now. I am only thinking about calling Adele."

***

After turning the Humvee into the motor pool, Bobby ran to the phone room. He punched in 011-854 before the Beauchamp's local number. He closed his eyes, tightened his lips, and looked upward. "Please, Adele. Be there."

The receiver clicked on the sixth ring. "Hello."

"Erica. You answer every time I call." He forced himself to chuckle. "I know your voice by heart. It's Bobby, calling from Iraq. Please tell me that Adele is home."

"I'm sorry, Bobby. She's out. I would be happy to leave her a message."

"No, Erica. This is serious. Shit is happening fast in this hellhole. I love Adele so much. I need to connect with her, Erica." Bobby closed his eyes and pursed his lips. "I killed another man today. I had no choice. Two men charged at me and Fuller with knives."

"Bobby. It was self-defense. Remember what Jesus said about the Roman Centurion. You're a soldier and a good one."

"Yeah, I know, and I believe in Jesus. But I keep asking myself, would they have tried to kill us if we didn't invade their country first? 'W' and the media sold this as a war of liberation. That's an even bigger lie than the weapons of mass destruction. We're here as occupiers. Who benefits? I don't know."

"Bobby, listen to me. The Romans were an occupational force in Judea at the time of Christ. They occupied Jesus's own country and his own people. Roman soldiers didn't benefit. Only the Roman wealth and power elite benefited.

Yet Jesus regarded Roman soldiers as professionals and worthy of forgiveness and salvation. Remember how he praised the faith of the Centurion? The Romans did some brutal things to the Judeans. On the other hand, they did improve their infrastructure, and their presence lowered crime. Serve honorably, and the good will outweigh the bad. So, keep the faith, Bobby. May God protect you and bring you home to Adele safely. I hope to have little nieces and nephews."

"It's not that, Erica. The problem is that I feel no guilt. What is coming over me? Has the Army finally succeeded in turning me into a remorseless killer? How do I deprogram myself from this when I get home? You're friends with Fuller's wife, Inez. You shop at Walmart together. I can imagine Chuck going into Walmart and spotting someone a hundred pounds overweight, with purple hair, covered in tattoos, and wearing revealing pajamas. I never imagined it before getting sent to this place, but now I can picture Chuck pulling out his Glock and blowing her away, thinking he's taking out the garbage. I know how I feel when someone cuts me off in traffic. Will I snap, kill someone, and catch a life sentence? It's good that you had dinner at Inez's house. Why you and not Adele? Anyway, Fuller only wounded his assailant. He begged for mercy. Fuller seemed to enjoy finishing the job. Fuller went bass fishing with Garth and me once. He was never like that. I mean, the man caught a two-pounder and released it, and he never accepted our invitation to go deer hunting. He even rescues opossums and raccoons. I get it—Fuller's right. A wounded animal is a dangerous animal. I'm a deer hunter. Am I now supposed to view human beings as game?"

"No one who isn't in your situation will ever understand, no matter how many fancy degree letters follow their name. I am here to listen to you and pray with you. Make an appointment with the chaplain. See if he will join us in a call. Give me the time, and we can all pray together."

I appreciate that you care, Erica. I really do." Bobby fidgeted with the phone cord. "But you're my future sister-in-law. I've been here for how long? I seldom get to speak with my fiancé. I need to express my love to her and feel her love in return. It's the only way I can cope with the hate."

"Don't worry, Bobby. She loves you. She got your letter and was deeply touched. "I'll tell her you called and explain your situation. I'll make sure she understands."

"Thank you so much, Erica. I love her so. Well, the other soldiers are lining up for their turn at the phone. I'd better go."

***

Trevor awoke first. He reached over and grabbed Adele's phone. '*Perfect. It's not locked.*' With a tight-lipped smile and narrowed eyes, he disabled the alarm feature. '*Uh oh. Sun glare.*' He strolled to the windows and closed the shades and curtains. '*She's still sleeping.*' He went to the bathroom and combed his hair with gel, leaving not a single follicle out of place. After brushing his teeth, he raised his lips and examined them like a horse veterinarian. He stood back from the mirror, turned, and patted his waist. '*Flat as always.*' Trevor returned to bed and lay beside her. He looked at the ceiling and grinned.

***

Adele awoke and turned to Trevor. He was looking upward. "Trevor."

He turned to her. "Well, good day, my morning glory." He pecked her lips.

110

Adele laced her arm around him and kissed him with an open mouth. "Hmm…What a way to start the day. But I'd better brush my teeth, so I taste better. You taste delicious as always." She climbed out of bed and took her cellphone from the nightstand. "Oh my God! It's ten-thirty! I'm so late for work."

"Relax. Breakfast is open until eleven-thirty. You'll find their smoked salmon, Austrian sausages, and Omelets made to order, along with fresh fruit and a flute of orange juice mixed with champagne, much better than an egg McMuffin on the run."

"But Trevor. My job."

"If the Chanel number five I bought you, along with what God gave you, did the trick yesterday, it will again on Monday."

"I'd better at least call in."

Trevor reached out, took Adele's phone from her, and closed it. "Oh, come on, my angel of the morning. Haisley's the devil of the afternoon. You think a dirty old bastard like him ever changes? Today is Friday. Enjoy a three-day weekend. We'll stop at the clothier on the way back. If Haisley wants to cause trouble, I'll buy you something that will stop him in his tracks. I have the room until tonight. They have an indoor pool with tropical plants. Isn't that better than your cubicle?"

"Yes…But…"

"But nothing." Trevor glanced at his Rolex Datejust 41 watch. "Shall we make love before or after breakfast."

"Huh…Well, I need to shower first."

"Perfect." Trevor stripped off his bathrobe, took Adele's hand, led her to the shower, and joined her.

Chapter 9

The 878th had lined up their vehicles for the day's mission: an Abrams M1A2 SEP Tank with Lenguan bridge-laying gear in place of a turret, a five-ton M925 cargo truck, and four Humvees. The unit stood in formation in front of the convoy. The morning sun cast glare into their eyes and had already pushed the thermometer to 96 degrees Fahrenheit with more heat to come. Sweat flowed down the soldiers' brows and cheeks, yet they remained firmly at attention.

Captain Duckworth walked before the unit. "At ease, troops." The Captain paused so the soldiers could wipe sweat from their faces. "You have been briefed, and you know what to do. We're putting down a Lenguan tactical bridge on Route Dragonfire, approximately forty-five clicks after it branches from Route Predator. Three days ago, the area got its first rain of the year. The flooding eroded a deep gorge. It's imperative for the 3rd Infantry that we get it spanned promptly. I will be going with you in the five-ton. Before we go to it, our XO, Major Whitehead, wants to address you."

Captain Duckworth saluted Major Whitehead. He returned the salute. The 878th Executive Officer stood before the unit. "Attention! Most of you appreciate the hard work I do behind the scenes. Those of you who don't appreciate it should especially give me your undivided attention. The President of the United States has said you're not going home until the mission is complete. I can assure you that I will do everything possible to keep you here until I make Lieutenant Colonel. That only happens if you perform your duties the right way." The Major wiped sweat from his neck. "And the right way is my way. Most of you want another stripe. That goes through me. So, you'd better shape up or you will have nothing to show for your deployment." He turned to Captain Duckworth. The Captain saluted. Whitehead returned his salute and walked back to the headquarters building.

"At ease men." Captain Duckworth addressed the unit. "I won't waste any more of our time. Let's get it on."

***

"Here it is. The turnoff to Route Dragonfire." SSG Sand steered onto a road forking to the right, following the convoy.

"Do you and Fuller think the insurgents will allow you to earn another medal?" SFC Mathews asked.

"Earned is right." SGT Fuller clenched his teeth. "I'm not Muttley begging Dick Dastardly for a medal. Dastardly was a bumbling screw-up who caused chaos at every turn. But Whitehead, he's a piece-of-shit of a different order. The kids laughed at Dastardly, and Muttley always got over on him. I still remember the episode on Dastardly and Muttley in Their Flying Machines. Dastardly promised Muttley a medal. He opened his jacket. It had a bunch of medals pinned on the liner. He gave Muttley the smallest one. Muttley later got his revenge." Fuller leaned forward to address SSG Sand. "I heard from the unit clerk, Specialist Harnich, that Sergeant Major Rothrock put us in for ARCOMs with a V for Valor. She told me that Whitehead changed it to just a regular ARCOM. She told me that Whitehead did it because it didn't involve enemy fire. Enemy fire, my ass!" Fuller clenched his weapon. "A knife will kill you just as sure as a bullet."

"I heard about it." SSG Garcia turned to SGT Fuller. "She told me that Whitehead was pissed off because you two didn't fill out the tag on the bodies properly."

"Fill out the tag properly?" Fuller scowled at Garcia. "Why should we even need a tag? Who cares if they have a gun or a knife? I'll say it now, and I'll say it again. If we kill

113

them all and let God sort out the rest, we won't have to worry about what weapon they're using or have to tag the losers."

"I'm starting to agree with you, Chuck." Bobby Sand gripped the steering wheel with both hands. "I can't figure out the reason for us being here in the first place, so who cares who we kill? I especially agree with you about Whitehead. Where does a REMF doing no more than push a pencil in an air-conditioned, barricaded building get off telling combat soldiers to shape up?"

"Yeah, pencil pusher is right." SSG Fuller imitated Muttley's grumble, "Sassafrassuh rassa-frassin piece-of-shit Whitehead." Fuller bit into a chunk of beef jerky. "Do things his way? Whitehead barely knows the way to the shithouse. As the great philosopher Classy Freddie Blassie once said, 'He's nothing but a pencil-necked geek."

"I'm a 'Mouth of the South,' Jimmy Hart fan." SSG Garcia laughed. "After Dastardly screwed up, he would shout, 'Do something, Muttley! And Muttley always came to the rescue, even if he did something to make it worse. Fuller, I can't imagine you ever coming to Whitehead's rescue."

"How the fuck can I, Carlos?" SGT Fuller scowled. "The chickenshit never leaves headquarters to get himself in any danger. I'm itching for a chance to keep on a dancing and a prancing on Whitehead's face."

***

Adelle wore the outfit that Trevor bought for her inevitable summons to Jeffery Haisley's office. She closed her eyes and looked back to Friday afternoon. *I can't wear this.* She held up the ultra-short, slitted skirt. *I'll feel like a whore. And this blouse,* She grabbed a white blouse with one hand. *This material is so thin. It's almost transparent.*

'Don't sell yourself short. No whore at any price ever looked as good as you or fucked as good as you. The treasury can't print enough money to meet your market value.' Trevor chuckled. *'You've trusted me thus far, don't stop now. I know Haisley's type. I told you my mother's a dowdy. A frump. Do you think a man of my father's wealth would stay faithful to that? Of course, what woman would voluntarily be with an old, bald geezer like him? He's the same as Haisley, but with money. Believe me. I know the type. Now wear that outfit to work tomorrow. Don't wear a bra and unbutton your blouse as low as possible. And be sure to swath your breasts and inner thighs with the rest of the Chanel Number 5 that I bought you.'*

Adele sat in her chair and slid under her desk until her abdomen hit the edge. She put her hands over her legs and her skirt's slit. She looked around, moved her hands from her lap, and grabbed a file. She held it over her cleavage. Glancing over the file, she looked upward and pondered the imperceptible movement of the clock's minute hand. The phone rang. After returning the receiver to the base, she took a deep breath. "You're on Adele." She applied a second coat of red lipstick, checked her eye shadow, and brushed out her blonde hair. She sprayed the final droplets of her Chanel Number 5 bottle into her armpits.

***

'You can do this, girl. Who's more successful than Trevor? Who can read people better? If he said this would work on Haisley, it will work.' While Adele strolled into Jeffery Haisley's office, she unfastened yet another blouse button. She stepped into his office. His stern countenance shifted to a leer the moment they made eye contact.

"Miss Beauchamp." His lips quavered. "It's not my decision. I'm only the messenger." His eyes narrowed as he licked his lips.

'*I'm used to him peering at my chest, but he quickly looks away. He's staring at my skirt as if his focus could melt it away.*' Adele took a step back.

"Computers, not people, now run the show." He turned his gaze upward to her chest. He inhaled deeply through his nose. "You're chronic unexcused absences," he took off his glasses and wiped the lenses. His hands tremored. He dropped his glasses onto the floor. Nervously, he stood and bent over to retrieve his glasses, not without looking up her skirt. '*Lacy panties, I see a hint of...*' He stared for three seconds... '*Better not.*' He jerked his head away, shifting focus to her gossamer blouse. '*Her nipples; her areolas...Lovely, lovely, lovely.*"

Adele squeezed her legs together and put her hands over her chest. She almost tipped over in her black spiked shoes.

He walked in front of his desk. After licking his lips, he said, "As I was saying, our computers have documented your unexcused absences. This comes from up top, unfortunately…" He stared into her hazel eyes and perused her fulsome, red lips. His mind went blank. "Hmm, mmm, mmm…" He lurched over, embraced her, and smothered her in kisses.

"Stop!" Adele turned her head away. "Stop!"

"No. No." He pulled open her blouse. "Yes. Yes." He stuck his nose in her cleavage. She grabbed what was left of his greasy hair and forced his head away and downward. He grunted in pain and flailed his arms while falling to his knees. With an adrenaline rush, he tackled her around the ankles. She fell backward. He started kissing her inner thighs; his head moved closer.

"Ahh!" She struck his temple with the side of her fist, knocking him away. She stood and took a fighting stance.

Haisley remained on his hands and knees. He looked up at her. "I'm sorry. I'm sorry. I don't know what came over me. Please don't say anything. Please. I have a wife. Three kids. A granddaughter. A mortgage. Please. Adele. Please." He rose to his knees. "I'm sorry. Please don't say anything." He steepled his hands.

Adele folded her arms over her chest. "Well, that depends. What about my job?" She buttoned up her blouse.

"I told you, please believe me, it's out of my hands. It's computers. The computer alerted Human Resources of your no-call, no-show, unexcused absences. The computer terminated you automatically. The county is scared to death of minority activists, grievance lawsuits, and bad publicity. They do what the computer says, so they can prove they treat everyone equally. It's not me."

"So, I'm fired."

"It's not like that. It's computers." Haisley remained on his knees. "Reapply. I'll do what I can."

Adele bit her lower lip. She took three breaths, each progressively deeper. Her brow furrowed; she gritted her teeth. "Ugh!" She grunted as she kicked him in the gut. Haisley groaned. He rolled onto his side and gasped for air. Adele stormed from his office. She grabbed an overcoat from her cubicle's standing coat rack, covered herself, and marched to her car.

***

Adele paid no attention to her speedometer or red lights. Her fraught nerves blurred her vision. Several automobiles blared their horns at her. Twice, drivers swerved to avoid collisions. She pulled into a driveway, trudged to the front door, and banged on it like Gestapo or KGB agents.

"Adele! What's this all about?" A young woman opened the door. "Oh, girl, what happened?"

Adele started crying. Jenny Carter hugged her and kissed her cheek. She took Adele by the hand and led her to her living room. "Let me make you an iced tea."

"Better make that a Long Island Iced Tea."

***

Jenny handed Adele her drink. It shook in her hands; droplets splashed over the glass's edge. "It's my job, Jenny, I lost it."

"There's something more you're not telling me, girl." Jenny sipped her Long Island Iced Tea. "You hated that job. You always complained about it being boring and low-paying. You also said you hated Haisley and how he was a lech and a dirty old man."

"Jenny," Adele lowered her head. "He attacked me. Sexually."

"Oh my God, Girl! He didn't …"

"No. I stopped him. Thanks to having you as a gym partner, I can handle that old bastard. He didn't get far. But my job's gone just the same."

"No, Adele, your job is not gone. I've been seeing a lot of Hank. His law firm can make short work of the likes of Haisley."

"No, Jenny. They fired me based on a computer readout. All a lawsuit can do is punish Haisley."

"Well, it doesn't take a legal eagle to know that the county may settle out of court. They'll give you your job back in lieu of paying a tort because of Haisley."

Adele gulped her drink. "I don't want to go back there. Besides, it's not his wife's fault that her husband's a creep. Look, Jenny, I don't care what Donald Rumsfeld says about collateral damage. Haisley's kids and grandson are innocent parties." Adele stood and smiled. "Remember our Tae Bo classes?" She lifted her right foot and performed a kicking motion. "Whatever pleasure he got out of attacking me, I gave him ten times more pain."

"You go girl!" Jenny laughed. "As for a job, I shouldn't offer it because you'll attract all the guys and get all our tips." Jenny chuckled. "I'll set you up with a waitress job at the Pussy Cat Lounge. A waitress is not the same as a stripper. But if you play it smart, you'll make just as much money." Jenny put her hands on Adele's shoulders. "Tell me, girl. Have you heard from Bobby?"

Adele lowered her head. A tear formed in her right eye. "Jenny. I've been seeing a lot of Trevor. I think I'm in love with him."

"Huh? I never would have thought." Jenny bit her lip. "But it's okay, girl. I will always love you. I just want you to be happy." Jenny and Adele hugged. They pecked lips.

***

Horrible Hank's Tavern was located two miles down Spruill Avenue from The Brocton Copper Works. The joint featured a coin-operated pool table with a Miller High Life aluminum billiard light overhead. The owner displayed a large bowling trophy and autographed roller derby skates on a shelf behind the bar. A signed photo of the tavern owner with professional wrestling champion Rick Flair hung on the wall by the entrance. The coin-operated juke box played *Beer for My Horses* by Toby Keith and Willie Nelson. Trevor Brocton and Henry Sawyers sat at a corner table. "At least they have this stuff." Henry held up his Heineken beer bottle.

119

"Everyone else here is drinking PBR, Miller High Life, or Bud. Otherwise saying, they're drinking piss from the horse the juke box record is singing about."

"Relax, Hank." Trevor sipped his Johnny Walker Black on the rocks. "It's the closest joint to my plant. I get VIP treatment as I have a say in the next round of layoffs."

"You mean your father's plant, and they think you have a say. My father told me about your little screw-up with Picardi Developments. Their big boss, Alex Picardi, was pissed. You're lucky my father respects your father; otherwise, they were going to sue."

"Well, we own 48 percent of Picardi Developments," Trevor folded his hands behind his head. "Let's see who gets the last laugh. When we own 50.1 percent, old man Alex's head will be the first to roll."

"What does your father say about taking it over?"

"Screw the old bastard." Trevor clenched his fists. "I wanted to short their stock and then have our agents buy up the remaining shares. But my father is living in the past. My day will come, and when it does, look out." Trevor wagged his finger. "Just remember, when I decide I want something, I get it. One way or another, I get what I set out to get. And that includes women."

"Speaking of women, remember that cute blonde with the ponytail we met at Rosa's Cantina?"

"Yeah, Jenny. She's Adele's best friend."

"Well, Jenny is far more than I thought. She's more than just cute; she's perky and friendly, and much smarter than you might think. I thought meeting a chick in a bar, who works as a waitress at the Pussy Cat lounge, would be just another tart. But she's so much more than that. I even introduced her to my family. Believe it or not, my father approves of her." Hank smiled. "He's always pressured me to settle down. Anyway, Jenny is so much fun. I don't think I will ever tire of her."

"It sounds like you're pussy whipped. I'm telling you, act like a doormat and they'll walk all over you." Trevor brushed him off. "I thought the one you wanted was Erica. You couldn't even get in the batter's box, much less get a hit off her."

"I remember from Rosa's Cantina how much you liked her sister, Adele, the soldier's fiancée. Erica has never spoken about you and her sister." Hank chuckled. "It looks like our Dan Juan, Casanova, Hugh Hefner met his match."

"Oh, really," Trevor grinned. "Let me show you something." He opened a silver pill box. He put the box beneath Hank's eyes. A quarter-inch-long filament sat on a purple velvet surface.

"What is that?" Hank pointed.

"It's a cunt hair. I plucked it from Adele while going down on her." Trevor smirked at him. "I know what you're thinking. It's an exact match to her head hair, at least how it looked before that faggot Jude DePlume made her over. Any more doubt about who's the man and who's the love-struck puppy?"

"You're gross. How can you do that?" Hank gasped. "Have you no respect?"

"Respect is earned, Romeo." Trevor closed the pill box. "How about I teach you what a man is all about. Care to bet five grand?"

"Five grand?"

"Yes. Five grand. You told me Erica is a stuck-up bitch? How about we bet five grand? My five thousand says I add her auburn pussy hair to my collection."

"You disgust me. Nevertheless, we all know what walks and what talks. You may have stolen Adele from the soldier, but you'll never get her sister. You're on."

Hank and Trevor shook hands.

Chapter 10

1991

"Get us another beer," Jimbo McClenahan shouted at his wife.

"You mean my beers!" Marcia McClenahan leaned on a mop. "After I'm done scrubbing your filth, I'm drinkin' 'em myself."

The McClenahans' single-wide trailer sat on Toogoodoo Road, on the rural outskirts of Charleston, South Carolina. Rusted auto parts, two junk cars, and knee-high weeds covered their yard.

Thirteen-year-old Steven 'Spike' McClenahan sat at the edge of the couch, avoiding a fabric tear and loose spring. He looked at his father and held up his empty bottle of Milwaukee's Best beer.

"You go get us two more." Jimbo sat in an adjacent chair. The paint on its wooden top back rail was chipped and faded.

Spike walked toward the kitchen.

"Oh no, you don't, you filthy little pig." Marcia blocked the entrance with her mop. "I just finished mopping. You're not trampling mud and dog shit onto my kitchen floor."

"Get out of the way, Mom." Spike lurched forward two steps. "Dad told me to get us some beers." He marched past her.

"Gaw dammit!" Marcia swung her mop ferociously, hitting the side of Spike's head. He saw sparks mingling with mop water. "You're too damn young to turn into a drunk like your worthless father."

Spike staggered back to the living room, massaged his head, and collapsed onto the couch.

"Dammit, woman!" Jimbo sprang toward the kitchen. "Get out of our way." He grasped his wife's cheeks and shoved her. He opened the refrigerator and grabbed two bottles of *Milwaukee's Best*. He walked back to their living room and handed his son a bottle. Marcia threw her mop at them like a spear.

"What the hell, woman!" Jimbo picked up the mop. With two hands, he broke it over his thigh. "Here, mop your damn kitchen with this." He threw the mop halves at Marcia. "Come on, Spike. We're out of here." As they walked out the door, Jimbo glowered at his wife. "And don't look back, Spike, or you'll turn into a pillar of salt."

***

Jimbo walked back from the office refrigerator and handed Spike a bottle of *Milwaukee's Best* beer. "Here is where men belong. McClenahan's Auto Body and Repair. Someday this will be yours, son."

Spike swilled some beer from the bottle.

"Just keep your nose clean, son. I don't care nothin' about how you do in English or History. Just don't get expelled. Your school's got a good auto mechanic class. I'll teach you all the math you need to know so you can cook the books like a pro. Here comes Julio. It looks like he got something for us." Jimbo gave Julio the signal to drive around to the back of the yard.

Julio climbed out of a 1978 Buick Century sedan. "I took this from the Stepford Mills parking lot." Julio stood shorter than the top of the car and carried twenty pounds of excess bodyweight. He held up his palm. "How much?" His eyelids twitched.

"The usual, and that's doing you a favor. While there's a decent demand for this model in Mexico and Colombia, lately, Carruthers down at the docks is paying less.

Unfortunately, you've got stiff competition. It's worth more to me to strip for parts."

"How much?" Julio kept his palm extended.

"Five hundred dollars." Jimbo put his hands on his hips. "Take it or leave it."

"I go to yale if they catch me. Come on, Amigo. Dame mas. How much?" Julio raised his upright palm to Jimbo's chest.

"Sí, Señor Imbecil. You go to *jail*, not Harvard or Yale. I also get locked up if I'm caught buying this from you. Five hundred. Take it or leave it."

"Sí. Sí."

"Spike. Go to the strongbox and get Julio five Benjamins. Here," Jimbo tossed Spike a set of keys. "Take Julio home in the tow truck. If you see an abandoned car on the way back, hook it up and bring it here."

Chapter 11

The Pussy Cat Lounge had two small stages at the north and south ends. The main stage was in the center, with four rows of tables surrounding it. Each stage had a pole in the center. Adele wore the Pussy Cat Lounge's waitress uniform: pink short shorts and a low-cut, white linen blouse tied behind the back, exposing her naval. She wore garters on each thigh. Both of her garters had cash stuffed under them. "Get us four beers," a customer wearing denim slacks, a flannel shirt, and a John Deere billed cap shouted to Adele. "Spend some time with us," he held up two twenty-dollar bills, "and this is yours."

Adele walked over to them. "What kind of beers do you guys want?"

"PBRs."

"PBR?" Adele chuckled. "And I'm supposed to believe you're big spenders?"

"Dance with me in the VIP room." He pulled out two one-hundred-dollar bills. "And I'll do some big spending on you."

"You and your posse are getting four PBR beers," Adele smirked at them. "No more."

"Well, come a little closer."

Adele walked over to him.

"This is yours just for being so hot." He put two twenty-dollar bills in her garter belt.

Jenny intercepted Adele on the way to the service bar. "See, girl," she put her hands on Adele's shoulders. "There's nothing to this. The customers aren't allowed to touch you, and you don't have to take anything off."

"I've already made twice what they pay me for a day in the county slave galley." Adele grinned. "And the customers here are nowhere near as lecherous as Haisley."

"You did a number on him." Jenny laughed. "In here, the bouncers will take care of it." Jenny grimaced. "Uh, oh, trouble just walked in."

Adele gasped.

Spike McClenahan entered the club. His black hair extended below his shoulders. He wore denim pants and a black leather vest, exposing heavily tattooed arms. "Well, Adele, welcome to where you belong. It took every trick in the book to bed you." He laughed. "Now I only have to put money in your garter belt."

"I'm a waitress," Adele put her hands on her hips, hunched her shoulders, and glared at him, "not a dancer or a whore."

"Not a whore? It's all over town that you're cheating on soldier boy with rich boy. You think people in this town ignore the Broctons?" Spike laughed at her. "Is this how much it takes to relive the good old days?" He put a twenty-dollar bill in her garter before moving his hand to her buttocks and clamping her right butt cheek.

Adele slapped him.

"You bitch!" Spike massaged his left facial cheek. "Dammit. You never got over me. I know it, and you know it." Spike stood and wrapped his arms around her, putting both hands on her buttocks. He started kissing her neck. "Mmm…Smells so good. Did rich boy buy you that delicious perfume?"

Adele scratched his cheek. "Get off of me!" She pushed him away.

Spike grimaced and touched his cheek.

Two bouncers approached. The bald, black bouncer wore black slacks and a tight black T-shirt, showing off bodybuilder arms. The white bouncer was a hundred pounds heavier and wore denim farmer overalls. His red hair and beard were overgrown. "That's the last straw, McClenahan." The white bouncer prodded at him. "Get out and don't come back."

"Otherwise, wise saying, you're banned." The black bouncer grabbed Spike's arm. "Let's go. You're outta here." He pulled Spike toward the exit.

"Take your dirty hand off of me, nigger."

The black bouncer released his grip and punched Spike in the gut, causing him to keel over and gasp for air. The white bouncer wrapped his arm around Spike's neck and twisted his arm behind his back. The bouncer forced him to the door and shoved him face-first to the pavement.

Spike climbed to his hands and knees; he spat out pebbles and dirt.

A man approached him. Spike only had time to notice his shiny black leather shoes before he heard him speak. "For such a bad boy, you're not much of a fighter. First soldier boy and now the bouncers."

"Huh?" Spike looked up at him.

"Come on, let me help you up. I have business to discuss with you."

Spike took his hand and allowed him to pull him to his feet.

"Let's talk in my car." He pointed. "It's the black Porsche Carrera GT."

Spike and Trevor sat in the car. "I think you know who I am."

"I know who you are… Trevor." Spike wiped dirt from his face. "I surely don't know what you want."

"You're among the better cannabis dealers in the area. But it's only a supplement to your chop shop income."

"How do you know about that, and what could you possibly want with me?"

"Well, you did once have Adele. If you can land a babe like her, I know there's more to you than meets the eye."

"Is that what this is about? Adele? Well, I'm over that tramp, and I don't care how hot she looks." Spike bit his lip. "You can have her."

"Actually, the one I want is her older sister, Erica. I know that she's hated your guts from day one and has banned you from the Beauchamp residence. Just like you just got yourself banned from the Pussy Cat Lounge. Don't worry about the Pussy Cat Lounge, though. After I grease the palms of the owner and the bouncers, they'll roll out the red carpet for you." Trevor smiled at Spike. "I want to make you a big-time offer, as in making you a big-time dealer. Forget about cannabis. Smuggling it is difficult, and it makes little profit. Moreover, people grow their own as easily as growing tomatoes. I have something far better coming across the Mexico-California border and sometimes even Charleston Harbor." Trevor straightened his collar. "It's called Fentanyl. Fentanyl itself is a powerful, synthetic opioid. Under strict doctor's care, it is legal to treat severe pain. I'm sure you know that, and you're familiar with its street slang. Bottom line, my lab uses it to create heroin."

"I don't get this. Your family is among the wealthiest in the Carolinas. That's not even counting what your family is worth back in California. Why do you need to deal heroin?"

"Yes, Spike, you're correct. I've had money from the day I emerged from my mother's pussy. Let me answer your question. What I've never had is power. My family is not backing my political ambitions; therefore, I need to build my political war chest. Power. Power is what I don't have, and power is what I want. Those who know me can tell you I will do whatever it takes to get what I want. I couldn't care less about issues or ideology. If I run for office here, it will be as a Republican. If I run for office in California, it will be as a Democrat."

"What do you want from me?"

"I want to give you a chance to make more money than you've ever dreamed of having. I am offering to make you my right-hand man. You know the streets. You can get more of my drugs to the people. You already have connections from dealing pot. You won't have to do any dirty work. You'll manage the street dealers and keep track of the profits and inventory. Work for me, and you get twenty percent of the take." Trevor chuckled. "I think you know that will be considerable. Moreover, what job offers twenty percent commission?"

Spike shrugged.

"Well, are you in?" Trevor extended his hand.

Spike shook it.

"And don't think you can take more than twenty percent. I get my wholesale from some highly unsavory people," Trevor grinned, "If you know what I mean."

Spike nodded.

Chapter 12

Adele awoke in her bedroom. She heard the sizzle and sniffed the aroma of ham and cheese omelets, bacon, and biscuit gravy. *'Erica's up early again.'* Adele sat up. A wave of nausea struck. She stumbled out of bed and ran into the bathroom. Through hazy vision, she viewed its bare blue tiles and dim fluorescent light. *'Am I in the death chamber I saw on the true crime TV show? Except this time, it's with a toilet instead of a wooden chair with a skull cap, straps, and wires.'* After kneeling over the toilet, she gazed into the mirror. *'I look like I stuck my head in a vat of white flour.'* She licked her fingertips and rubbed the dark shadows under her eyes. She had suspected it for several days: the strange heaviness in her belly, the way her skin felt hot and foreign, a subtle change in gravity. Picturing herself back in Walmart's feminine hygiene aisle, she thought about her investment of one dollar and ninety-eight cents. *'The price of truth.'* Her past and a possible future swung like Poe's pendulum in the form of a urine-soaked plastic stick.

A two-minute wait.

She remembered Bobby boarding the military aircraft with his unit, bound for a possible one-way trip. She clenched her jaw and thought of her previous life. *'Cheap clothes, budget meals, community college rather than a university, a dull house in a dull suburb.'*

"Oh my God!"

She gazed at the pink line beneath the plus sign.

'Plenty of soldiers have gotten Dear John letters. Bobby will survive.'

She patted her abdomen before wiping away a cold tear. *'The finest schools, big time connections...the best of everything...For both mother and child.'* Adele managed a faint smile. She sat on the closed toilet seat and took a deep breath.

***

"I've got news, the good, the bad, and the ugly." SFC Mathews sipped from a cup of orange juice. "What do you want first?"

"Hit us with the bad news first, Matty." SSG Sand finished his cup of coffee and slid his plastic mug aside.

"The first bad news is that there's no good news. Here's the second bit of bad news. Carlos went to sick call. The medic gave him the day off. Now for the ugly news. Whitehead is taking his place."

"You've got to be kidding!" SSG Fuller leaped from his chair.

"No. I'm not. I wish I were." SFC Mathews folded his arms. "From what I understand, he's required to leave the compound once a month."

"Let's first give Carlos a blanket party." Fuller pursed his lips. "It's bullshit that he gets to stay in the barracks and jack off to his centerfolds and porno DVDs while we clear Route Predator of IEDs with that chicken shit REMF in his place." Chuck threw up his hands. "I'm glad I bought all those life insurance policies for Inez. Leave it to Whitehead to kill us before the enemy can." Fuller pointed to the foreign civilian kitchen staff standing behind the chow line. "Those coolie cooks finally got my eggs right. Whitehead just stole my appetite." Fuller marched out of the Dirty Bird Café without returning his tray.

***

Douglas Whitehead stood in front of the team's Humvee. He jabbed his finger at it. "What the hell is this?"

132

"It's a sticker of Muttley," SGT Fuller grinned, "the cartoon dog."

"I know what it is, Sergeant Fuller." Major Whitehead jutted his head. "Or soon shall I call you, Specialist Fuller? I want to know what it's doing there."

"Muttley's our mascot." Fuller nodded. "He's got guts and attitude. Two things a soldier needs in this place."

"Each one of you has violated my orders." Whitehead wagged his finger. "I denied your request to rename yourselves Team Muttley. I told you that you are Team Falcon. Until I say otherwise, you are Team Falcon. Am I understood?"

"Yes, sir," the team replied.

Team Falcon boarded their Humvee. SSG Sand pulled in front of Team Black Mamba.

"What the hell are you doing, Sand? Tell Team Black Mamba to go first."

"Major Whitehead, sir," SSG Sand turned to the Major. "When we're assigned a two-team mission with Team Black Mamba, we rotate who goes first; the first vehicle in a two-vehicle convoy is in greater danger of getting hit with an IED or taking sniper fire. Today is our turn to go first."

"You think I don't know that? Buck Sergeant Sand? You tell Team Black Mamba to go first, or I'll make that demotion stick."

***

Team Falcon rolled down Route Predator behind Team Black Mamba. SSG Sand drove; Major Whitehead sat next to him. SFC Mathews took SSG Garcia's place in the back seat. The Major glowered at the driver, "Don't follow so damn close, Sand."

"We have to keep it tight so no enemy vehicle can sneak between us."

"You have a pretty fiancé back home. I'm sure you want to get to her before Jody does. That's up to me. I approve or disapprove of your leave. Now don't drive so close, Sand, understood?"

"Yes, sir."

"And you're steering is too tight and stay away from the curb." Major Whitehead looked up at Specialist O'Connor, seated in the gun turret. "Look more alert. You're the first soldier the enemy sees. If they think you're sleeping up there, they may shoot at us, and you're the first target. I don't plan on serving as the second target because of you." Major Whitehead looked back at Sergeant Fuller, "What the hell is wrong with you? Waving your weapon in each direction."

"It's how the Third Infantry taught us."

"Fuller!" Major Whitehead prodded. "That's the last time you do it your way instead of my way."

"It's not my way; it's the Third Infantry's way."

"You're with the 878th Combat Engineers, and I am the executive officer. You do it as I tell you. Understood?"

"Yes, sir." Once Whitehead looked away, Fuller inaudibly muttered, "Sassafrassuh rassa-frassin."

***

Trevor drove Adele in his Porsche Carrera GT on the feeder road toward her home. She put her hand on his leg and leaned forward. "Honey, I wanted to wait for the right moment to tell you my wonderful news." She kissed his cheek and reached into her handbag. "I love you, Trevor. I love you forever. Our love has made something wonderful." She showed him the blue plastic stick with the pink line.

"I'm pregnant. We're having a baby together." Adele beamed.

Trevor slammed on the brakes. The car screeched and swerved to the right. "What the Hell?" He released the brakes and glowered at her.

"A baby." Adele's spirit dropped into her stomach. "You're going to be a father. Aren't you happy?"

Trevor looked into Adele's eyes. Her tears were his political ambitions swirling through a funnel and into oblivion. "You're getting rid of it." He scowled as he spat the words out. "And you're going to keep your mouth shut."

"No!" Tears stung her eyes. "I love you!" Adele wailed. "It's our bay-bee! I thought you loved me." She grabbed his arm and shook him.

"Love you?" He pushed her arm away. "You're a hot piece of ass and it was fun fucking you, but that's as far as it goes."

"But those things you brought me?" Tears shrouded her face. "I thought you loved me."

"You think those," he skewed his voice in a mocking tone, "things I bought you, put a dent in the Brocton fortune? I've tipped bartenders more than what both you and that stuff are worth."

"You said I'm beautiful." Her heart palpitated; she put her hand over her chest. "Don't you want a daughter beautiful like me or a son tall and handsome like you?" Adele bawled. "Please, Trevor! Don't do this to me! Tell me you love me and that you want to be a father."

"Look, you." He pinched her cheeks hard enough to hurt her. "I am going to run for high office. I will need a wife who's up to Brocton standards. In both class and pedigree." Trevor gave her a loathsome look. "A waitress at a tittie bar...Dressing you up is like putting lipstick on a pig. Now you're getting rid of that thing you're carrying, and you're going to keep your white trash, gutter mouth shut." He shoved her head.

"No! It's a baby! A beautiful baby. I don't care what you do or say. I love you, and I'm keeping our baby! I have rights. You're going to support our child."

Despite her tears and wailing, Trevor read only resolution in her face…

…Eleven-year-old Trevor sat at the breakfast table.

His mother stood by a picture window. 'Trevor, it looks like Cookie got run over. Before Ernesto drives you to school, make sure he properly disposes of her. I have guests coming over. I can't have roadkill in front of the house.'

'What? Cookie?' Trevor almost heaved his breakfast. He ran to the window. 'No! No!' He bolted out the front door and sprinted toward the ghastly sight. 'Cookie! Cookie!' Trevor kneeled over the dead Cocker Spaniel and bawled.

'What the…' His mother muttered, grimaced, and followed him.

'Mommy! Cookie! I want Cookie, mommy, I want Cookie!' He looked at his mother; her face looked sculpted from frozen putty, and her eyes like alabaster stones. He flinched before she even raised her hand.

'You bastard!' His mother slapped his face as crisply as ringing a bell. 'How many times are you going to humiliate me? You stop that now! What's worse?' She prodded at him. 'Roadkill in front of the house, or you making a spectacle of yourself. Go to the car! Seeing you can't do as you're told, I'll have Ernesto dispose of this mess…'

Trevor massaged his stinging cheek. 'But Mommy…Cookie…Cookie.'

His mother slapped him again. 'I don't have time for this. I can't keep a nanny because of you, and I need to get ready for the luncheon.' She prodded. 'Now, get in the car!'

"…Don't fuck with me, Adele. Although it's not on me to dispose of it, I'll have an associate call Planned Parenthood. They'll be expecting you." He prodded. "You better show up, and you better keep your mouth shut about it."

Adele slapped him. Hard.

Trevor saw Adele in blood-red pixels. His head felt like a pot over a flame. "So, you wanna play rough, bitch." Trevor leaned over Adele and opened her door. He braced his back against his door, put his foot on her, and kicked her out of the car at 30 mph.

A loud thud shook every part of Adele's body as she hit the pavement. She lost consciousness during the next two bounces. Four seconds later, she was lying on the roadside in a fetal position.

***

"Why are you stopping?" Major Whitehead wiped sweat from his brow. "I didn't tell you to stop."

"Major," Bobby kept both hands on the steering wheel. "Team Black Mamba gave me the hand signal. They see something suspicious up ahead." Bobby pulled their Humvee next to Team Black Mamba's Humvee.

"Look," SPC O'Connor peered down from the gun turret. "See the wires sticking out of that thing? It's barely hidden in that dead dog. It's an IED if I ever saw one."

SFC Mathews got out of the vehicle, stood next to SFC Grant of Team Black Mamba, and looked at the suspected IED through binoculars. He lowered the binoculars and looked at Major Whitehead. "Specialist O'Connor is right. It is an IED."

"I'll call it in to headquarters." Major Whitehead grasped the SIGNAR radio receiver.

"No!" Bobby Sand grabbed Major Whitehead's wrist. "Don't do that! You might set it off. We'll call it in after we get out of its blast zone."

"Don't touch me again," Whitehead wagged his finger, "or I'll have you breaking big rocks into little rocks at Leavenworth. Okay," the Major nodded, "You know so much about IEDs, you go and investigate it. We're not backtracking and calling in a false alarm. Not on my watch, anyway." He looked back. "And take Fuller with you. He also thinks he knows more than I do.

***

Erica stepped outside her house. Migraines had afflicted her mother, Monica, keeping her awake. It was past midnight. *'Adele's car is here even though she's not home. At least she didn't park me in. Mother is out of Sumatriptan. The Lee Street Walmart has a 24/7 pharmacy.'* Erica put her key in the door of her 1996 Chevy Caprice. *'What's that at the end of the road? It looks like a cloth dummy.'* Erica looked closer. Her heart stopped. She choked on her breath. "No!" She covered her eyes; tears sluiced through her fingers. "Oh Lord Jesus, sweet Jesus." Erica jumped into her car and turned the ignition key. A metallic grind. "No. No. Please, Lord, please." She again turned the key. Her car started. She sped down the road, hit the brakes, and jumped out of her car. Adele's clothes were shredded. Scrapes and abrasions covered her face and body. Her lips were twitching. Erica heard an incoherent murmuring.

"Adele, Adele." Erica hugged her head. "My beautiful sister." Erica started kissing her bloody cheek. "I love you; I love you, my beautiful sister. My beautiful sister." Erica closed her eyes. *'Heavenly Father, in the name of Jesus,*

138

please, please, please, help my Adele.' Erica braced her arm under her sister, lifted her into her car, and drove away. "Don't worry, Adele. If God is with you, who can be against you? Let the Holy Ghost comfort you. We're on our way to the hospital. You're going to be fine. I know it. I love you so much, Adele. I know sometimes we fought. But it's going to be okay. Keep praying, Adele. Keep praying."

***

Trevor turned around and drove back to the scene. *'You idiot, Trevor.'* He hit his forehead with his palm. *'Not that she didn't deserve it, but if she lives, she talks. Bye-bye, political career. What if Daddy fires me, or worse, does to me what he did to Edgar? Edgar was a faggot. I don't know if he'll hate this even more.'* He spotted Erica helping Adele into her car. "Oh shit." *'Adele is still alive. She'll tell her stuck-up bitch sister what happened. Surely, she'll tell the cops.'* Trevor followed at a safe distance as they turned onto Brinsfield Road. He hit the speed dial on his cellphone. "Spike," Trevor spoke into his cellphone. "Here's where the huge bucks begin. How does fifty grand cash sound to you?"

"Fifty Grand!" Spike squeezed his phone and beamed. "Talk to me."

"You've assembled untraceable cars from stolen parts. Time to put one to work. It's Adele and her sister. I know you hate them both. Adele dumped you, and she humiliated you at the Pussy Cat Lounge. Erica treated you like a leper and stopped you from getting her sister back. They're driving on Brinsfield Road. I want them to have a fatal accident. Do it now, and I'll make it Sixty Thousand."

"You want me to kill them? Why? I've never killed anyone before. You're right. I hate them both. But enough to kill them? Besides, it's life in prison or Old Sparky if I'm caught."

139

"Cut the sentimentality. You're running my fentanyl operation. Do you know how many people die of an overdose every day? You've already done enough to get life, and if you talk, the cartel will kill you, and it will prove far slower and far more painful than Old Sparky. We don't have time for chit chat. I said sixty grand if you do it right now. The clock is ticking. Yes or no?"

Spike gritted his teeth, looked up, and closed his eyes. He took a deep breath.

"Well?"

"Okay. Make it sixty-five grand and I'll do it."

"I don't have time for this…" Trevor pursed his lips. "All right. You got it. Sixty-five."

***

Bobby Sand and Chuck Fuller shuffled over to the suspected IED.

"Whitehead is insane for making us walk over to this thing." Fuller grimaced. "He's a total retard. Matty got a close-up with his binoculars. It's a damn IED. Why does Whitehead have a problem with that?"

"Yeah. It's an IED all right." Bobby Sand pointed at the object. "Look at the wires and transistors connected to the cylinders. Let's get out of here before one of the maggots on the dead dog sets it off."

"Yeah, that roadkill smells worse than Carlos's farting and Whitehead's breath." SGT Fuller pinched his nose. "Of course, Whitehead doesn't do enough work to break a sweat and need underarm deodorant."

Bobby made eye contact with SFC Grant of Team Black Mamba. The tall, lanky black team leader stood outside his Humvee. Bobby showed him and SFC Mathews, now sitting next to Major Whitehead, a clenched fist followed by a slow point, signaling that it was an IED.

Major Whitehead grabbed the SIGNAR's receiver. "I'll call it into headquarters." The Major put his thumb on the talk-to-call button.

"No!" SFC Mathews screamed and grabbed Major Whitehead's arm.

***

Erica sped at close to 90 mph down Brinsfield Road. Her sole focus was getting her sister to the hospital. She didn't notice the headlights gaining on her. Ten seconds later, the car pulled up beside her on the driver's side. Without warning, it sideswiped her. "Ahh!" Erica screamed. The car hit her again. She squeezed the steering wheel, regained control, and sped forward.

Spike lost control of his car for two seconds. Now he was behind the sisters. He slammed on the accelerator and rear-ended them.

Erica and Adele were thrust forward.

Adele grunted in pain. "It's okay, Adele. It's okay." Erica floored the accelerator and leaned back. Spike continued to hit her car from behind. On top of the engine roar and crunching metal, Erica heard bells and a horn blast. Looking ahead, she saw flashing lights. A freight train was barreling toward the level crossing. *'I have one chance. Beating the train puts him behind me, and I can get away.'* She gritted her teeth and sped toward the level crossing.

She and the train finished in a tie.

***

Major Whitehead pushed the SIGNAR's call-to-talk button.

141

Bobby and Chuck saw a flash of light before total silence. The blast knocked SFC Grant to the ground. Team Falcon's Humvee shook with enough force to dislodge SPC O'Connor from his gun turret perch. He landed on SFC Mathews. Major Whitehead bawled and cried out to his mother.

***

The train hit Erica's car, slamming it across the tracks like a fiery basketball. It came to a halt twenty yards away on the tracks. The train struck again, sending what remained of the car into a ditch. The flaming car ignited the nearby weeds and bushes.

Spike pumped the brakes and turned his wheel completely to his left. "Shit! Shit! Shit!"

His car did a 180-degree spin before stopping. "Yes!" He thought of his sixty-five thousand dollars windfall without knowing a third of his car sat on the tracks. The boxcar's wheels ran over him, exploding the gas tank. He threw his melting arms in front of what remained of his face.

END OF PART ONE

PART TWO

Chapter 1

Erica stood on Brinsfield Road. The shrill of police sirens, ambulances, and fire engines confused her more than her weightlessness. She spotted a television cameraman focusing on an attractive woman. She wore a pantsuit and talked into a microphone. Multiple red and blue flashing lights, television production lights flooded the area with luminescence, and the flames of two burning cars and a brush fire blinded her, but through her squint, she saw a baby with wings fly upward.

"What's happening here?" Erica asked a policeman. He ignored her. "Officer, please, tell me. What's going on?" She grabbed his arm. He did not react. Her grip failed even to crease his uniform. The policeman remained oblivious to her. He walked over to another officer. Erica followed him. "Officer, Please! It's my sister. She needs medical help." The cop did not look back. He spoke to his partner. Their voices were garbled. Erica ran to a fireman. "Please help my sister. She was hit by a car. Please! She needs help!" The fireman ignored her. Floating rather than walking, still not knowing why, she drifted to an ambulance and investigated its open back door. *'Empty.'* Seconds later, she saw the scene from twenty feet above.

She heard a voice. "Erica."

A floral aroma supplanted the stench of burning rubber and flesh. Erica stood before a woman wearing an immaculate white gown, cut in a "V" over strikingly bountiful and gorgeous breasts. Her shocking white feathered wings reflected the police, fire, and ambulance lights like rays from a pearl. Shades of subdued violet shone from the mysterious woman's indigo tresses, flowing like a mountain stream past the small of her back to a textured end.

Her forehead was as wide as her jaw. Matching in thickness, her upper and lower lips were the color of Romanee-Conti wine. A mid-sized celestial nose was aligned with her rounded cheekbones. Set an eye width apart, her blue eyes appeared deeper than the ocean and tilted upward at the outer edges ever so slightly. Erica looked into her eyes and saw a tear. A wave of comfort swept over her. "Who are you? Can you tell me what's happening? I am so confused. Help me! My sister was in a serious accident."

"Erica, I am Isolde Maria. Heaven sent me as your guide to the afterlife."

"Afterlife?" Erica raised her arms. "I don't understand."

"Erica, your spirit is alive. You have a mission to accomplish before you reach your final destination."

"I don't understand any of this." Adele shook her hands. "Please help my sister."

"Adele is not part of our plan."

"No. Please. You must help her."

"Erica." Isolde Maria floated over to her. She extended her long, toned arms and gently held Erica's shoulders. She looked at her with soft, wide eyes. Their kindness cloaked all gloom. A teardrop slid down her cheek.

"Isolde Maria, I'm confused. What's happening? And why are you so beautiful? You're more beautiful than anyone I could ever imagine. Is it a reflection of your goodness, or is it to lure me to destruction? Is it to soften your telling me something awful?"

"Erica. The ultimate evil was committed against you, your sister, and your niece. If you trust me, things will improve beyond anything you can imagine."

A wave of fear crystallized Erica. "I'm starting to remember. Another car was crashing into me… The train," Erica started to shake, "The train…"

"Erica," Isolde Maria kissed Erica's forehead. "It's over now. It's okay." She hugged her. Erica returned her embrace and held her close. Isolde Maria softly stroked her cheek. "It was no accident, Erica. Fear not, I am with you now, and powers much higher than me love you, will protect you, and deliver you from evil." Tears now streamed from Isolde Maria's eyes. "Erica, your mortal body, along with your sister's and her baby's mortal bodies, were murdered."

"Murdered? No. Wait. You said something about a Baby? What baby? Adele doesn't have a baby. I don't have a niece."

Isolde Maria held up her hand in a halt gesture. "You will learn about that later. Now is not the time."

"Are you saying that I'm dead?" Erica covered her eyes with her hands.

Isolde Maria tightened her lips and nodded.

"No! No! No! I don't want to be dead. I wanted to go to law school. I never got to be a wife or a mother. No! No! Bring me back." Erica bawled. "What am I? A ghost? I don't want to be a ghost." She gazed deep into Isolde Maria's eyes. After three tearful gasps, she lunged forward and embraced the angel. Erica held her with all her energy and strength. Resting her head on the angel's shoulder, Erica rubbed her cheek against her cheek. She grabbed a lock of her hair, held it to her eyes, and soaked the angel's hair with her tears. After five minutes, she stood back. Erica and Isolde Maria faced each other while holding hands.

"Erica, life on Earth is tragic. Mortals will never find true happiness as individuals or as a society. You must look to Heaven. Erica," tears welled in Isolde Maria's eyes. "Your sister's fiancé, Bobby, is also now one of us."

"You mean…?"

"Yes, Erica, he was killed in Iraq." Isolde Maria pulled one hand away but kept a firm grip on Erica's other hand.

"He also lives on. Fly with me. We are going to greet him at Dover Air Force Base."

"Yes, take me to Bobby. Will you tell him about Adele, or shall I?"

"He is not ready for the entire truth."

"The entire truth?" Erica shook her hands. "I don't understand."

"When the time is right, you both will know everything. For now, it's enough for him to find out he's dead and now a ghost." Isolde Maria smiled. "We will tell him together. I belong to both of you." Isolde Maria nodded. "Let's fly now, Erica."

Erica squeezed the angel's hand. They flew higher and above. The scene below faded away. They became one with the night sky.

Chapter 2

Erica and Isolde Maria stood on the tarmac of Dover Air Force Base. Erica spotted the Boeing C-17 Globemaster III aircraft's descent. She cried. Isolde Maria put her arm on her shoulder and rubbed her back. "I'm sorry, Isolde Maria, I've experienced the pain of grief before. I mourned my father for months. I'm confused, Isolde Maria. I feel guilty…How can I say it?" Erica sniffled? "I'm mourning my own death."

"I live in the world of the living and the undead. I understand." Isolde Maria kissed Erica's cheek. "Even though you live again, you suffered a horrific loss. I am with you. You're not alone. We can mourn the loss of your unborn children together."

"What about my mother? Who's going to care for her now that I'm gone?"

"Worry not, your mother is in Heaven's hands."

"I trust you, Isolde Maria. I can feel it. I've never felt love like what I feel from you." Erica put her hands on the angel's shoulder and looked into her eyes. "Now I understand the Bible teaching that Jesus, the Father, and the Holy Ghost love me. As much as you love me, I know Jesus loves me even more. I can't comprehend it, but I know it's true."

"He created us both, Erica." Isolde Maria smiled. "He gave me the capacity to love you with a love beyond a mortal's capability. But it's nothing compared to the love of the one who sent me to you. You will realize it more when you reach your final destination. Smile Erica. Faith is a belief and confidence in the unseen and unknown. If something were proven beyond a reasonable doubt, it would no longer be faith. It's good for mortals to harbor doubt; otherwise, it would result in fanaticism. Meanwhile, Earth's greatest scientists have never disproved God and eternal life. Some may think they have." Isolde Maria chuckled. "But professing themselves wise, they became fools." She held Erica's right hand. "So, all beliefs or lack thereof, require a measure of faith. But you...How blessed is knowing for certain that you live forever?"

"I love God even more for sending you to me. I am no longer afraid. Look," Erica pointed. "The plane is about to land. Must I also mourn for Bobby? I was so happy when he got engaged to my sister. She became a better person while involved with Bobby, and I knew being a mother would change her even more."

"Erica," Isolde Maria braced her shoulders and gazed into her eyes, "I am going to reveal part of a secret. Adele was never going to marry Bobby, and they were never going to have children together. Bobby is almost here. He needs you, Erica. I know you're strong enough to help him. Remember how you pulled yourself together after your mother's stroke? You can do the same for Bobby. Don't worry. I will guide you. Bobby is a strong man, but ultimately, he will need your strength as a woman."

Erica lowered her head. A sole tear fell from her eye. Isolde Maria's hands remained on her shoulders. Erica gazed into her eyes. She kissed the angel's lips before embracing her. "Yes, Isolde Maria." Erica kissed her ear before speaking. "I can do it."

"Erica, many things must remain a mystery until this phase of your afterlife is complete." Isolde Maria beamed. "But when the time is right, Heaven will be even richer with your presence."

Isolde Maria and Erica held their embrace. Ten seconds later, the angel vanished. Erica stood alone and faced the now-landed Boeing C-17 Globemaster III aircraft.

***

150

'My leave. At last. I wish I didn't have to return to that shithole, but, hey, the Army gave me two weeks at home.' He pictured Adele and imagined making love to her. *'In a moment, Adele. In a moment, I will see. In a moment, I will feel. In a moment, I will tell you how much I love you and I'll show you with a kiss.'* Bobby walked on the Dover Air Force Base tarmac. He looked around. *'What am I doing here? My leave was supposed to be a charter flight into Atlanta, not an Air Force Base. Where is everyone?'* Bobby spotted a familiar female and smiled, the edges of his lips almost reaching his ears. *'It's Erica! Adele must be close by.'* "Erica!" He shouted and waved.

"Bobby!" Erica waved and jogged over to him.

They gently embraced.

"Erica, I am delighted to see you. No offence, but I'd rather see Adele. Where is she?" Bobby looked around. "For that matter, where are we? I thought we were landing at Hartsfield-Jackson Airport in Atlanta. This is an Air Force Base. Are we at Joint Base Charleston? Where is Adele? You have no idea how much I missed her. And my parents? My brother and my sister? Didn't they come to greet me?"

Erica took Bobby's hand and walked with him. She tried in vain to prevent a tear.

"There's something you're not telling me." Bobby yanked his hand away. "Did Adele leave me for another man? She made me suspicious; she was never home when I called. Tell me! I have a right to know."

"Bobby," Erica dropped her head and cried. She looked up. Bobby's distress was palpable. "It's nothing like that."

"Nothing like that? She's not here, and you're crying." Bobby spread his arms. "What is it? Tell me. I feel weightless. I can't even feel my heartbeat. Something is wrong. I'm a man; I'm a soldier. I can take it. Tell me."

Tears drenched Erica's face. She felt herself crystallize; she realized she was not breathing air. "Bobby, we're at Dover Air Force Base."

"No." Bobby shook his head. He gasped on seeing the opening cargo doors of the Boeing C-17 Globemaster III aircraft that transported him. Eight military personnel representing the Army, Navy, Air Force, and Marine Corps stood at attention in full dress uniform. Their next movements were deliberate, synchronized, and silent as they removed each flag-draped transfer case from the aircraft and into awaiting hearses. He turned to Erica. His lips quavered. "You mean, I'm…"

Erica nodded.

"No. It can't be. I have my whole life ahead of me. I want to be a civil engineer: designing railroads, highways, and bridges. I want to be a father. I want a family with Adele." Bobby started to float skyward. A wave of panic swept over him as the vista became smaller and more distant.

"Bobby! Bobby!" Erica reached upward. "Come back."

Bobby lost control of his movements and thoughts. The scene became more distant; the stench of jet fuel and rubber remained.

"Bobby! Bobby!" Erica covered her head and eyes. "No! No! Come back. Come back."

The aroma of a flower garden swept over Bobby. He felt a warm, reassuring grip on his hand. Isolde Maria lowered Bobby back to the tarmac. He stood still and pondered the depth of her oceanic eyes. *'She's so beautiful…No. Beyond beautiful. Her wings. I must be in Heaven.'*

"Bobby. I am Isolde Maria. I'm yours and Erica's angel guide. I know you had other plans. Heaven has a different purpose for you. I will help you fulfill it."

"You're more beautiful than anyone I've ever seen anywhere, even in art, movies, or photos. But Adele has my heart. Where is she?"

"Bobby, I would never try, nor am I able, to take Adele's place. As a Heavenly Angel, I can't marry or be given into marriage."

"You can't marry? I'm a man, and you're beyond gorgeous. No offense, it's a lovely offer, but I want to marry Adele."

"No offense taken." Isolde Maria chuckled. "I can't marry anyone. I am here as your guide. When the time is right, you will find something far better than a wife. The spiritual world harbors many mysteries. Not all is for you to know right now."

"But Adele? Where's Adele?"

"Bobby. I am here for you. You must give me your full trust and confidence. When you were deployed to Iraq, you knew it could happen." Isolde Maria nodded. "I know it's hard for you to come to terms with what happened. Erica faces the same storm."

He turned to Erica. His finger jittered as he pointed. "You mean, you're also…"

"Yes. Bobby. I'm also dead. We're both ghosts. But where is Adele?"

Isolde Maria held up her arm in a halt gesture. "You and Adele were never wed." Isolde Maria grasped Bobby's shoulders and gazed into his eyes. "Even if you were, marriage is until death do you part. I'm sorry, Bobby. Your bond with Adele is broken. Death has permanently ended your romantic bond."

Bobby closed his eyes and lowered his head. He squeezed his eyelids shut in a vain attempt to withhold tears.

"Bobby, you have a wonderful heart and a great capacity to love. I know how much you loved Adele. Love doesn't die overnight. I have never experienced the pain of romantic heartbreak; I can, however, understand and comprehend it. The pain will fade in time. Until then, know that I love you. I will help you and I will guide you." Isolde Maria kissed Bobby's forehead. They embraced. He breathed deeply through his nose, imbibing her delicious fragrance. She stood back. "You and Erica share the same mission." Isolde Maria looked at both Bobby and Erica. "Take my hands." She extended both hands. Bobby took the angel's left hand; Erica took her right hand. "Let me take you both to your new home." Isolde Maria flew Bobby and Erica away.

Chapter 3

Erica and Bobby walked across expansive, manicured green grass grounds. "I see it, but I don't believe it."

"After all that's happened," Erica wore denim jeans and a white blouse, "I'm ready to believe anything."

"Yeah, the Wilton Manor was a dilapidated mess for as long as I can remember." Bobby was still wearing his desert camouflage US Army battle dress uniform (BDU). "Additionally, the grounds were a weed-choked, trash-strewn mess."

"Everyone was afraid to visit because it's haunted. It's so creepy even the vandals left it alone." Erica pointed at the antebellum manor house. "The county owns it. I know the Civil War Historical Society wanted to buy it and restore it, but they never raised enough donations. But now look. It's sterling! I can't believe it!"

"At this point," Bobby chuckled, "I'm ready to believe anything."

A petite young woman in her early twenties opened the front door and stood on the main portico. Whitewashed columns supported the wide porch, shading the mansion and impressing as a Southern interpretation of a Greek temple. Brick chimneys rose from each end of the three-story mansion's hipped roofline. Ornate shutters shielded floor-to-ceiling windows. "Erica, Bobby, welcome. We are expecting you."

"She looks and sounds friendly enough. Her Southern accent is genuine. And the place sure doesn't look haunted anymore." Bobby turned to Erica. "Shall we proceed?"

"Do we have a choice? My woman's intuition detects only good vibes from her. Moreover, Isolde Maria dropped us off here. I trust her with all my heart."

Bobby and Erica stepped onto the main portico.

The young woman raised her outstretched right hand with her fingers gently curved. She fluttered her hand. Erica touched her hand and slightly bowed. Next, Bobby took her hand. The belle kept her elbow close to her body while yielding to Bobby's firm handshake. "Greetings. I'm Margarette." She smiled warmly. "I am your hostess." Margarette's blue eyes sparkled. A wide-brimmed hat topped her shoulder-length blonde hair. She wore a powder blue, cotton dress with elbow-length sleeves and a modest neckline. "Oh, aren't you just a picture of loveliness?" She held Erica's hand while her eyes quivered. "Oh, your green eyes and auburn hair, you must make a gentleman's heart bloom like a summer magnolia. And to be tall like you, did you step off a pedestal?"

"Thank you, Margarette." Erica blushed and lowered her head. "Those were lovely things to say."

Margarette closed her eyes. "Please speak again. I do declare your accent is true Carolina. And you," she looked directly at Bobby, "a tall, handsome soldier is always welcome at Wilton Manor." She extended her slender arm and took Bobby's hand. "Come inside."

Bobby had once entered Wilton Manor with two teenage friends on a dare. They lasted less than a minute in its dust, cobwebs, and darkness. The first rattle and moving shadow had the boys running out screaming. This time, Margarette led them through a framed sidelight, double door opening to a vast entrance hall with a sweeping staircase, high ceilings, and ornate European chandeliers. The rooms and furniture were of another age, yet pristine and immaculate. Men wearing military uniforms and women in semi-formal attire sat in velvet-upholstered settees positioned by mahogany tables. "You got here just in time. Tonight is our military ball. You and Erica will represent the Iraqi conflict." Margarette arched her eyebrows, "You two will join fallen veterans from many different wars and conflicts."

"What's with those two?" Erica pointed to a black man wearing a Civil War Union uniform and a White man in a Confederate uniform. "Isn't the Civil War over?"

"Oh, those two." Margarette chuckled. "They killed each other in battle during the Siege of Charleston. They're best friends now." She touched Erica's shoulder. "Don't take them too seriously. They enjoy arguing. Let me introduce you to them." Margarette led Bobby and Erica over to the Civil War soldiers. "George, James, this is Bobby and Erica. He came to us after dying for his country in Iraq."

"Good afternoon, Madam." The black soldier stood and bowed to Erica. "My name is George. I escaped slavery from these parts, took the underground railroad up North, and joined the Union Army to free my people."

"Well, I'm James. I never owned a damn slave and damn-well never wanted to. You damn Yankees hit us with the Morrill Tariff. That forced us to pay more for industrial imports, hurting our agricultural economy while feeding Yankee industry."

"He's spouting hogwash. Ask him if he ever objected to slavery."

"Don't bother listening to him." James pointed at George, "He was stupid enough to bring a knife to a gunfight."

"Well, my saber did a number on you." George pointed back.

"Yeah, what number from one to ten? It didn't stop me from pulling the trigger." James laughed. "What good did killing me accomplish? Look where you are. Living in a manor house.”

“Ha. Ha. Ha. This time, I have the master bedroom while you have a guest room.”

“Ignore those two.” Margarette laughed. “They always carry on like a couple of rascals. Look around you. You will even see soldiers and sailors from so-called enemy armies too. We are all in this together. We all died before our time. We do what we can to fulfill our purpose so we can move on to our final destination. Meanwhile, you two will live here with us. Let me take you to your room.” Margarette led Bobby and Eric to the top of the stairs and took them down a second-story hallway adorned with oil paintings and mounted oil lamps. She led them into a room with a teak desk, two mahogany, velvet-padded chairs, and a large, framed canopy bed.

“Is this my room or his?” Erica pointed at Bobby.

“It’s both of yours. Aren’t you two a married couple?”

“No. Just good friends.”

“Lord have mercy! I can’t permit an unmarried couple to share a bed. I’m afraid this is our last room. This is a manor house.” Margarette pointed at Bobby. “You can’t flop in a living room like a drifter.” She bowed her head. “And I can’t ask a gentleman to sleep in the servant’s quarters. I’m sorry, Bobby. You’ll have to find a home elsewhere.”

“You can’t do that to him. He is new to this ghost thing.” Erica placed her hand on Margarette’s shoulder. “He has no idea of where to go.”

“Well…” Margarette bit her lip. “He’s a soldier who died for his country with honor, so I can’t cast him out like a stray. I’ll let him sleep on the floor.” Margarette folded her arms. “For now, anyway.”

"Margarette." Erica smiled. "I have an idea. Bring us extra pillows. We'll erect a barricade between us. Additionally, Bobby and I can take turns standing outside the room when we change clothes."

"That's a peculiar arrangement, but I can tell by how he talks and conducts himself that he's a true Southern gentleman who will always respect a lady and her virtue. I will allow it." Margarette beamed. "And you," she placed her hands on Erica's shoulders, "so pretty. But you can't wear denim to a formal ball. Bobby's uniform is just dandy. But we should make you the belle of the ball, or as you will say a century later, the queen of the hop." Margarette chuckled.

"I'm afraid 'Queen of the Hop' is also before my time." Erica laughed.

"Oh, Erica, but your beauty is timeless. If I didn't know better, I'd say you stepped right out of a portrait, and you're as graceful as a swan but twice as fair. Would you grant this one-hundred-and-fifty-eight-year-old Southern woman the honor and indulgence of dressing into ravishing creature of my time?"

"Of course, Margarette. How can I say no after how nice you've treated Bobby and me?" Erica smiled. "You've given us more than a place to stay, you've given us a home."

"Splendid!" Margarette beamed and raised her hands. "Let me show you what we have." She walked over to the closet and opened the door. It creaked open, wafting in the aroma of pressed violets and cedarwood. "How about this?" Margarette held up an ivory satin gown. It matched Erica's subdued hourglass form, including an off-the-shoulder neckline and short, puffed sleeves."

"Huh," Erica put her hands in front of her face. "It's lovely. I'd be right pleased to wear that gown of uncommon loveliness."

"Well, I declare. I'd be right pleased if I could make your precious auburn hair bloom like a chrysanthemum bouquet, fix you up with my makeup, and share my jewelry with you. Come to my room," Margarette took Erica's hand. "We'll have guests spanning two and a half centuries trip over themselves upon seeing you."

***

Bobby sat in the main ballroom with Jason, a fallen Vietnam War veteran. He wore his dress-green uniform, battle ribbons, and a green beret with a 10th Special Forces Group flash. He held hands with Sunbeam. She wore strappy leather sandals and a tie-dyed T-shirt without a bra. Her long blonde hair was parted in the middle; her beaded headband held three daisies. James extended his glass of bourbon to Jason. "I salute you. For some odd reason, Americans made you into the bad guys. I identify with you."

George guzzled his bourbon. "Ain't no odd reason you're hated, Jimbo. You were traitors who rebelled against the established and standing United States government, all to keep my people in bondage."

"Traitor?" James stood up. "We fought for our constitutional right to succeed. Look up Article IV, Section 3. It will teach you something about States' Rights. While you're at it, look deeper into your Commander in Chief. Talking about jumping out of the frying pan and into the fire. Lincoln wanted to move you from the plantation to the boat back to Africa."

Bobby, Jason, and Sunbeam snickered at their arguing. Jason adjusted his green beret, "In my time, they would've killed each other by now."

Sunbeam guffawed. "They already killed each other once. We've all come a long way as ghosts. They've progressed to good-natured verbal sparring."

"You're right. Besides, back in our day, you shouted insults and threw stuff at the military. Now look at us." Jason kissed Sunbeam's lips. Sunbeam kissed him back.

A tinkling bell caught the attention of the entire party. Margarette stood by the foot of the stairs. "Ladies and gentlemen. I welcome y'all to our military ball. Many of y'all gave your lives to your countries. Win or lose, regardless of the cause, y'all are heroes. Our newest member of the Wilton Manor family is Staff Sergeant Bobby Sand of the United States Army. Won't you please stand and take a bow?"

Bobby looked around. James, George, Jason, and Sunbeam nodded to him. Bobby stood to the applause of the gathering.

"Our veterans left loved ones behind. Let's raise our glasses to those who stayed behind, waited patiently, and kept their families intact." Margarette paused. "I also wish to salute those of you who were not a fallen warrior's partner in life but have become a partner in death. Please stand. Sunbeam, three other ladies, and one gentleman stood." Margarette nodded for them to sit. "Ladies and gentlemen, I now wish to introduce our newest guest. While she wasn't Staff Sergeant Sand's partner in life, she is now his partner in death. If y'all would please shift your gaze to the top of the stairs. First- hold on to your seats. The vision of charm, grace, and beauty you're about to behold may come as a gentle breeze…or knock you over like a hurricane. With great pride, I present Charleston's own treasure, Miss Erica Beauchamp."

The room fell into stunned silence. She glided down the sweeping staircase in ivory satin slippers. A warm summer draft fluttered her matching Ivory colored gown's skirt. She didn't need a corset for its gold frills to hug her waist. Gold straps held the gown over bare shoulders. Puffy short sleeves enriched her long arms, tapering to an elegant gold cuff bracelet worn over a silky white glove. The gown framed her breasts like a portrait in a world-class art gallery. Her auburn hair was parted down the center with precision and swept back into a braided chignon, low on her neck. A single-strand pearl necklace adorned her round neck. Her cheeks had the perfect amount of makeup to enhance her heart-shaped face, high cheekbones, and subdued chin. The gathering remained breathless.

"Bobby," Margarette smiled and nodded to him.

Bobby stood. He took a deep breath. His nerves tingled. He floated over to Erica. She extended her gloved hand to him. He took her hand and walked her over to their table. The silent gathering at last stood and applauded. Bobby and Erica sat at the table with James, George, Jason, and Sunbeam. Erica took off her gloves, folded them, and placed them on the table. "Tonight, we're getting treated to live entertainment."

Sunbeam smiled. "Yes, Erica, and best of all, it could be anyone from the last two hundred and fifty years."

"I'm hoping for Jimi Hendrix, Janis Joplin, or Jim Morrison." Jason sipped his bourbon.

"In that case, I'd like to see Kurt Cobain," Bobby grinned.

"All I see is a piano. Jerry Lee Lewis, Fats Domino, and Little Richard are still alive, so we probably won't be rockin' and rollin'." Erica turned to George and James. "Who would you guys like to see?"

"Music is something we agree on." James smiled. "I'm hoping for George's favorite. It came along after we passed to the ghostly realm. I hope Margarette got us Fats Waller."

"And I could live with, oops, that didn't come out right," George laughed, "James's later favorite. George Gershwin. I hope he plays something from Porgy and Bess."

"Shh." Sunbeam put her finger over her lips. "It looks like Margarette is about to introduce our entertainer."

Margarette tinkled a silver bell. "Ladies and gentlemen. I know y'all didn't come to hear me ring a bell and talk. So, I proudly introduce y'all to our singer and piano player."

"Oh my God! Erica," Sunbeam grasped Erica's hand. "I here I thought you were just about the most beautiful woman I'd ever seen. No offence, but she's breathtaking."

"Don't worry. I love you and only you." Jason squeezed Sunbeam's free hand. "Nevertheless, I never saw anything like her while alive or dead."

"I second that," George's jaw dropped, "and she's not even black."

James kept his eyes on the woman. "George, I'm too enchanted to respond to that."

High black spikes enhanced her tall stature. The ballroom fell into a trance. She wore an ankle-length red gown with posh sequins. An inch-wide band on her shoulder's edge secured her gown. It had a ruffled heart-shaped cut over her breasts and tapered slightly to her waist, enhancing the contours of her figure. A modest pearl necklace reached the edge of her cleavage. Her wavy indigo hair cascaded down her back. "I am Isolde Maria. I was invited to be the entertainment for your ball. Am I at Wilton Manor, or did I get lost along the way and end up in a graveyard?" She beamed. "I've faced dead audiences before, but never fossils. What does it take to dig all of you up?"

The gathering laughed gaily.

"I can start by taking two hundred and fifty years of song requests, but that may take yet another century." Isolde

Maria paused for the get-together's laughter. "Some of you have waited a long time, and I mean a long, long time, so let's bring this party to life."

The assemblage applauded.

"I want Staff Sergeant Bobby Sand and his breathtaking partner Erica to have the first dance."

Bobby froze. Erica stood and took his hand. "What's the matter, Bobby? You've looked into the whites of enemy combatants' eyes, but now you're afraid to dance?" She pulled Bobby to his feet.

Bobby looked back and forth before allowing Erica to pull him to the dance floor. Isolde Maria played the instrumental prelude on the piano. Bobby put his left hand on Erica's waist and his right hand on her shoulder. *'She's Adele's sister. I know Adele would never object to a friendly dance.* He closed his eyes. *'Yet just touching her waist and arm is far too delightful.'*

Erica and Bobby swayed to the piano music without fully embracing. Erica put both hands around the back of his neck. She looked into his eyes. *'I always wanted him for my sister. She needed a strong, silent type to help her mature and grow.'* Erica gazed into his eyes. *'I don't think she ever appreciated how handsome he is.'* Erica unconsciously brushed his cheeks with her fingers.

'Erica, like Adele, was always pretty, but I only saw her as the older sister. Now she looks drop-dead gorgeous. I guess she was too busy helping her mother and Adele, and perhaps a tad too modest, to show her radiance to the world.'

Isolde Maria addressed the audience, "You two are ghosts, not zombies. Are you afraid the other might devour you if you get too close?" She paused for the crowd's laughter. "This song is meant to be danced cheek to cheek."

Bobby and Erica glanced into each other's eyes before embracing and swaying together.

Isolde Maria sang,

"Midnight with the stars and you.

Midnight and a rendezvous.

Your eyes held a message tender,

saying I surrender, all my love to you."

"Bobby, her voice is mesmerizing. Her tone is so lovely and serene." Erica tilted her head back and looked at Bobby's lips. "Now I know everything is going to be okay."

Bobby gazed at Erica's high cheekbones and fulsome smile. "The sirens hypnotized sailors with their voices." Bobby chuckled. "Look at what happened to them."

"Silly." Erica laughed. "That was mythology. Has anyone ever heard a siren song? We're listening to her right now. Besides, the sirens destroyed men. I'm a woman. I sense only purity and goodness in her voice."

"Erica, I don't know how to say this. I faced death every day in Iraq. Adele was never there for me. I stood on my own, as a man should. But this time…Erica…I need you."

Erica and Bobby tightened their embrace. They rubbed their cheeks together as they danced, and Isolde Maria sang.

"Midnight brought us sweet romance.

I know all my whole life through,

I'll be remembering you, whatever else I do,

Midnight and the stars and you."

Chapter 4

Bobby and Erica sipped coffee spiced with chicory and sugar from French Limoges cups. Margarette strolled over to them. "A warm good morning to my favorite sweet pair." She winked. "Seeing y'all waltz last night was like watching a story unfold. There was enough heat between you two to set the stage on fire." She raised her fan and gave it a playful flutter. "I do declare, letting an unmarried couple share a bed with only a pillow separating y'all is right peculiar." She chuckled and fanned Bobby and Erica. "From now on, it better be a brick wall or you're sleeping on the floor." She giggled and tapped Bobby on top of his head with her fan before walking away.

Bobby turned to Erica. "Well, I do hope my snoring didn't keep you awake."

"I must admit, sleeping in the same bed with my sister's former fiancé," Erica winced, "was a bit unsettling, even if the pillows fell somewhere between the Berlin Wall and the Great Wall of China."

"I sense a 'but' coming."

"Yes. But…" Erica took a deep breath. "I admit, I enjoyed the rhythm of your breath." Erica blushed and lowered her head. "And the pillows couldn't block your warmth."

"May I confess something?"

"Well, it is your turn." Erica laughed.

"Your fragrance was the air of sweet dreams."

Erica and Bobby held hands and inhaled deeply through their noses. The aroma of a lush bouquet of gardenia, jasmine, lilac, and roses delighted their senses. They felt a gentle hand on their shoulders.

"Huh," Erica gasped.

Isolde Maria stood before them. She wore a doctor's white coat, light blue slacks, and a medical headscarf that covered her luxuriant, indigo tresses. The proportions and contours of her face still radiated. "Bobby, Erica, I have to take you someplace."

"Will you bring us back?" Erica looked around the room, her eyes wide. "The other ghosts are doing so much to help us adjust to…well, being ghosts."

"Of course, Erica." Isolde Maria chuckled. "This is important, and it will put you even more at peace." Isolde extended both hands. Erica and Bobby each held one of the angels' hands. They dissolved into particles and floated away.

***

Bobby and Erica found themselves in the hallway of the Good Shepherd Hospice. Isolde Maria led them through an open door. Tears immediately sprang from Erica's eyes. "Mother! But, but…You look so..."

"Erica!" Monica Beauchamp walked over and hugged her daughter. "I am thrilled to see you. I hope you are also thrilled to see me. Look at what Dr. Isolde Maria did for me! She found a miracle cure. I look and feel thirty years younger."

"I don't know how…" Erica glanced behind her. Isolde Maria had vanished.

"You know that medical technology is not my thing," Monica beamed. "So, let's not ask the good doctor too many questions. All I know is that I'm healthy and I'm looking like a beautiful woman again."

"You were always beautiful, mother."

"Oh, you're still too polite, Erica. You know, I was a decrepit old lady before Dr. Isolde Maria's treatment. But you, Erica," Monica placed her hand on her daughter's shoulder, "sacrificed everything for me. You even gave up your dreams of law school."

"Oh, Mother, you've laughed at the lawyer jokes. Isn't the world a better place because of a mother like you rather than another lawyer?"

"You're too kind, Erica." Monica's eyes opened wide. "And Bobby! You're back from the Army. I am so glad you came. Where is Adele? I know she is in good hands now that she has met a gentleman like you." Monica smiled. "Promise you will take good care of her."

Bobby glanced at Erica before holding both of Monica's hands. "I promise."

"Erica, now that you don't have a sick old lady to worry about, I hope you can find a good man like Bobby. I am hoping for at least one grandchild."

Isolde Maria walked into the room wearing a stethoscope around her neck and a manila folder in her hand. She chuckled. "I have another special surprise for you."

"Dr. Isolde Maria!" Monica beamed. "What more can you possibly surprise me with? And Erica, I couldn't be prouder of you. But you know I couldn't do it alone. Charles was a wonderful father and a wonderful husband. I never stopped loving him. Dr. Isolde Maria promised to take me to him."

Isolde Maria braced Monica's shoulders and kissed her forehead. She moved her head back enough to gaze into her eyes before kissing her lips. "Come with me, Monica." She took her by the hand.

The room's walls became like cumulus clouds. A staircase with white steps and a gold balustrade appeared. A blindingly bright light shone at the top. Isolde Maria led Monica to the top of the stairs. They vanished together.

Erica bawled. She embraced Bobby, buried her eyes on his shoulder, and soaked his desert BDU uniform in tears.

Chapter 5

The Wonderer's Inn was secreted away on Edgecombe Drive, a side street off Brinsfield Road. The motel's location was ten minutes away, in different directions, from both the Pussy Cat Lounge and Horrible Hank's Tavern. The Wonderer's Inn had a dozen free-standing units. Each unit had a 170-square-foot bedroom, and an untiled bathroom with a sink, toilet, and bathtub with a shower nozzle. Trevor Brocton had rented cabin number twelve. It was at the end of the driveway, after the paving ended, and next to a swamp. He rented it monthly, using a fake ID. He knew it was unnecessary, but as insurance, he bribed the manager and his staff to stay out of the unit. The manager took the money and asked no questions. Trevor lay in bed with Cloretta, who danced as Thais at the Pussy Cat Lounge. She turned onto her side and faced Trevor. "I know you're paying me for this. Yet, still, you couldn't treat me to something better?"

"Relax, babe." Trevor got out of bed and walked to the bathroom mirror. Rather than smash a small cockroach scurrying up the wall, he secured a stray hair follicle with another dab of Oribe Gel Serum. "I've scoped out the place. There's nowhere for Mr. Bates to make an unwelcome entrance. Would you rather I shorten the cash stack I left on the table, or do you want me to spend it on a fancier room?"

"Why do you have to cheapen me? I know you never would've taken Adele to a dump like this." Cloretta sat up and pulled the top sheet over her breasts.

"Cheapen you?" Trevor marched into the bedroom. The towel around his waist fell to the floor. "A dump like this? I should rather screw you under an I-26 overpass. Whores like you should appreciate having a mattress with a roof over your head. You're good value for money. Let's leave it at that. You know the truth."

"You bastard!" Cloretta spat.

Trevor took three deep breaths. His rage increased with each inhalation. He scowled at her; narrow eyes underscored his fiery complexion.

She curled her shoulders inward, arms crossed tightly over her chest, wishing she could fade into the wall.

"I'll teach you what you're worth." He lurched over, put his right hand on her throat, and pinned her head to the bed. With his left hand, he plucked one of her pubic hairs. She shrieked. He held it in front of her. "Ha! Ha! Ha!" He laughed sinisterly. "Does this not speak a thousand words as to your net worth?"

Sweat and tears covered her face.

Blood rushed to his penis. "You want another hundred dollars? How about I pluck a few more? What do you say? Answer me bitch." Trevor pinched her cheeks, his fingers and thumb against her flesh and teeth, and shook her face. He reached down and plucked another pubic hair.

Cloretta screamed. With a burst of adrenaline, she pummeled him with spasmodic punches. Trevor grabbed her wrists. He looked her over. '*Pathetic. How dare she strike a Brocton?*' He pinned her arms to the bed and violated her. Hammering. Hammering. "Ahh…Yes…My nectar of life," he muttered as he climaxed.

She bawled.

"Shut up. Stop blubbering. I want to watch this. Trevor got up and turned up the volume of the TV. It was tuned to a press conference.

"Good afternoon, I'm Grady O'Malley, Sheriff of Charleston County." Two South Carolina state police, one in plain clothes and the other in uniform, flanked the

Charleston County Sheriff. "The Sheriff's office and the South Carolina state police have concluded our investigation into the crash that took the lives of sisters Adele and Erica Beauchamp and Steven McClenahan. Our investigation included crash scene forensic evidence, interviews, and the testimony of the train operator and the locomotive's event recorder. We have ruled the deaths of Adele and Erica Beauchamp a double homicide, and Steven McClenahan's death an accident. Evidence beyond a reasonable doubt is that Adele Beauchamp and Steven McClenahan were once romantically involved. Multiple witnesses at Adele's place of work, The Pussy Cat Lounge, where she was employed as a waitress, have testified that Adele Beauchamp physically rebuffed Steven McClenahan for inappropriately touching her. He reacted violently. The venue's security has testified under oath, backed up by eyewitnesses, that he resisted their efforts to eject him from the premises. Jealousy, anger, and revenge motivated McClenahan to commit this heinous crime. Skid marks and the testimony of the train operator prove that McClenahan followed the sisters in an automobile. An unregistered vehicle that Investigators determined he constructed from stolen parts. He used this vehicle as a weapon to deliberately hit the sisters from behind, forcing them into the locomotive's path. Afterward, McClenahan lost control of his vehicle and skidded under a moving boxcar. All three bodies were incinerated." The Sheriff nodded to the reporters. "Charleston County Sheriff's Office and South Carolina State Police have concluded our investigation. Thank you." The reporters shouted questions as the Sheriff walked away. The TV network returned its feed to the studio and its male and female news anchor pair.

"Yes!" Trevor shook his fist. "I just saved myself sixty-five thousand big ones." He looked at Cloretta with a wide smile and bright eyes.

"You're a monster!" She lay on the bed, weeping and sobbing. "How can you be happy? I loved Adele. Besides, she was your girlfriend." Cloretta wiped away tears with her hand. "What do you mean you saved sixty-five thousand dollars?"

"Oh, so you loved her, huh?" He held one of Cloretta's pubic hairs three inches in front of her eyes. "Did you munch on one of these? I have a few of hers. If you behave, I can give you one to chew on."

"You're sick!" She prodded. "I'm a dancer and only on occasion do a job on the side. You know I also like girls, and Adele was hot, but she didn't swing that way. Plus, she was a waitress, not a dancer. Some of the girls hated her because they were jealous of her looks, and she made more tips. But she was my friend. I loved her and I miss her." Cloretta broke down. "I thought you loved her!" She prodded. "I know she loved you."

"I've tolerated enough of your bullshit. Here." He walked over to his trousers hanging on the back of a chair and pulled out his wallet from the back pocket. He took out two one-hundred-dollar bills. "I'm sure you've had freaks before, but none that tipped you with two big ones." He handed her the bills. "This is in addition to your regular fee sitting on the table. I'm sure this also buys your silence, not that I must buy it. After all, it would be the word of a stripper, drug addict, and whore against a Brocton. So, take my money and shut the fuck up." Trevor returned to the bathroom and re-combed his hair, adding another dab of Oribe Gel Serum. "Get dressed. I'll drop you off at the club." He walked over to her and held up her pubic hair. He kissed it and put it in a silver pill box. "To remember you until next time. And there will be a next time. You may not want to do it." Trevor smirked at her. "But you're a single mother. Soon you'll go broke and have no choice but to take whatever work you can get."

Cloretta again pulled the top sheet over her and wept.

"I don't have all day. Hurry up. I have a meeting with Picardi Developments."

***

George and James wore semi-formal, albeit out-of-fashion, civilian clothes. They sat at a high table at the Hooters on King Street. A college football bowl game was on the TVs. "I love this sport." George pointed at the TV.

"We had baseball back in our day, but nothing like this. Yes!" James raised his arms and cheered as Alabama scored a touchdown. "Roll tide!"

George folded his arms and shook his head. "Okay. Your boys tied the score. Michigan is about to get the ball." George smirked at James. "Your cheers are about to turn to tears."

"Another mint julep will put a smile on both of our faces."

"It's your turn for the next round."

"Here comes our waitress." James waved to her. "Miss Ronni, if you would please, may we have two more mint juleps?"

"Yes, sir," the twenty-year-old brunette smiled. "Coming up," she jotted down their order on her notepad.

"Not only did we not have football in our time." George finished his mint julep. "No respectable place has such roses among thorns on display." He beamed. "She's a vision of loveliness."

"I thought you preferred black women."

173

"I do." George grinned. "Just because I like cherry pie more than peach pie doesn't mean I dislike peach pie, and our waitress is one ripe peach."

"Ain't that the truth. As gorgeous as Erica and Margarette looked in their ball gowns…Mmm…Mmm…God bless the future. Miss Ronni sets the house on fire in those short shorts and a T-shirt."

"Hey! Look! The TV." George pointed. "They interrupted the game for a police report. Isn't that our Erica?"

"Yes. It is. And that photo must be of her sister. She's just as pretty."

"Will you get a load of that guy?" George pointed at the TV. "Look at those Satanic tattoos. He would be strung up in two shakes of a lamb's tail back in our time. I remember sailors having an anchor or something like it tattooed on them, but that?"

"Goodness gracious. According to the sheriff, he murdered our Erica and her sister."

Ronni returned with her tray of mint juleps. George and James had vanished. She turned to another party. "Hey, do you know where the two gentlemen who sat at this table went?"

A stocky male wearing an Alabama Crimson Tide jersey spread his palms. "No one was sitting at that table."

"What do you mean?" Ronni set her tray of mint juleps on the table. "How can you miss them? A white man and a black man. They dressed funny and talked funny. They drank mint juleps. No one orders those anymore." Ronni scratched her head. "And they were so polite and well-mannered. How can I forget them?"

A female also wearing an Alabama football jersey shrugged. "I'm sorry, Ronni, he's right. No one sat there."

"Yes! Go! Go! All Right." A patron wearing a Michigan Wolverines jersey and cap stood. "Hey, Ronni, no one was sitting there," he pointed at the empty table. "I'll tell you what, I'll celebrate Michigan's twenty-yard gain by buying those mint juleps from you."

Chapter 6

'What's a matter, Trevor? You dropped her off unharmed.' Trevor drove out of the Pussy Cat Lounge parking lot. *'Nothing to worry about, Trevor. Nothing to worry about. She's a stripper and a whore. Even if she talks, who will believe her? Even though I did it for her own good, she can still make you look bad. You did the right thing, Trevor. Getting caught silencing her is a bigger risk.'* Trevor turned onto the feeder road toward I-26. 'Oh shit!' He glanced at his Porsche's dashboard clock and banged on the steering wheel. 'I'll never make my meeting with Picardi Developments.' He gritted his teeth. *'Fuck it. Rather, I drown it out. The boys should be finishing work about now.'* Trevor picked up his cellphone.

***

Trevor sat at a table in the corner of Horrible Hank's Tavern, away from the bar and the door to the restrooms. "Over here." He waved at Henry Sawyers and Michael Evans as they entered the tavern. They walked across the peeling linoleum floor to Trevor's table. "Damn, Trevor. What's with this dive? The only thing missing is sawdust on the floor." Henry sat. "Why not a trendy place on King Street?"

"I'm doing you a favor," Trevor smirked at him. "Now you can see how your lowlife clients live."

"Need I remind you, the William Crane Law Firm is a corporate practice. We don't do criminal law."

"Corporate? Criminals?" Trevor laughed. "Same thing. Different methods."

176

"You seem in good spirits. You must be heartbroken after losing Adele. What a tragedy. Not just Adele but her sister as well."

Trevor placed his palms down on the table. "Adele was just a game. She posed a greater challenge than most. After all, she was engaged, stealing her away from her fiancé posed an added challenge. Nevertheless, at the end of the day, no woman can resist the Brocton charm?" Trevor grinned.

"Yeah, and the Brocton money." Michael chortled.

"Trevor, you know that Adele was Jenny's best friend." Henry pursed his lips. "Jenny is shattered. If any good came out of this, the tragedy has brought us closer. I told you that my family approves of her. I've got big news." He beamed. "Jenny and I are engaged."

"What? Henry Sawyers, a scion and member of Charleston's most prestigious law firm? Engaged to a waitress at a tittie bar? You've got to be kidding. And here you castigate me for inviting you to a dive bar."

"I resent that, Trevor. Just because we're at a low-life bar doesn't mean you have to act like a low-life. Adele was gorgeous, and she loved you. You also took her from a fiancé who loved her and served our country. Why the sick game?" Henry pointed at Trevor, "Okay. The McClenahan guy was no loss, but her sister was also a looker. She never harmed anybody. At least show some respect for the dead."

"Who canonized you?" Trevor laughed. "You weren't calling my game sick when I passed my sloppy seconds on to you. You think you'd get Jenny without me breaking the ice? Besides, Adele's so-called fiancé bought it in Iraq. He already got full military honors. The city of Charleston renamed a city park after him. They're also going to erect a statue of him in front of his old high school. So, enough about honoring the dead, and speaking of the dead, you're lucky Adele's stuck-up sister got it too. Otherwise, you'd be out five grand."

"Let's not go there." Henry shook his head.

"Why not? You have the gall to call me a low-life? You not only made a low-life's bet, but you would've lost." Trevor smirked and placed his interlocked fingers behind his head. "You doubt it?" Trevor reached into his pocket and pulled out a silver pillbox. He grinned and opened it. "A pussy hair, courtesy of Thais, the hottest dancer at the Pink Pussy Cat. You know, the tall brunette with ass and legs that go on forever, and now you have proof that I got between them."

"That's disgusting." Michael stood. "Why do you have to do that? What do you have to prove? Hollywood would be hard-pressed to find a leading man as handsome as you. I'm only five-nine. You're six-three. You've got the Brocton fortune, you're a slick talker, and you know how to dress. We all know you're a ladies' man. What more do you have to prove? Why do something so crass and crude?"

"Who is *we* white man?" Henry jabbed Michael in the ribs. "You may think he's a ladies' man, but I know he was never enough of a man to bed Erica. She has too much dignity and class for…a low-life like him." He pointed at Trevor.

Trevor ignored Hank's barb. "Dignity and Class? Erica shared a three-bedroom house in Bayhaven with her mother and sister. They had to wait in line just to take a piss." He kept his palms down on the table while standing and leaning toward Henry. "Try Stuck-up and fridged." Trevor laughed. "Maybe even lesbian, but that never stopped me."

"Whatever." Henry threw up his palms. "You're not invincible. You weren't gonna nail her, regardless. Hey, listen. The jukebox is playing an old Carl Butler number. Now this honkytonk's got some atmosphere. Let's change the subject. I'll get us some shots of Jack and a pitcher of beer."

Trevor slowly, deliberately smiled. He tightened his jaw and tilted his head at Henry. Trevor lowered his eyes and pressed his lips tightly to stifle his laughter.

Chapter 7

"Did you sleep well?" Erica smiled at Bobby.

"Even though I slept next to a pillow barricade, the nearness of you beats the crap out of a cot in Iraq with Sergeant Fuller's snoring and Sergeant Garcia's farting." He chuckled and gave Erica a friendly hug.

"Well, I would hope so." Erica patted Bobby's back while prolonging their embrace. "Let's get some breakfast. I can smell Margarette's eggs and bacon from here."

***

"A good morning to Wilton Manor's sweetest pair." Margarette wore a light cotton wrapper dress with a floral motif. She had a matching ribbon in her hair and embroidered slippers on her feet. "I hope y'all kept those pillows between you, but based on what I see, I do declare, I best build y'all that brick wall." She chuckled and took Erica's hand. "I may dress like I did about a hundred and fifty or so years ago, but that doesn't mean I've slept the whole time since. You're here by special invitation. I'm your hostess during your stay, and it's my sincere wish that I make Y'all's stay as pleasant as possible." She grinned delicately. "Rest easy. The good Lord never sends more than your souls can bear. Wilton Manor is nothing like the popular song from your time, *'Hotel California'*. You're checked in, but you can come and go as you please." Margarette braced Erica's arm and waved at Bobby. "I know y'all are new at our ghostly thing. George and James want to fill you in on something." Margarette nodded. "It's serious, so I think you should give him your ear." Margarette offered Erica her arm. She gently held it while Margarette took them to George and James.

Both Erica and Bobby did a double-take upon seeing James wearing an Alabama Crimson Tide football jersey and George wearing a Michigan Wolverines jersey. Their demeanors were serious. Margarette held Erica's hand and nodded to her to sit. Bobby followed.

"Good morning." James first nodded to Erica and then to Bobby. "Firstly, Margarette is more than our hostess. She is the mistress of the house."

"Otherwise, saying, we're one big ghost family; she's our matriarch." George sipped a cup of coffee. "Although our angel guides outrank her."

"Matriarch!" Margarette laughed. "I do declare, if someone looks up to me as their matriarch, I prefer they be younger than me."

"Well, Miss Margarette, we did speak to you first about this." James nodded. "I wouldn't speak to them about this matter without your approval. The four of us, the rest of us actually," James looked at Erica before motioning to the rest of the guests, "are in this together." He looked directly at Erica and Bobby. "We don't outrank you. But through over a hundred and fifty years of experience with this, George and I have gained more knowledge about our powers and limitations."

"In this house, we are vivified with human bodies. Outside of our Wilton Manor sanctuary, we are unseen. If we concentrate enough, we can transport to other places as specters." George slid his coffee cup and saucer to the table's edge. "We can muster the energy to vivify and even talk to mortals temporarily."

"We are not empowered to communicate with people who knew us while living without the approval of our angel guide," James added.

"Yes," Erica beamed. "Isolde Maria, the woman who played piano and sang for us, is our angel guide."

"That enchantress is your angel guide?" James stood. "What did you do to warrant her? My angel guide is a black man named Joshua Magumba."

"And what's so bad about a black man?" George stood and faced James. "He treats you far better than you deserve." George grinned and pointed at James. "Besides, you're just jealous because Aurelia is my angel guide, a beautiful black woman."

"Yeah, well, I bet she likes white guys."

"And I bet if Joshua Magumba wanted, he could woo a pretty white lady." George held up his hand. "Okay. Let's not go there right now."

"Agreed." George sat. "We'd better tell Bobby and Erica what they need to know."

James nodded to Margarette before speaking. She nodded back. "As you are aware, Wilton Manor houses spirits from even before its construction. You just arrived from the turn of the 21st century. Your new friends, Jason and Sunbeam, died in the late nineteen-sixties."

Margarette looked at Bobby and Erica. "As I reckon you've come to realize, Wilton Manor remains just as it was before the War Between the States—unchanged, untouched…as if the years never dared set foot inside."

George added, "That means no TV or electricity. Therefore, James and I transported ourselves to Hooters on King Street to watch the Alabama versus Michigan football game."

"It's like Margarette told you, we're not prisoners in place or time." James folded his hands. "We know what goes on in the outside world. As the great English writer Charles Dickens wrote during Margarette, George, and my day, 'It was the best of times, and it was the worst of times'." James laughed. "That applies to our time and this time. Hooters would be scandalous in our time, but George and I love that it's respectable in this time."

"We all died differently." Margarette fluidly brushed a loose strand of hair behind her ear. "We all share that we died before our time. Bobby," Margarette tapped his hand. "You, James, George, and Jason were killed in combat. I was thrown from a horse as a young lady. Sunbeam died of a drug overdose. Y'all are not judged by how you died, but the contents of your hearts when you lived and what death prevented you from accomplishing."

"What I want to tell you is…" James took a deep breath, closed his eyes, and tilted back his head. "Erica, we saw on TV how you died."

Erica squeezed Bobby's hand and gasped. Her face froze as she looked at James and George.

"I consulted with Margarette and my Angel guide, Aurelia." George steeled his expression. "You were murdered and murdered by someone you knew."

"Murdered." Erica's voice jumped an octave. "By whom?"

"Steven McClenahan." George gritted his teeth. "He forced your car in front of a train. He wanted revenge against your sister. You happened to be in the wrong place at the wrong time."

"Dammit!" Bobby stood. "I knew that asshole was nothing but trouble." Bobby smacked his forehead with his palm. "If only I weren't deployed. I could've looked after her."

Erica grabbed Bobby's arm. "It's not your fault."

"Yes, it is. He was waiting for me to leave."

Erica wept.

"The veil's been lifted, and I reckon the truth is almost too much for your heart to bear." Margarette squeezed Erica's hand. "But you have Bobby, and you both have each other's differing strengths. Although you have many new friends here who understand, I think y'all should have private time alone. George. James. Would Y'all be so kind as to teach our precious new friends how to transport?

After Margarette left, George addressed Bobby and Erica. "Close your eyes and count each breath, inhaled and exhaled, until you reach ten. Concentrate on your angel guide. Picture her, but don't call her name. Now count your breaths, inhaled and exhaled, but do it with the letters A through J. Bobby. The three of us are military. You can use the radio telephony alphabet, alpha through juliet. Afterward, concentrate on where you want to be. Your angel guide will take you there without appearing to you."

"First, both of you must make certain of where you want to go." James laughed. "It's a big World out there, I'm sure you want to go to the same place."

***

Erica and Bobby walked together on Folly Beach. Bobby turned and faced Erica but hesitated to hold her hands. "Erica, what is stranger?" Bobby snickered, "Our lives or our afterlives?"

Erica laughed. "I guess laughter is our only medicine. Thanks to Spike McClenahan, I'll never be a mother or give my mother a grandchild. I wish I were alive to go to law school and prosecute him." Erica chuckled. "I know what you're thinking. Well, not for murdering me and my sister, but for any number of things that miscreant may have been doing."

"Is it ironic or coincidental. This is the spot where I got engaged to Adele. Of course, it was a warm summer night.

Now here we are alone on the same beach on a cool, early Spring dawn."

"Bobby, I have so much to be grateful for. I had a wonderful mother and father. Father's dying hurt both Adele and me. I think it affected Adele more. After our mother suffered her stroke, I was the only one left to look after her." Erica gazed piercingly into Bobby's eyes. "I was thrilled when Adele met a man like you. I knew from then on that she would set herself right."

"I am now sometimes angry at W and his puppet-masters for getting us involved in Iraq. I believed in it. I thought I was going to change the world and make it a better place for Adele and our future family. All that happened is that I went away, and the door for McClenahan to murder Adele and you opened."

"Please, Bobby." Erica touched his hand. "You must not blame yourself, or anyone else for that matter. Spike was evil. I sensed it the first time I met him. McClenahan, and McClenahan alone, is to blame for the murder."

"I'm sorry, Erica." He lowered his head. "It's just that I am one to take responsibility for my actions."

"Bobby," She took his hands and pecked his lips with a closed mouth. "Not only are you not responsible for our murder, but do you realize that you not only gave your life to your country, but you care more about me and Adele's lives than your own?" She smiled at him. "You gave your oath to your country and the Army. They were putting you through Engineering school. Even if the cause was not worth killing others for or dying for, you fulfilled your obligation. Unfortunately, the enemy also had their obligation."

"They weren't my enemy until the politicians made them my enemy."

"That goes for every war, Bobby. Jason got drafted. He was compelled by penalty of imprisonment or exile to fight in the tropical heat, seven thousand miles away, and for what? How about George and James? Brother killed brother in their war."

"Wow! Erica. You confirmed what I knew and felt all along. I always found you attractive." He grinned, "and not just for your looks, you had a woman's wisdom and an inner beauty that glowed. Right now, its brightness is blinding."

"Thank you, Bobby." Erica blushed. "That was kind of you to say. Of course, Adele and I were sisters and looked alike." Erica chuckled. "So, I guess that's par for the course."

"It wasn't quite like that. You were admirable while Adele was adorable. I know she looked up to you." Bobby gazed into Erica's green eyes. "I know I did."

"Thank you again, Bobby." Erica smiled. "I admired everything about you. You carried yourself with assurance and confidence. You were a hard worker with a vision for the future, not just for yourself, but also for others. I thought you were everything a man should be, and perfect for my sister." Erica nodded. "Now I know you are."

"I'm going to confess something, Erica. At times, even though I was only two years older, I felt more like Adele's big brother than her lover." Bobby raised his hands. "That doesn't mean I wasn't crazy attracted to her. She was as sexy and appealing as any girl I've ever met. I couldn't get her off my mind when in Iraq. Her rarely taking my calls upset me horribly."

"Don't worry, Bobby." Erica squeezed his hands. "I know exactly what you're saying."

"When I was in Iraq. It wasn't Adele who consoled me. It wasn't Adele when I needed a woman's special strength in addition to a woman's empathy, understanding, and compassion." Bobby released Erica's right hand and turned to the oceanic horizon. "When I proposed to your sister, there was a full moon. It shouted to my heart. Now that the moon slumbers, the stars whisper your name."

"Bobby, it's amazing how my death and rebirth as a ghost have opened my mind. Now that we're spirits, scripture comes to light. *'Hear now this, O foolish people, and without understanding; which have eyes and will see not; which have ears and hear not.'* Erica faced Bobby and placed his hand on her shoulders. "I also hear the stars whisper. I can hear them say, Bobby. Bobby. Bobby." Erica closed her eyes and lowered her head. She opened her eyes, looked up, and braced his shoulders. "Isolde Maria brought us together for a reason. I don't know exactly what it is yet, but it's no coincidence."

Bobby reached out and held Erica's shoulders, his arms touching her arms. "Isolde Maria released my heart from Adele. But I am a man, and the sting of betrayal hurt. Yet here I am with you. The stars no longer whisper your name. Now the rising sun sings 'Erica' in a choral rhapsody. Margarette is right. We have each other."

"Bobby, you were more than the perfect man for Adele; you are the perfect man for me."

"Erica, I knew this all along. I wanted to be sure, you know, that I wasn't just transferring my love for Adele to you. Now I know for sure." He tightened his grip on her shoulders and gazed deep into her eyes. "I love you, Erica."

"Bobby, I love you too."

They embraced and kissed. Their tongues mingled with the lub dub cadence of the surf breaking and washing over their feet.

Chapter 8

Trevor flounced into the offices of Brocton Copper Works and sat on their receptionist's desk. "Good morning, Miss Moneypenny. What can I do you for?"

"Right now, you'd better call me Miss Hutchinson or at least make sure your father hears you address me as such." She looked at him with steely eyes and not a hint of a smile.

"What's wrong?" He slid closer to her. "Not enough Brocton charm this morning."

"It's not that, Mr. Brocton."

"Mister? So why the formality? I thought we advanced to sweetheart and honey."

"It's not me, it's your father. I didn't suddenly turn cold. You know how much I like you and what your words and charm do for me. That's not going to change anytime soon. I want to get you in a serious state of mind. Your father wants to see you. I'm letting you know. He's not happy."

"Seeing that I've slayed dragons for you, I think I can deal with an old man." Trevor strolled into his father's office.

Thomas Brocton II held a manila file in front of his face. "Close the door."

Trevor closed the door with his foot and sat in front of his father's desk. He crossed his legs in a figure-four position, with his right ankle on his left knee. He folded his hands behind his head.

"Who gave you permission to sit?" The senior Brocton put the file away and placed his palms down on his desk. "Stand up."

"Oh, come on," Trevor smirked. "Who put the bug up your ass?"

Thomas Brocton sprang to his feet. "When I tell you to stand," he prodded, "you stand!"

Trevor slowly stood. He kept his posture purposely relaxed.

"I just met with accounting. You took sixty-five grand from the company for no apparent reason. Care to explain?"

Trevor blanched.

Thomas blinked slowly and sighed. "I thought so. That's embezzlement. If you weren't a Brocton, I'd have you up on felony charges, and you'd be facing at least a decade behind bars. Just because this family doesn't need another scandal," he prodded, "doesn't mean you're getting off scot-free."

Trevor spread his palms and shrugged. "I took the sixty-five thousand to protect the Brocton name."

"Ha! Ha! Ha!" The senior Brocton's laugh was void of humor. "Yeah, I bet from a mess you created." He scowled. "Here's yet more fallout owing to your uselessness. See this?" He shoved a document into Trevor's face. "It's a legal brief. Your lawyer buddy, Henry Sawyers, wrote it up on behalf of Picardi Developments." Thomas jabbed it in Trevor's nose. "He's almost as worthless as you, so his uncle wouldn't have him write it up unless it was a slam dunk. Take it. Read it."

Trevor turned a whiter shade of pale as he read the brief.

"As you can read, and I wasted enough money on private schools to teach you how, Picardi Developments has canceled their contract with us for non-performance. My legal team has confirmed what I already knew. There's nothing I can do to fight it. It seems you were a no-call, no-show for an important meeting. You also caused us to miss yet another shipment. Now I'm stuck with a bunch of copper pipes and no buyer. You have also, once again, damaged our reputation. Your mother is right. I got rid of the wrong son."

Trevor slumped. He closed his eyes…

…On his father's orders, he had turned around and bent over. Each lash of the belt made him wince, but he refused to cry. His father turned over his belt so that the buckle would strike him. He now whipped him on his lower back rather than the buttocks.

The pain caused Trevor to collapse on the floor. He went into a fetal position and covered up as best he could.

'Don't you dare cover up.' His father put his hands on his hips, holding his double-over belt in his right hand. *'If I want to punish you, I'll damn well punish you, and I will do it as I please and when I please.'* He smiled and cracked his belt like a whip.

Trevor saw his father's sadism clear as day.

His father laughed as he continued the assault…

… "Straighten your posture when I talk to you!" Thomas Brocton prodded. "This is the last straw. You're not getting away with it this time. You are unofficially no longer part of Brocton Enterprises. I say unofficial. If I were to fire you officially, it would cast more shadow and scandal on us than you've already caused." He paused. "You will report to your office…" He glared at Trevor and prodded. "On time!" He paced behind his desk. "We will keep up appearances. Spend the day playing video games or reading comic books. I no longer care. You no longer have anything to do with the operations of Brocton Copper Works or any other business involving Brocton Enterprises. Your salary is canceled. It is now an allowance. I will be deducting part of my sixty-five grand weekly. I am already in discussion with my lawyers about disinheriting you. I won't cut you off completely. Word getting out that you're living in a cardboard box under an overpass would bring down the Brocton name. I will try to keep our business in the family. Maybe I'll adopt a winner and leave it all to him."

Trevor's lips quavered. "B-But father…"

"Stop calling me, Father!" Thomas shoved the files from his desk. They thudded against the floor. "From now on, it's Mr. Brocton. And another thing. When you come to work, I mean, the office, you will no longer speak with Miss Hutchinson. She has class. Use your allowance on cheap tarts. Am I understood?"

"Yes, but…"

"But nothing! Get out of my sight! You make me sick."

Trevor again regressed to a beaten ten-year-old. He walked out of the office, head down, hands laced together. Trevor heard the door slam behind him. He saw a dab of moisture in Miss Hutchinson's eye, although she looked away from him. His mind went fuzzy and blank as he trudged to his car.

Slowly, he felt his lips tense and his jaw tighten. *'Henry Sawyers. You worthless, chicken shit coward. You could've asked your uncle to talk Picardi into honoring our contract. And where did you get the notion that I couldn't seduce Erica Beauchamp? You never gave me the credit I deserved for stealing Adele from Soldier Boy.'* Trevor broke into a tight-lipped smile. *'It's time you learn a lesson in respect. You're about to discover what a real man is all about, and it ain't you.'*

Trevor broke out in maniacal laughter. He spoke aloud, "Dearest Mom and Dad. You think I don't know what you did to Edgar? Turnabout is fair play. We'll soon see who will be running Brocton enterprises."

Trevor pulled into a Mobile gas station. He walked over to a payphone, took a calling card out of his wallet, and dialed the one-eight-hundred number. After a prompt, he punched in the card number. He next punched in country code 57, followed by 2, and then a seven-digit number.

"Juan, it's Trevor Brocton." He listened for 90 seconds. "Everything is fine. Our operation is doing well. I'm making you money, and you're making me money. I need something personal, and I need it fast. I know, it's going to cost me. If you can deliver, I'll pick it up following our usual procedure."

"Si."

Trevor beamed.

***

Trevor parked in the Pink Pussy Cat Lounge parking lot. He poured water from an Evian bottle into his hand and rubbed it into his eyes. After lighting a cigarette, he placed it in front of his eyes so the smoke could irritate them. He strolled into the Pink Pussy Cat Lounge and spotted a leggy female wearing pink high-cut shorts and a thin white cotton shirt. She had threaded her blond hair through her pink ballcap's ponytail opening. Trevor frowned and waved her over. "Jenny," Trevor pretended to cry. "Oh my God, Jenny. It's Adele. I miss her so much. I loved her, Jenny. I loved her." He hugged Jenny.

Jenny embraced him and cried. "She was my best friend. I loved her so much, and she loved you. I miss her like there's no tomorrow."

"Why does God always take the good ones?" Trevor cried.

"I don't know…I don't know…God also took Erica." Jenny broke down. "I know he wanted them both. Who wouldn't want them?" Jenny rubbed her eyes on Trevor's shoulder. "I want them back so badly. But I know…I know…" Jenny bawled.

"The Devil got McClenahan. At least he's not coming back." Trevor bobbed his head. "But Adele?" Trevor cried without tears. "I'm sorry, Jenny. I can't be seen crying here. Can you get off work? Let's go where we can cry our eyes out together and honor our dear departed Adele, whom we both loved so much."

"My shift ends in twenty minutes. I'm sure I can leave early."

***

Trevor pulled up to cabin 12 at the Wanderer's Inn motel.

"Why are you bringing me here?" Jenny braced herself against the car door. "Take me away. I've heard certain girls from the club bring tricks here. This place has a reputation. I can't be seen here. After all, I'm engaged to an attorney."

"Relax. You're with a Brocton and you're sitting in a Porsche Carrera GT." Trevor grinned. "Ain't nobody going to consider that disreputable. Besides, no one is here to see us." Trevor reached under his seat and grabbed a silver and gold flask and two shot glasses. "This contains Macallan single malt Scotch. It's as classy as it gets." He poured Jenny her shot. With the guile of a master illusionist, Trevor slipped white powder into her glass. He handed her the cocktail before pouring himself a shot. "Cheers." They tapped glasses. "Bottoms up." They downed their shots in one gulp. "The parking lot is empty." Trevor took the glass from Jenny. "Coast is clear. Let's go inside."

Jenny stumbled. Trevor held out an arm, letting her steady herself.

"This room is disgusting." Jenny pulled her face. "Adele told me you took her to the Wentworth Mansion. I wouldn't board my cat in this dump."

"Adele." He cried without shedding tears. "I miss her so much, Jenny. Please stay and have another drink with me."

"Only for Adele. I die every time I think about her, Trevor. We both loved her." Jenny wept and sat on the bed. "Something's wrong. I feel so woozy."

"Another drink should help." He handed her a shot of Scotch whiskey.

Jenny gulped it. Her world became a fuzzy, swirling whirl. Trevor pushed her onto her back. "What's happening? What's happening? I can't move." Black pinpricks only blurred Trevor pulling off her blouse. It scratched her eyes as it went past her face. "No. No. Please don't. What's happening to me? What are you doing to me?"

"Lovely, lovely." Trevor buried his face in her cleavage. "These are as nice as your friend's." He sucked her right nipple.

"No. No." She muttered while trying to raise her hands. She wanted to clutch his gel-slicked hair and pull his head away, but her arms were unresponsive.

Trevor kissed her abdomen, licked her naval, and unfastened her shorts.

Jenny's impaired senses still detected that he was pulling down her shorts. She tried to kick him, but her brain's synapses failed to reach her legs.

"Thank you, Jenny. Trimmed, but you left me enough length."

Jenny's deadened nerves still registered a stinging pain.

"One for my trophy case. Ha! Ha! Ha! Well, my Jenny babe." Trevor leered at her. His eyes seemed to telescope from his skull like antennas transmitting evil and malice. "I think you know what's coming next." Trevor took off his clothes and mounted her.

"No, no, no," Jenny mumbled as he violated her. "No, no, no." Sweat, saliva, sticky breath, and the repugnant object inside her sickened her. Her '*no's*' were reduced to faint thoughts. Her soul died again, again, and again.

"Ahh…Here comes my ultimate gift." Trevor climaxed. "The nectar of life."

Afterward, Jenny lay still, murmuring and sobbing. Trevor sat in a chair, legs crossed in a figure-four. He lit a cigarette. After twenty minutes, Jenny partially regained consciousness.

"I know what you're thinking." Trevor laughed at her.

Jenny managed to sit, her eyes still glassy and her face partially paralyzed. "You. You…"

"Yes. I drugged you and I fucked you. Ha! Ha! Ha! For a near corpse, you were good."

"No…No…I didn't want it. You raped me. I hate you!"

"Do you, now? Too bad it had to be this way. It would have been just a matter of time until you did it out of love, just like your dead friend. Unfortunately, I don't have the time to go through the same routine. You will be far more responsive for our next round."

"You drugged me! You raped me!" With great effort, she raised her hand and prodded. "You're a monster! I'm going to the police. You're going to prison."

"It will be the word of a waitress at a tittie bar against a Brocton. And how will lawyer boy's family react to the publicity? How will they deal with the talk?" Trevor folded his hands behind his head. "Get ready to go again. Otherwise, I have something to show your big-shot lawyer boyfriend." Trevor got off his chair, reached onto the bedside table, and held a silver pillbox in front of her eyes. He opened the box and showed her a filament. "Does that look familiar? I know it will to Hank. You either have sex with me consensually, or I show him. Ha! Ha! Ha! Even if he believes you, he will still know, one way or another, that you intimately knew my purifying penis. Consider the ways his mind will conjure it. Soon, more doubts will infiltrate his imagination, oh, yes, Jenny, those lingering doubts. Henry's weak, a god-damned sissy. He does what his father says, as he says, and without question. He'll tell his father. You know how he'll react. Face it, his father's approval and your future life hang in the balance of this little cunt hair. You know it, and I know it. This tiny hair determines your big dream."

"You bastard!" With a burst of energy and adrenaline, Jenny slapped his face. She left a red handprint on his face. The silver pill box went one way; its intimate content the other.

Trevor's eyes narrowed and reddened. He furrowed his brow. His expression became twisted like barbed wire. "Cookie! Cookie! Mommy! I want Cookie!" Trevor bared his clenched teeth and mounted Jenny.

She kicked his privates with her shin and grabbed his face, digging in her fingernails.

Trevor knocked her arm away, throttled her, and squeezed with demonic strength.

"No. No. Oh God, please. Help me."

"Yes. God. I'm God. And I have the power of life or death. I can take or keep the life of whomever I want." He snapped her head up and down as he strangled her. He heard her hyoid bone crack; two seconds later, her cricoid cartilage fractured. Jenny lay lifeless. Blood surged to his penis. "This will bring you back to life." He violated her warm corpse. "Ahh, my nectar of life." He got up and stood next to her dead body. He reached down and weaved his fingers into her pubic hair. He pulled as if extracting crab grass and put the contents into his silver pillbox.

Afterward, Trevor covered her body with sheets and a thin blanket. He tucked her in and kissed her cheek. "Sometimes the nectar of life takes longer. I'll be back, Jenny dear. We'll soon love each other again."

Trevor locked the door behind him and drove away.

Chapter 9

Sergeant Charles Fuller stood at port arms with his M16 rifle in Philadelphia, Pennsylvania's Washington Square, part of Independence Hall's grounds. Here lie the unmarked graves of fallen War of Independence soldiers. Unfortunately, grave robbers and ghouls once plagued the grounds. Leah, the ghost of a young Quaker woman who served as a nurse in George Washington's army, once guarded their graves. Sergeant Fuller now had the honor. He stood by a gathering of Revolutionary War soldiers. An orchestra was playing a Haydn symphony. A colonial soldier approached Fuller. "I wish you had joined us in our time. If you could go back and give us a bunch of those weapons," he pointed at Fuller's M-16. "We could've beaten the bloody Redcoats in eight weeks rather than eight years."

"I would've also brought back a battery-powered boom box and treated you guys to AC/DC." SGT Fuller laughed. "It would be louder than that orchestra, and it would rock."

"We've heard everything over the last two hundred and thirty or so years. I agree, AC/DC, as you say, rocked. But Haydn was Mozart's mentor and Beethoven's teacher, so we'll stick to the music of our time."

"I surely appreciate the sacrifices you guys made to create our great nation." Fuller lowered his weapon and saluted. "It's an honor to guard your graves, even if the ghouls went out of business years ago."

"Maybe no ghouls, but you scare away the crackheads and mad vagrants." The colonial soldier chuckled. "Besides, you also made the ultimate sacrifice. Otherwise, you wouldn't be here watching over us."

"I miss my wife and family and many other things, but I've learned more than I ever imagined about duty, sacrifice, and valor from you guys."

"I don't know how long you'll be with us or what ultimately awaits you. No offense, but we miss Leah. You're one of a series of her replacements. Leah guarded our graves for about a hundred and eighty years. An angel more beautiful than any human art could ever depict came down in 1961 and made Leah a mortal so she could marry a mortal man."

"Yes. The beautiful angel! Isolde Maria! She brought me here." Chuck laughed. "Well, getting used to this ghost thing takes time. I was a married man. Even though marriage is until death do us part. I'm not looking for Isolde Maria to hook me up with anyone."

The colonial soldier grinned. "I know your favorite band, AC/DC, plays rebellious music, and we're the ultimate rebels, but tonight is a special occasion, and, as you can see and hear, we're treated to an orchestra. You probably don't know what they're playing." He laughed. "Haydn's London Symphonies. As you 21st Century guys would say, "In your face, Lobster backs.""

"I bet AC/DC would rattle them more." SGT Fuller laughed.

"Here, here, Sergeant Fuller." The Colonial Soldier laughed and slapped Chuck's arm. "But ghost ladies are coming to join us for a grand military ball. I doubt they're ready for your time's hard rock, so Haydn it will have to be. You're one of us now, you've worked hard guarding our graves, and, as we all know, the ghouls are out of business, so why don't you put your M-16 down with our muskets and join us as soon as the lady ghosts arrive?"

"Thanks. I think I will."

***

Sergeant Fuller stood at attention in a straight, shoulder-to-shoulder line with War of Independence soldiers. The Orchestra played the second movement of Haydn's Symphony No. 94 in G major, *The Surprise*. Two immaculate white Landau coaches, each pulled by a team of four white horses, arrived at the grounds. One by one, women wearing white Robe 'a l'Anglaise ball gowns gracefully exited a carriage. One by one, a soldier broke ranks to greet her with an extended arm. She would take it and allow him to escort her to the orchestra, where they danced a Minuet. The third woman to exit the carriage had slightly below shoulder-length, ash-blond hair. While waiting his turn, Fuller noticed the chesty woman's hazel eyes. *'She looks familiar. But how would I know? I'm not 250 years old.'*

Chapter 10

Bobby and Erica held hands as they walked across Wilton Manor's polished walnut floors.

Margarette waltzed over to them with small, precise steps, revealing only a subtle hip sway, "Good evening, my sweetest pair." She delicately placed her hand on Erica's shoulder. "Just one of you brightens my parlor. The two of you together set it aflame." She extended her graceful arm in the direction of a pair of couches. "Won't you join us?"

Jason took a daisy from Sunbeam's headband and sniffed it. He returned it to her headband, squeezed Sunbeam's hand, and kissed her cheek. He turned to Bobby and Erica. "Good evening. I can see by the sand on your feet that you two did some beachcombing."

"I saw where George and James taught you how to transport." Sunbeam braced her arms on Jason's thigh and leaned toward the couple. "You can leave as you wish, but I'm glad you chose to return."

Bobby and Erica sat on the couch. They continued to hold hands. "Margarette has given us a home." Erica smiled. "What more could I hope to find?"

"Don't thank me." Margarette blushed. "Your angel guide, Isolde Maria, brought you here."

"Your kindness and generosity have gone above and beyond what anyone, human or angel, living or dead," Bobby chuckled, "could ever hope for. Thank you, Margarette. Erica is right," Bobby kissed Erica's cheek. "You have given us more than a place to stay. You have given us a home."

Jason stood. "You won't believe what I found. Come and have a look." Jason walked them to a table in the main drawing room. It looked like a box with a hand crank. A polished brass horn topped it, twice the height of its base; it stood high and proud, reflecting evening shadows. "It's not the original Thomas Edison. I place it as being from the twenties or thirties. This gramophone is set to 78 RPM." Jason smiled and nodded to the Lady of the House. "Margarette permitted me to make some alterations. I modified its internal gearing to play at 33 RPM. I also lightened the tone arm and sanded down the stylus needle so it could handle modern albums."

"I permitted him only after he convinced me that my favorite song was performed even better by a group called the Flamingos. I loved the song ever since George and James took me to an early talky picture palace and I heard Dick Powell sing it to Ruby Keeler. So be careful, Sunbeam," Margarette delicately extended her arm and touched Sunbeam's shoulder. "Jason's a persuasive one."

"Don't I know it, Margarette." Sunbeam kissed Jason's cheek. "How else could a peacenik like me fall so madly in love with a Green Beret?"

"Oh, come on, Margarette. It took George to second my endorsement of the Flamingos to convince you." Jason took a 12-inch vinyl record from an album cover with the wording, *'Doo Wop's Greatest Hits.'* He cranked the gramophone and played the record. Sunbeam took his hand, pulled him to the center of the room, and led him in a slow dance. Several other ghostly couples joined them, dancing to the Flamingos' rendition of *I Only Have Eyes for You.*

Bobby nodded to Erica. He twitched his head in the direction of the dancers. He extended his hand to Erica. She took his hand. Bobby embraced her and swayed her to the music. "I don't know if the stars are out tonight, but I do know the sunny and bright is the glow in your eyes."

"Oh, Bobby, hold me close and never let me go." She pulled his pectorals into her breasts. "The garden reminds me of our Isolde Maria, and the avenue is crowded with other ghosts, but at this moment, you're the only one on Earth, and I'm the only one with you." Erica gently kissed his lips, accompanied by a flicker of her tongue.

Bobby touched his nose to hers. They imbibed the fragrance of their breath. He softly, gently nibbled her lower lip before kissing her. "I had so much to live for, yet moments like this are more than worth dying for."

"I always knew you as the strong, silent type." Erica chuckled and gazed into his eyes. "So, I guess some dry, even gallows humor goes with the territory." She pressed her cheek to his cheek.

"Oh. The softness of your cheek, Erica. Only having eyes for you now excludes everyone who ever lived…"

"Shh," Erica put her finger over Bobby's lips. Bobby sucked and nibbled on her finger. They kissed until the record finished.

Sunbeam rang a small bell. "Ladies and Gentlemen. I can see that the newest members of the Wilton Manor ghost family only have eyes for each other. So, let's clear the dance floor and give them center stage. This record was recorded shortly after I joined all of you. It helped me to understand my new entity. Bobby, Erica, I want to play this for you." Sunbeam laughed. "Why did you two let go of each other. You can slow-dance to this. I know what you're thinking," Sunbeam chuckled. "If I'm introducing it, it must be hippy music. "Sort of, but it's much more than that. It's by a group called Renaissance. Jason, sweetheart, crank up the gramophone and play the record.

The song began with the sound of an eerie wind rustling through forest trees. After ten seconds, a gentle triangle ringing joined the breeze. After ten more seconds, it drifted into a piano introduction…

Erica embraced Bobby and whispered into his ear. "Her voice. It's so mysterious, ethereal. Her tone, her delivery, it's enchanting."

"Erica, we've experienced so much together. I now realize I need you more than ever. Whenever I am at a loss for words, I have you to express it for me."

"Sunbeam is right. This song is helping us accept and thrive in our new ghostly realm."

Bobby and Erica danced to the recording of Renaissance and their lead singer, Annie Haslam.

"Travel the days of freedom,

Roads leading everywhere,

Come with me now and show how you care.

Follow the dying embers,

Cross on the paths they lay,

Breath of the past, the earth's yesterday.

Changing the order slowly,

Leaving the mist of time.

Clear your mind, maybe you will find,

That the past is still turning.

Circles sway, echo yesterday,

Ashes burning, ashes burning."

Bobby and Erica held each other tighter. They pressed their chests and cheeks together as they swayed to the record.

"Imagine the burning embers.

They glow below and above.

Your sins you won't remember,

And all you will find there is love.

Ashes are burning brightly,

The smoke can be seen from afar.

Ashes are burning the way."

The gathering applauded Erica and Bobby after the record ended. Bobby and Erica stood still and shared a kiss.

***

Bobby and Erica returned to the couch. The other guests' banter melted into a blur of white noise. Bobby and Erica smiled at each other and kissed before tapping glasses and finishing their drinks. Erica stood first, took Bobby's hand, and helped him stand. They walked hand in hand to the top of the stairs. Each of their steps seemed to suspend the laws of gravity itself, and perhaps for them, it no longer existed. The hallway portraits and landscapes became foggy white dots, blending with their thoughts. They entered their room and stood by their bed. "Do you want me to leave so you can change first?" Bobby nodded to Erica.

"No thanks, Bobby." Erica beamed at him. "Stay. I need your help undressing. First, let me take care of something." She leaned over the bed and tossed the pillow barricade to the floor.

Chapter 11

Trevor sat on a couch in the Brocton mansion's living room. He sipped a bottle of Schorsbock beer.

"Enjoy that beer. It's the last I'm buying," Thomas Brocton growled. "After I deduct your installment of my sixty-five grand, you'll have just enough left to guzzle Pabst Blue Ribbon."

Trevor cocked his right hand and middle finger, but thought better of flipping it. Instead, he quickly scanned his father up and down and tightened the corner of his mouth in derision.

"Don't you smirk at me, boy." Thomas prodded. "Your mother and I are leaving for the Yacht and Mariner's Dinner in Hilton Head. If you were a Brocton in good standing, you could accompany us. As it is, you'd better enjoy the last of that beer while you watch wrestling and roller derby on TV."

Trevor's mother glanced at him and raised one side of her mouth in a sneer before turning her back to him.

Trevor laughed after they were out of sight. "Bon Voyage to both of you." He held his beer bottle in the direction that they exited…

…That night, Trevor had set his alarm for 0400 hrs. No need, he lay awake until the time. Trevor donned a rubber protective suit and headgear taken from the plant. *'It cost me much of the sixty-five thousand that I borrowed from my business, but it was well worth it. Juan, you came through in spades, hombre.'* Trevor crept into the garage. The door to the Rolls-Royce Limousine was opened. He climbed in and cautiously opened the cylinder that he had brought with him. He took a deep breath and steadied himself. Using a brush of Kolinsky sable hair, Trevor applied Novichok to the limousine steering wheel.

***

Thomas and Georganne Brocton said nary a word to each other as their chauffeur drove their limousine southbound on I-95. They looked straight ahead, not noticing their driver's discomfort. He had been attempting to ignore the putrid smell filling his nose. He shook his head, struggling to keep his eyes focused when a wave of nausea rose from his gut, and along with it, a burst of metallic-tasting saliva filled his mouth.

Dizzy, dizzy…

His head struck the steering wheel. His arms fell slack, dangling to his sides as the weight of his now limp body pressed down on the accelerator.

The Rolls-Royce swerved from the left lane to the right lane in a split second.

The Broctons screamed, clinging onto the seat, the handle, the seatbelt, anything they could find. Their eyes widened upon spotting the semi. Its horn was blaring, its lights flashing. They took a final, sharp breath and closed their eyes.

A speeding semi-truck broad-sided their car, sending it rolling and bouncing end over end until it exploded.

The trucker slammed the brakes, but it was too late. His semi jackknifed, sending the trailer barreling towards a car with a family. The trailer slammed the car off the road and over an embankment. The tractor unit skidded to the side, slammed head-on into a tree, and ignited.

Chapter 12

Brocton Enterprise's major shareholders and executives silently waited around a large, rectangular teak table. Six sat on one side, and another six sat across. Trevor Brocton straightened his posture, jutted his chin, and steeled his expression as he entered the boardroom and stood at the head of the table. "Good afternoon, ladies and gentlemen of Brocton Enterprises. I am still dealing with the horrible and unexpected loss of my parents. It's something from which I may never fully recover, and, of course, we lost our chief executive officer. I am sure each of you shares in my pain and grief stemming from this terrible loss. Nevertheless, my father would want us to keep a stiff upper lip and do everything possible to keep Brocton Enterprises at the top of the standings. Many of you are fearful of change. I can't say I blame you. I can assure you, your jobs are safe, and as your new CEO, I will make every effort to ensure that any transition runs as smoothly as possible. I will not radically change the company's culture, but changes are inevitable."

Harold Shannon, an executive vice president with Brocton Enterprises, asked, "Mr. Brocton, what changes do you propose?"

"I'm glad you asked, Mr. Shannon. Firstly, Brocton Enterprises will expand our property development operations. Brocton Copper Smelting supplies builders across the nation. We can increase the profitability and share value of Brocton Enterprises by working hands-on in construction and development. We can garner greater profits and, at the same time, undercut our competition by building with supplies and materials that we manufacture. Ms. Greenwell, as our Chief Investment Officer, get with Walter Long, of the Davis Investment Group. Work together to short-sell Picardi Development stock. You both know the procedure. Picardi Developments has been ripe for a hostile takeover for some time now. They're teetering on the ropes. We've played rope a dope long enough. It's time to go for the knockout. My father was reluctant to hit 'em with a haymaker. Well, now I am both wearing the gloves and working the corner. Do any of you have any objection to a hostile takeover of Picardi Developments?"

"No objection, but what next, Mr. Brocton?" A tall, slender junior executive wearing tortoise-shell glasses leaned forward.

"I am glad you asked. After we take over Picardi Developments, I am targeting Evans and Carlton Construction. Eventually, we'll corner the market as the sole property developer in the Southeast with Brocton Copper Smelting making our metal building supplies." Trevor opened his hands. "Otherwise, it's business as usual at Brocton Enterprises. Do I have any more questions?" Trevor stood still for five seconds. "Very well. Let's get back to work and keep Brocton Enterprises on top." Trevor maintained his erect posture and left the room with measured steps.

Chapter 13

Bobby awoke facing Erica. He kissed her lips and gently flicked her tongue.

"Mmm…What a delicious way to start the day." Erica slid over and embraced him, kissing him with vigor. "Bobby." She touched his nose. "Before we get too carried away, and your kisses and warm body surely carry me away, something is lying heavy on my mind."

"What's that, darling?"

"It's Adele." Erica got out of bed.

"It can't wait until after breakfast? I can hear the bacon sizzling, and I can smell the biscuit gravy."

"No, Bobby, this is serious." She got out of bed and donned a robe and slippers. "It can't wait any longer. I know your feelings for her were in our previous life, and that we belong to each other in this life. Trust me, Bobby. I feel no jealousy. At first, I'll admit, it felt funny, and, yes, I harbored guilt. That's over. I love you without reservation. What will never end is that she is my sister, and I love her dearly. Bobby, we now know how to transport. I want us to look for her."

"Look for her? Where can we possibly start? She may be in a whole different dimension."

"Please, Bobby, we must." She shook her hands. "We have to at least try."

"We can summon Isolde Maria. I am sure she knows."

"I'm also sure she knows." Erica tensed her lips and tightened her eyelids. "The problem is that I don't think she will tell us."

"Erica!" Bobby sat up. "You know we can't go against her. You know she follows God's will. You need to be patient until God tells her the time is right. Besides, she's been so kind to us. You know her timing is the right timing."

"I thought you would understand, Bobby. Adele's my sister." Erica shook her hands. "I need to find her, right now, and I'll do so with or without you."

"Do you know what you're saying?" Bobby got out of bed and put his pants on. "We still have much to learn about our predicament. I'm happy and at peace now. I love you more than I thought a man could love a woman. So, I'm telling you out of love. You're up against forces we don't understand. You can put yourself in grave danger."

"Danger? You never backed down from danger or a fight. You willingly went away to Iraq. Why not now go the extra mile with me?"

"You really want to know?" Bobby put his hands on his hips.

"Yes, Bobby." She nodded. "Tell me."

"I went away to hell on earth, otherwise known as Iraq. Adele was all I thought about. My love for her kept me and my fellow soldiers alive. Yet the whole time, Adele was cheating on me with that low-life creep Spike McClenahan. And what did her cheating get you? Killed." Bobby prodded. "Just like the enemy forces did to me. As far as I'm concerned, Adele can burn in Hell with him."

"I can't believe you said that!" Erica furrowed her brow. A tear strayed from her eye. "That's the most despicable thing I've ever heard, in life or death. I gave my heart to you in part because I was touched by how much you loved my sister. Now I don't know. I just don't know." She scowled and shook her head. "What I do know is that I must find Adele, and I'm now going to do it without you. Don't try to follow me." Erica marched out of the bedroom, slamming the door behind her.

Bobby sat down on the edge of the bed. He put his chin in his hand.

Chapter 14

Trevor Brocton entered the Picardi Developments boardroom flanked by two security guards, both as tall as himself. One was a Pacific Islander with a sumo physique and wearing martial arts attire, while the other was a muscular Caucasian with a shaved head and dressed like a Secret Service Agent. Eleven Picardi executives and major shareholders sat around an oval, oak table. Their founder, Alex Picardi, sat nearest the table head. "Good afternoon. Although you know who I am, let me introduce myself anyway." Trevor licked his lips. "I am Trevor Brocton. Your new chief executive officer."

"How dare you strut into my boardroom like you own it!" Alex Picardi stood and prodded.

"Ha! Ha! Ha! I do own it, old man."

"Old man?" Alex continued prodding. "You insolent son-of-a-bitch. You backstabbed me and everyone in this room."

"Sit down, old man. Short-selling your stock was perfectly legal. Call it what you want. Bottom line. I now have a controlling interest in this company."

"You don't tell me what to do. What is legal is not always ethical. I founded Picardi Developments back when you were pooping your diapers. I don't have to put up with this."

"You're finally right about something." Trevor raised the right side of his mouth halfway. "You don't have to put up with it. That's because, effective immediately, you are retired."

"That's bullshit!"

"You're over 65 years old. Ethical or not, I'm now in charge, and my first order of business is establishing sixty-five as our mandatory retirement age." Trevor looked to his side. "Security. Show this man the door. He's a retiree and no longer works for the company. This is a confidential meeting discussing company business."

The security officers each grabbed one of Alex Picardi's arms and forced him toward the door. "You bastard, you!" He vainly shook and squirmed in the guards' grips. "You're not getting away with this. My attorneys will have something to say."

"Your attorneys work for me now. Complain to the nurses and orderlies at the retirement home." Trevor turned. "Security, please close the door behind you once Mr. Picardi is removed."

The remaining board members murmured incoherently.

"If any of you has an objection to my ascendancy, now is your chance to leave voluntarily, without the help of my security detail."

The executives and shareholders ticced their heads. A man in his early sixties with graying temples stood and walked out the door. A middle-aged woman wearing a beige pantsuit followed.

Trevor waited until his security detail closed the door. "Let me quote the President of the United States. Either you are with me, or you are against me." Trevor paused to look at each of the remaining eight individually. "Very well then. The Brocton and Picardi Construction board meeting shall now commence. My second order of business: I have found an ideal site for a lower-middle-class housing development. It's the site of the dilapidated old manor house and grounds known as Wilton Manor. First, we need to acquire the property. Next, we demolish the house, clear the land, and construct a hundred-and-ten, two and three-bedroom villa units. Brocton Copper Smelting will supply piping and wiring materials. Charleston County will build roads, water, sewage, and electrical infrastructure at public expense. Accounting will document the projected profit in writing. I don't think we need this to realize our profits will be considerable."

"Sir," A young executive wearing a gray jacket a size too large and a red tie four inches too long raised his hand. "Our acquisition team has tried to get that property over the last three years. We planned to develop it with executive homes on acre-sized stands."

"McMansions," Trevor smirked. "That's a new trend, I'll grant you that. Nevertheless, bigger and faster profits are in the pockets of McDonald's restaurant customers." Trevor pointed. "If erecting tract mansions was such a good idea, why didn't you do it back when you were Picardi Developments?"

"Sir, Malcolm Haisley, the County Planning Director, thwarted our every attempt. He claims it's on hold for possible declaration as a national historic landmark."

"Malcoln Haisley, huh." Trevor pinched his chin. "And none of you could get past him? I will handle this personally and show you that under my leadership, Brocton and Picardi Construction is a can-do organization. Once I acquire the Wilton Manors property, I will call another meeting to discuss detailed plans for the new Wilton Manors."

***

Trevor walked into a business without knocking. The company was not a storefront or office, but a single-wide trailer in a residential park. "I can smell what you're smoking, but I can't place it. Colombian? Mexican? Homegrown?"

"I know you. Aren't you Trevor Brocton? What are you doing here?" Bernard Poindexter took off his wire-framed glasses, wiped the lenses clean, and put them back on his thin nose.

"Is that how you greet a potential, high-paying client? And when was the last time you showered? Last week? It looks like you change your clothes as often as a homeless bum. I stood here for five minutes, but you didn't look up from playing World of Warcraft to notice."

"I'm sorry, sir…It's just that…"

Trevor held up a stiff arm in a halt gesture. "I hope I didn't stop you from breaking your high score." Trevor chuckled. "Don't worry, Bernard, I didn't come to pick on you. I'm sure you've had enough of that already. I'd move some of those manuals and papers from that chair and sit, but I might get a stain on my new Giorgio Armani slacks. If you had a modicum of self-discipline, you might have joined the ranks of Bill Gates and Steve Jobs."

"I'm sorry, sir."

"Stop apologizing. In an off-hand way, I just complimented you." Trevor disarmed him with a smile. "Okay. You're socially awkward. Shit happens. I don't hold it against you. But I'm not here to be your therapist and discuss your parents or your childhood. I doubt you could develop a good physique even if you had the discipline to work out, and you couldn't help being born clumsy. We can't choose our parents. Where you scored in the gene pool is your brain. I compared you to Bill Gates and Steve Jobs for a reason. You know computers better than anyone I know of. Unfortunately, few others are aware of your expertise. Work for me, come through, and you will be a legend in the tech community, if not famous with the public. Money goes with the territory. Money makes up for a lot of shortcomings when it comes to the ladies." Trevor picked up a stray pornographic magazine and looked at the centerfold. "I do see that you like the ladies." He tossed the magazine aside.

"Okay, sir. I'm listening."

"I want you to hack into the computers of Charleston County planning director, Malcolm Haisley. I know his weaknesses. The man is a lech."

"I can do it. His work Email is public domain. Most computer experts would use Wireshark or Cain and Abel to get his IP, hack into his work computer, and track him to his home computer." Mathew beamed and jutted his chin. "But I've written an even better program. I call it Hacksmart. I'm afraid to market it because I know someone will steal it."

"You use it for me, and I will not only pay you generously, but I can also hook you up with an honest lawyer to ensure you obtain an ironclad copyright."

"Did you say, 'honest lawyer'?" Bernard laughed. "Isn't that an oxymoron?"

Trevor laughed with him. "Do we have a deal?" He extended his hand.

Bernard wiped his hand off with a rag and shook Trevor's hand.

"Get to work." Trevor scribbled on the back of his business card. "That is my personal and direct mobile phone number. Call me ASAP when you get something."

***

Bernard waited for Trevor with his trailer door unopened. He sat with his knee over his thigh, leaned back, and locked his hands behind his head. He beamed at Trevor as he arrived.

"I can see by your expression and body language that you hit paydirt."

"Yes, and even better than you hoped. It seems your mark, Malcolm Haisley, is linked to the Mormons."

"Mormons?"

"Yes. He wants us to Brigham Young." Bernard smiled and shook his hands like an infant with a rattle. "Brigham Young? Bring 'em young. Get it? He's into young girls. Ha! Ha! Ha! I've tracked both his work and home IPs to a chat room called YSO. Young Seeking Old. You have to be eighteen to join. Some of the profiles are escorts; nevertheless, some are legit."

"I knew you would justify my confidence in you." Trevor cleared a chair of magazines and pamphlets and sat next to Bernard.

Bernard pointed to the screen. "His profile handle is lorne_a_20014. He's online right now."

"Let's post a fake profile. We won't reveal her age until he's swallowed the bait. Then we spring the trap." Trevor laughed. "Thirteen should do it."

"I'm already ahead of the game." Bernard smiled. "I hacked into the yearbook of John C Calhoun Middle School. I'm no pedophile. Nevertheless, this one is cute." He pulled up a photo of a blonde, eighth-grade girl.

"Perfect," Trevor beamed. "I'll call her kaylaprincess_94." Trevor slid up to Bernard's keyboard. "I'll title her profile, 'Young Girl ISO Daddy Love." Trevor turned to Bernard. "I think he'll bite."

Bernard posted the faux profile with the middle school girl's photo. Trevor and Bernard passed a hand-rolled cannabis cigarette back and forth. Bernard took a long draw. He dropped it into an ashtray and jabbed his finger at the monitor. "That didn't take long!" Bernard pointed at the screen. "Look. He's replying already."

> *Lorne_a_20014: 'Kayla, you say you're a princess? I agree. You look like you stepped out of a fairytale and into my dreams.'*

"He's making this too easy." Trevor typed.

Kaylaprincess_94: 'Ohhh UR 2 sweet. My daddy never says nice things like that 2 me.'

Lorne_a_20014: 'I wanna be your daddy king, I will love and protect you like the precious princess u r.'

Trevor smirked and nodded at Bernard before responding.

Kaylaprincess_94: 'My father only cares about work. He's never home, and when he is, he only talks about football and golf. He's always drinking beer, and whenever I try to talk to him, he yells at me.'

Lorne_a_20014: 'He sounds like an awful man. Does he ever give you hugs and kisses?'

Kaylaprincess_94: 'Oh no, never. He never shows me love.'

Lorne_a_20014: 'Let me be your king. Your royal daddy. I will love you like a princess deserves to be loved.'

Kaylaprincess_94: 'I'm scared. I'm only 13. Is that OK?'

Lorne_a_20014: 'It's okay if you keep us a secret. I can get in a lot of trouble, you know. A father should introduce his daughter to womanhood, if ya know what I mean.'

Kaylaprincess_94: 'But won't it hurt?'

Lorne_a_20014: 'I'm not some young boy. I'm a mature man. Your daddy, your king, ur my precious princess daughter. After I lick you and get you moist and ready, King Penis will meet Princess Vagina, and you will be my queen 4 ever. Do you want 2 meet King Penis?'

Trevor and Bernard laughed. Trevor quickly typed.

Kaylaprincess_94: 'First I wanna c.'

"Oh my God." Trevor slapped Bernard's shoulder. "He can't be that stupid. He sent it."

"I may not have big muscles." Bernard laughed. "But I do have something bigger than him."

Trevor laughed. "He should rename that thing Pauper Penis rather than King Penis. "He's typing." Trevor pointed at the screen.

Lorne_1_20014: 'Again, keep our luv a secret. You don't want the cops 2 take your true daddy away, do you?'

"Ha! Ha! Ha!" Trevor guffawed. "We got him. What do you say? We go for the kill. One of my vice presidents is in on the plan. He's letting me use his house. His daughter is a freshman theater major. She's a petite five-one. She's nineteen but can pass as a thirteen-year-old and has agreed to play decoy. I have a TV production crew on call. Here goes." Trevor typed.

Kaylaprincess_94: 'Never. R Secret is sealed with a kiss...I can't wait. My parents r out until past midnight. Can you come over 2night @ 8ish? I live @ 388 W. Ridge Rd. It's just off I-26, exit 14.'

Lorne_a_20014: 'Okay, but first delete your archives and remember my Princess Kayla, I luv you more than anything. 2night at 8, your sugarplum fairytale dreams come true.'

***

"He's here, Casey." Trevor motioned his decoy. "You're on."

Malcolm Haisley strolled up the walkway to the front door. A petite, long-legged young lady in high-cut dark blue shorts and an armless brown blouse stood at the doorway. An olive baseball cap topped her long, brown hair. She had the gentle, sculpted face of a model. Casey opened the door. "Hey. I'm glad you could come. How are you?"

"I'm good, how are you?" Malcolm Haisley strolled in and plopped into a plush, reclining chair.

"Comfortable?" Casey, the decoy pretending to be Kayla, sat on the arm of another chair. "It's a massage chair." She pointed. "There are three buttons. One for your butt. The other for your lower back. And the other for your upper back."

"Yes. It feels great. But I thought you had blonde hair."

"That was my yearbook photo. I dyed it myself. Do you like it?"

"It looks pretty. Very pretty."

"Thank you. Well, what do you want to do?"

"Let's start with a kiss." Haisley scrunched to the side of the massage chair and patted the seat. "Snuggle up next to me."

"I'm more comfortable sitting at the edge of this chair for now. You just got here. Let's talk first."

"Okay. But one kiss speaks a thousand words." Haisley leered at her.

"You know where a kiss will lead. That's why you came over. Right."

"Of course, my precious Princess. I came to love you like you deserve to be loved."

"So, did you bring condoms?" Casey grinned and opened her hands.

"Yes. I did."

"Where are they?"

"They're out in my car."

"What good are they going to do in the car, if we're in here?"

"Well, yell at me, why don't ya," Haisley replied.

Trevor walked into the room. "Pretty comfortable there, Mr. Haisley. Are you a Bonanza fan?"

Haisley jerked in his chair. "Yes." He squirmed. "Umm," his jaw chattered. "I love Westerns. Bonanza was my favorite show. Lorne Greene was my favorite actor."

"That explains your screen name." Trevor held several sheets of paper. "Interesting chat log you got here. Is it appropriate to write to a thirteen-year-old girl, *'After I lick you and get you moist and ready, King Penis will meet Princess Vagina, and you will be my queen 4 ever. Do you want 2 meet King Penis?'*" The corners of Trevor's lips lifted slowly, deliberately. "Let me introduce you to King Penis." Trevor showed Haisley his webcam photo of himself exposed.

"Oh Cawd!" Haisley's stress and Southern accent mispronounced 'God.' He slapped his forehead, covered his face, and lowered his head.

"I'm Trevor Brocton, and there are some things you need to know. After Brocton Enterprises' hostile takeover of Picardi Developments, I'm now CEO of Brocton and Picardi Construction. You have committed multiple felonies. Where do I begin?"

"No. No. I'm sorry. I wasn't going to do anything. She has a mean and emotionally detached father. I was just stepping in as her surrogate father. I only wanted to mentor and protect her."

"Protect her by licking her and getting her moist so it won't hurt while you rape her? That's awfully white of you, Padre. If you want to be a little girl's father, this chat log is not something you would put in an adoption application, and, as the old cliché goes, one picture speaks a thousand words." Trevor shoved Malcolm's dick-pic in his face. "Sending that photo alone constitutes a felony." Trevor handed him the photo. "Your ticket to prison. Oh, and I'm sure you know how child molesters are treated in prison. The other inmates will pass you around like a rugby ball. Your career is over. When you get out, if you get out alive, you will spend the rest of your life as a registered sex offender. Combine that with your age, and you will be lucky to get a minimum wage job. You might as well check back into prison until you die. You're married, aren't you? How will this go over with your wife?"

"She'll divorce me." Haisley pressed his fingers over his eyes, vainly fighting tears.

"You have a daughter. How would you like it if a greasy, balding old pervert sent her dick-pics and then came over to rape her?"

"No. No. Please! Don't tell anyone."

"I didn't think you'd like that." Trevor looked up from the chat log. "And how will your kids react to all of this?"

"They'll never speak to me again." Haisley's face froze and drooped.

"You have, or shall I say, had a granddaughter. I don't think your son will ever let you near her."

"Please, please, Mr. Brocton." Haisley shook his hands and streamed tears. "I'll do anything. Please, just let me go. I'll get help. I'll never do it again. Pease," He steepled his hands. "Don't tell anyone." He raised and shook his arms. "Please!"

"Now you're catching on." Trevor moved inches from Haisley. "As CEO of a development and construction company, you can both approve a sale and approve development plans on a property that I want. The old Wilton Manor estate."

"I will get in trouble if I approve it. Higher-ups are discussing preserving it as a historical landmark."

"You'll get in trouble?" Trevor laughed sadistically. "Right now, you're facing a long prison sentence and a lifetime on a sex offender registry. I'm going to help you stay out of trouble with the criminal justice system and your job. Wilton Manors is a throwback to the days of slavery. Politically Correct is the current zeitgeist. Play the antebellum slavery angle. Getting the activists on your side will be easy. The press will follow. Once that happens, the higher-ups in the county bureaucracy won't dare fire you. Otherwise, well…" Trevor shoved Haisley's chat log and dick-pic in his face.

"Okay. Okay." Haisley shook his hands. "I'll do it."

"I know you will." Trevor beamed. "Oh, and one thing you won't have to worry about. I'll pay fair market value. I need you to keep your job. I will soon take over Evans and Carlton Construction as well. I will want other properties, zoning variances, and plan approvals." Trevor nodded to the entrance of an adjacent room. A man with a large video camera and another with a microphone entered. "Malcolm Haisley. I own you."

***

"Good afternoon, Florence." Trevor strolled into the Brocton Copper Works head office.

223

"What happened to Miss Moneypenny?"

"As you know, things have changed. Talk about a bittersweet moment. I have achieved another huge win for Brocton Enterprises." Trevor covered his face by pinching his nasal bone. "But my father is not with us to be proud. I have acquired the old Wilton Manor property for Brocton and Picardi Construction." Trevor turned his back and put a dab of saliva on his left eye. "I have no one to share my accomplishment with. I am sure wherever my parents are, they are proud of me."

"I know they would be very proud of you." Florence smiled.

"Florence," Trevor sat on her desk. "What do you say we celebrate together, over dinner?"

"Strictly business?"

"Sure." He spread his palms.

"Okay. I'll pick you up at seven. "Don't worry. I know your home address."

Chapter 15

Bobby sat in the Wilton Manor drawing room. His complexion looked as if he had dipped his head into a vat of white flour. His cup of coffee jittered in his hands; droplets spilled over the edge. It clinked as he placed his cup in a saucer. He then fidgeted with a teaspoon.

"Now hush that furrow in your brow, Bobby." Margarette sat next to him. "Everything's gon' be just fine. You cast that frettin' to the wind."

"Thank you, Margarette. I know you mean well. If this happened while we were mortals, I wouldn't worry. Erica is a strong and street-smart woman." Bobby bent the teaspoon in half. "But now we're ghosts. She doesn't have your experience with the spiritual realm."

"That's why the good Lord provides us with an angel guide. Wherever our darling Erica may be, Isolde Maria will find her and bring her back to us."

"Please be right, Margarette," Bobby steepled his hands and closed his eyes.

"You know what the Lord says in his Good Book, wherever two or more are gathered in thy name, I shall be with you."

"I know I need Jesus to go from ghost to angel. Erica found him long ago. I just hope that, wherever she is, she keeps the faith."

"I know you, I know our Erica, and I know your angel guide Isolde Maria." Margarette stood. "You need to trust your lady of the house. I've been a ghost for over 150 years and counting. I know there's no cause for concern, truly, let your mind be at ease. Let's hold hands in prayer." Bobby and Margarette silently moved their lips in prayer. Afterward, she stood. "Let me bring you a pitcher of cold, sweet tea. We'll sip it together with James and George and wait for our darling Erica to come home. I declare, will you look at that? Sunbeam must have read our minds."

Sunbeam walked over with a tray. It held a pitcher of iced tea and several glasses. She placed it on the table. Margarette poured Bobby, James, George, Sunbeam, and herself a glass of iced tea.

Jason walked over and placed his hand on Sunbeam's shoulders. He tilted his head back and exaggerated breathing through his nose. "I know that's not just the flowers in your hair, love. Margarette, did you just plant the Garden of Eden in your drawing room?"

Their next sight was speckled particles that began to form into two people. Two seconds later, it sharpened to crystal clarity. Isolde Maria appeared wearing a V-cut, shocking white gown. Her indigo tress splashed over her shoulders and chest, flowing to her waist. Erica gripped her left hand like a cliff purchase. Her complexion was even whiter than the angel's gown; her eyes were glazed, and her mouth was locked half open.

"The spiritual realm is not for either mortal or ghost. Erica ventured to where many angels fear to tread. I am a Heavenly Counselor. I had to summon a Seraphim to bring Erica back." Isolde Maria's blue eyes beckoned like lighthouse beams cutting through the fog. Although she gazed at the entire gathering, she connected with each one individually. "Bobby." She pointed at him with her right forefinger.

Bobby scrunched in fear. He pressed himself against the back of his chair.

"I have determined that you and Erica have a need to know. Stand, Bobby, approach me, and take my hand." The angel extended her hand. "I will take you and Erica to Adele."

***

Bobby held Isolde Maria's right hand while Erica held her left hand. They crystallized and spun through a flashing kaleidoscope of light. They landed on their feet. They first heard chirping birds and the babbling of a brook flowing over smooth stones. Large oak and magnolia trees shaded the brick Virginia-style mansion. It featured white columned porticos and floor-to-ceiling windows. Isolde Maria had vanished. Bobby and Erica spotted a woman in a light blue muslin dress with a delicate floral pattern. Although her attire was loose-fitting and modest, it could not hide the fullness of her figure and the generous curve of her chest. She wore a wide-brimmed straw sun hat with a floral band; her thick ash-blonde hair reached five inches beyond her shoulders. She gently pushed a young boy on a swing suspended from a thick elm tree branch. A younger girl wore a pink bonnet that left a peep of platinum blonde hair. She stood close to her mother.

Erica immediately identified the woman. She ran up to her while Bobby walked. "Adele! It's me! Your sister!"

Adele turned and smiled.

Erica did a double-take. Her younger sister now appeared four or five years older than herself.

"It's been a long time, Erica. Six years. I can see that you went to a different dimension. Time moves differently in eternity. The year is 1794. I am a mortal again in this realm. I will age naturally. Like all mortals, I will die once again. I am also spiritually born again. Someday, we will be reunited in Heaven."

"Mortal?"

"Yes. Mortal. These are my children. Richard and Martha. Your nephew and niece."

"Hi there, Richard and Martha," Erica waved. "I am your Aunt Erica."

The children were oblivious to her. Richard swung higher on his own; Martha clung to the hem of her mother's dress.

"They can't see you or hear you. They're mortals and you're a ghost."

Bobby arrived. His eyes opened wide.

"Hello, Bobby." Adele faintly smiled. "I've waited six years and thought I must wait another fifty to say, 'I'm sorry.' I was unfaithful to you. But all things work together for those who love the Lord. Erica was right for you all along. Deep inside, I knew it. But how could you ever get together if you were with me?"

"You never knew how much I loved you and how much I needed you while deployed in Iraq." Bobby winced. "As you can see, it turned out to be a one-way trip."

"I'm not excusing my behavior, but I was not ready for you or even worthy of you." Adele lowered her head. "You are now with a woman worthy of your love." Adele smiled at last. "Coincidentally, my husband is a soldier. His name is William. He was an officer in General Washington's Continental Army. He risked everything for his country. His wife died of cholera while he was fighting for independence and liberty. He is a good man, Bobby and Erica. As soon as America won independence from the British, he freed his slaves. Because he was always a good man, most of his freed slaves chose to stay. William pays them the same fair wage that he pays his white workers."

"Mommy, Mommy, look at me!" Richard flew higher on his swing.

Adele embraced him from behind on his return. "I'm proud of you, Richard. But you must be more careful." Adele took Martha's hand. "I am home now. This is a better time for me. It's less complicated and has fewer temptations." Adele nodded. "It's also richer. We listen to Bach, Haydn, Mozart, and Beethoven. Our library is stocked with great literature and poetry. Being a full-time mother beats working in an office cubicle for a pervert, or maybe worse, the Pussy Cat Lounge…" She chuckled. "Erica, Bobby, I wish I could chat with you more. I'd invite you inside for lemonade, but I see that your angel guide is here. I think she wants to return you."

Erica and Bobby turned to see Isolde Maria wearing the same white gown, but now with the addition of her luxuriant white wings. She stood across the lawn.

"Adele. I forgive you for everything that happened. You will always be my sister, and I will always love you with all my heart."

"I love you too, Erica." Adele hugged her sister. "We will be together again as sisters in Christ for eternity." Adele kissed Erica's cheek. "I will miss you until then."

Erica kissed Adele's lips. Adele vanished. The Virginian estate vanished. They stood together in a sea of light. Isolde Maria stood before Erica and Bobby. Erica lurched over, grabbed her gown's arm sleeves, and shook her. "It's not fair! It's not fair! I was the good sister. Why does she get a second chance at mortal life and get to be a mother?"

Isolde Maria pursed her lips and slightly narrowed her eyes. "I am disappointed in you, Erica. I thought you would be happy for your sister. Where is your faith, Erica? You and Adele were given different gifts that come with different expectations. Your purpose is the same as your sister's purpose, as both are identical to mine. We are to serve God.

He has great blessings planned for you." Moisture made Isolde Maria's eyes shine bluer than the star Rigel.

"I'm sorry, Isolde Maria. I'm sorry." Erica bawled and rubbed her eyes on the shoulder of the angel's gown. Isolde Maria disappeared. Erica ran to Bobby and embraced him. "I'm happy for her, Bobby. I truly am. Her children were adorable, and she seemed so happy and content. I'm going to miss her, Bobby. Hold me close." Erica squeezed Bobby tighter and closed her eyes. "I miss her already."

Bobby held Erica close to him and closed his eyes.

When they opened their eyes, they had returned to the Wilton Manor drawing room.

Chapter 16

Trevor picked up Florence Hutchinson at her apartment building. Trevor opened his car door for her.

"Wow! A new Ferrari!" Florence wore a white sundress with brown embroidery over the chest and shoulders. She wore gold hoop earrings and a gold necklace. She pushed down on her sun hat as she climbed into Trevor's car. "What happened to your Porsche?"

"I still have her. I've added this new Ferrari 36- Modena to the family. She's slick and stylish, isn't she?"

"Does that reflect your lady collection, new, slick, and stylish?"

"Au contraire. You're my vintage Rolls-Royce Silver Cloud."

"The tragedy hasn't cost you your charm. I'm unsure about getting compared to a car." Florence chuckled. "But if it's a Rolls-Royce, I know you mean well." She smiled at Trevor. "I'll take it as a compliment."

"What I have planned for us is worthy of a woman of your fine vintage and caliber."

"Now, Trevor, you know I could pass for your mother. This is strictly professional. I hope you didn't outdo yourself."

"The Brocton way is the best way—the only way—and that means treating you like a queen." Trevor pulled out onto the highway.

"Where are you taking me?"

"Close your eyes and dream. Imagine you're riding in a heavenly chariot and you're flying above the clouds to the sweetest destination."

"I've known you for how long? You have a way with words. Now I hope to know the real you."

Trevor grinned.

***

Trevor drove off the highway at exit 221, soon reaching Wentworth Street in downtown Charleston. Five minutes later, he turned onto the Wentworth Mansion driveway. "Oh, my goodness, Trevor. This is the Wentworth Mansion. I'm only an old receptionist. You shouldn't do this."

"Shouldn't I? Just a receptionist? You give Brocton Enterprises a heart and soul, a warmth that my late father, God rest his soul, could never bring." Trevor held her hand for three seconds. "I want you to realize it. You bring immeasurable value to the company." He held her hand again. "And to me."

After Trevor turned his car over to the valet, he extended his arm to Florence. She took it. Trevor escorted her to the elevator.

"Why are you taking me into the elevator? Aren't we dining at the Circa 1886?"

"Do they serve chateaubriand prepared by a top-rated French Chef?"

"No...but..."

"But nothing." Trevor walked Florence out of the elevator. "You'll have to trust me." Trevor opened a door. "Viola. The Grand master Suite."

"Trevor!" Florence covered her face. "It's magnificent. I never..."

"When I compared you to a Rolls-Royce Silver Cloud, I meant it. You'll never see a Rolls-Royce pull up to the McDonald's drive-through window. Just for you, I've hired Andre LePeau to prepare us a meal fit for royalty."

"Trevor, are you treating me to dinner in a private room because you don't want people to think you're a gigolo escorting an old lady?"

"Old? Style and class can't be taught, and it doesn't come automatically with age. If anything, I'm not at your level." Trevor held both of her hands. "So, let's put the age and work nonsense behind us and grab the moment."

***

"Trevor, I had never experienced a meal like that. And I mean experienced."

"For all these years, you worked for my father. Now you work for me. I wanted to show you, not just tell you, how valuable you are to me." Trevor poured her a glass of Valdespino sherry. "To new beginnings." Trevor and Florence touched glasses. "Ahh, you are like this fine sherry, you improve with age."

Florence chuckled. "Unfortunately, cheesy lines don't improve with age."

Trevor dipped his finger into the sherry and rubbed it onto Florence's lips. He kissed her. "Ahh, the finest vintage."

Florence lowered her head and blushed. "You probably kiss many beautiful, young ladies."

"None to match your fine vintage, my dear. Sip some more with me." Trevor lifted his glass of sherry. Florence and Trevor tapped glasses and drank. The second she placed her glass on the table, Trevor kissed her again, this time he gently flicked her tongue.

"Trevor, I confess. I know you were only playacting, but I really did have the same crush on you as Miss Moneypenny had on James Bond. Moneypenny never got her man. I worked for your father, and, besides, I harbored guilt just thinking about being with a much younger man."

233

"And now?" Trevor grinned.

"I don't know what to say."

"Say nothing." Trevor kissed her. He put his hand behind her neck to prevent her from pulling away. No need. She returned his wet kiss with vigor. Trevor, without relinquishing his lip lock, moved his hand under her thighs. He lifted her and cradled her. Florence braced her left hand around Trevor's neck and her right hand under his armpits. She kissed him as if passion alone could satisfy years of yearning. Trevor carried her to the bedroom and placed her on the bed. While kissing her, he unbuttoned her blouse. Florence helped him.

***

Afterward, Trevor poured Florence champagne into a crystal goblet. "To the new us." They tapped glasses.

"Oh, Trevor. I almost forgot what it was like to be a woman. Your father was rough and fast. You truly made love to me. I've never felt so good and in so many ways."

Trevor's brow furrowed, his eyes narrowed. His complexion turned red as if his skin were lava…

…Florence sat on her mother's lap. She gazed at her mother's kind, plumpish face as she read her the fable of Pandora's Box. Her mother kissed her cheek, opened a different book, and read to her from Robert Lewis Stevenson's Dr. Jekyll and Mr. Hyde, "He gave an impression of deformity without any nameable malfunction. He had born himself with a sort of murderous mixture of timidity and boldness…"

…Trevor's glare elicited more terror in Florence than when her mother read Dr. Jekyll and Mr. Hyde or even Edgar Allan Poe. *'His stare. He looks crazier than Manson.'* She lost control of her bladder. She tried to picture her words as a solid that she could grab and stuff in a box. Trevor's hands lunged for her throat. She knew that box could never be closed.

***

Trevor muttered to himself, "You've got to be more careful about this, Trevor." *'Even the best of the best, Bundy, Gacy, The Night Stalker, Son of Sam... got careless and got caught. Jeffrey Dahmer...'* Trevor pinched his chin. *'He awoke to a dead body in Milwaukee's Ambassador Hotel. He snuck out, purchased a large suitcase, and returned to the hotel. He was able to stuff the body inside and leave the hotel undetected. I'll wait until the swing shift comes on and get a large suitcase from home. If Dahmer could fit a man in a suitcase, I can surely fit this skinny old hag into one. But first...'* Trevor reached into his pocket and pulled out a silver pill box.

***

"That wasn't too hard." Trevor wiped sweat from his brow and admired the suitcase containing Florence's body. *'I'd better hurry. I can't leave the van parked in the back forever.'* "Okay, Trevor, you're on." Trevor first checked to ensure that the floor was vacant. He rolled the macabre suitcase to the service elevator and pushed the call button. "Shit!" *'I thought so.'* He realized that he needed a special key to operate it. "Okay, Trevor. Here goes." He pushed the passenger elevator call button. He stood aside as it opened. *'Nobody.'* He rolled the suitcase into the elevator. *'Better not go through the lobby.'* He pushed the button for the first floor. Trevor leaned against the back wall as the elevator descended. "Shit!" The door opened on the fourth floor.

An overweight middle-aged man with a bald pate entered. He loosened his blue and yellow striped tie and looked at the

235

suitcase. "Where are you going? An Amazon safari or crossing the Sahara?"

"I'm an Amway salesman." Trevor placed his hand on the suitcase's latch. "Can I interest you in some cleaning supplies?"

"No, thank you." He looked away and moved close enough to the door to press his nose on it.

Trevor exited the elevator on the first floor. He lugged the suitcase down two flights of stairs. He first scanned the utility room for closed-circuit TV cameras. *'None.'* As added assurance in case he missed a camera, he did not turn on a light. He bumped into a table and later kicked over an empty mop bucket. *'Shit, Trevor, alert the night maintenance staff or security, you idiot.'* He rolled the suitcase through the utility room and out the rear door without further incident. He sighed and rubbed his brow. "Still there," he spotted his unmarked, white van. He loaded the suitcase into the back. *'No one is chasing you. Don't speed or run any red lights.'* After fifteen minutes of driving, Trevor reached the Wanderer's Inn. *'Thank you, Satan, whoever owns this dump can't afford outdoor lighting. It's a good thing that what few customers this place gets only stay for an hour or so.'* He pulled up the unpaved driveway to cabin number twelve and the adjacent swamp. He took one final look, "No one," and rolled the suitcase into the cabin. "Good news, Jenny, I've got you company." Trevor pulled Florence's body from the suitcase and dumped it onto the bed next to Jenny's corpse. He felt a tingling and a blood rush to his penis. "Let me bring you to life with my nectar. I want you to enjoy your new lady friend." Trevor disrobed and violated Jenny's corpse.

Chapter 17

Bobby and Erica held hands while sitting in the Wilton Manor drawing room. "Don't be sad, darling. Isolde Maria let you say goodbye to your mother and Adele. I had two parents who loved me and raised me to the best of their ability. I also had a brother and a sister. You met my brother, Albert. Except for maybe my best friend, Matty, he was a fish's worst nightmare. I miss them all. But Isolde Maria said it best. Better I let them grieve in peace. She also told us that demons from Hell often imitate ghosts. She added that appearing to them may cause confusion and open the door to evil entities." Bobby smiled. "Our angel guide did assure me that I would see them again. I'll take solace in that."

"You're right, Bobby," Erica closed her eyes and bowed her head.

Bobby kissed her forehead. "Erica, what do you say we go away. We'll stay within the limits of our powers as ghosts. But let's be bold and go far away."

"After all we've been through, a vacation would serve us well." Erica arched her eyebrows. "What did you have in mind?"

"I was thinking an isolated beach on a Greek island."

"The Greek islands were always my dream while a mortal. But let's use our powers to avoid the cruise ship and tourist spots."

"I read that the Island of Anafi boasts breathtaking vistas and quiet beaches." Bobby took both of Erica's hands. "Let's concentrate on Anafi Island. Here goes." They counted each inhalation and exhalation from one to ten. Next, they counted each breath using the radio telephony alphabet.

Erica and Bobby dissolved and drifted away. "Bobby! I never imagined such a place."

Bobby and Erica were on a small stretch of a golden-sand beach. Porous rocks sculpted by the tides flanked one side of the cove. The wind and the sea flowing through them seemed like a song. The cliffs of Kalamos were behind them. "Let's climb to the top. Maybe if we visit the Monastery of Panagia Kalamoitissa, we can learn something about being ghosts that Isolde Maria isn't telling us?" Bobby pointed. "Look at that outcrop. Its perch is directly over the sea. I'm tempted to climb up and dive in."

"Seeing that you're already dead," Erica laughed, "Let's not tempt death a second time. You better ask Isolde Maria before you do anything too crazy."

"Ah, Come on, Erica. She's my angel guide, not my mother. Why do I need her permission to do everything?"

"It's not about getting permission. It's that she has quantum leaps more knowledge of the spiritual realm and our current state. We need to learn from her and trust her. I found out firsthand what can happen if we challenge the spiritual realm on our own. It was terrifying, Bobby. Please take my word for it. I don't want to relive it."

"Yes, and you had me worried sick, and you're right, Erica." Bobby raised his palms. "In the end, Isolde Maria took us to Adele. But Erica, the sea. It's breathtaking. It beckons us. It's turquoise at the shore, and a short swim away, it's cobalt—and calm as a pond." Bobby stood and held Erica's hand. "It's crystal clear, and I see no dark shadows hovering underneath or black fins cleaving the surface. Come on. Let's swim." He tried to pull her to her feet.

"Not yet, Bobby. Why can't we relax and soak up the sun? I know you're excited, but let's first take in the sight of

Mount Kalamos. I read that it's the second-highest monolithic rock in the Mediterranean, behind only Gibraltar. And the aroma of the sea mingled with the thyme bushes and sagebrush. I know Heaven above is grander. Yet we've found the next best thing here."

"Erica, Heaven is wherever you are." He chuckled. "Except Iraq. Even you couldn't redeem that place."

Erica moved her face inches from Bobby. "As beautiful as the landscape of this island may be, I prefer looking at your handsome face." Erica brushed her fingertips over Bobby's cheeks. "Rather, I smell your breath than the sea and natural spices." Erica touched her nose to his nose. "I'll take your lips to my lips over vintage Argyros wine." Erica delicately kissed Bobby, savoring every nanosecond of his tongue's tingle and flavor.

"Oh, Erica, I don't remember the blast that ended my mortal life. I do know that it can't surpass the power of your kisses."

Bobby and Erica sprawled on the golden sand. The sun and Erica's arms and hands warmed his back while her hamstrings and calves caressed his thighs. His strokes matched the gentle lapping of the tide. A breeze both cooled them and sang to them through the porous rocks. Erica's moans of pleasure delighted him beyond any siren song or symphony.

"Bobby." Erica nibbled on Bobby's ear. "I see a sailboat cruising into our cove. But I don't want to stop. I can't stop."

"Close your eyes, Erica, we can melt into our ghost mode, no mortal can see us."

Bobby and Erica transformed from matter to photons, from flesh and blood to spirit and soul. They wholly united and shared every conceivable sensation and emotion. Shared lights of every hue and magnitude flashed and streaked through their beings. Harmonious and melodic music chimed and danced with each loving movement, firing every possible pleasure neuron and impulse. Bobby and Erica had merged into one sentient entity. Only divine mystery stood in the way of cognizing this love beyond death.

Chapter 18

Bobby and Erica walked hand in hand through the Wilton Manor drawing room.

"I declare, could even the charge of the Light Brigade vanquish those smiles?" Margarette greeted them. "You're already my sweetest pair, but now y'all have created enough sugar to sweeten all the kingdom's candy. Rather, don't tell me about the spice that gave y'all your added joy."

Bobby and Erica chuckled. "It's not us," Erica took Margarette by the hand. "It's because of our lady of the house. You have made our afterlife a happy life."

"I'm sure I don't deserve such words, but I treasure them just the same." Margarette smiled, "After all, without our angel guides, I could never be a good," She laughed, "ghost host."

Bobby and Erica laughed with her.

"We still got you beat." James pointed at George. "The Crimson Tide has twelve national titles to the Wolverines' eleven."

"Yeah, as of now." George jutted his jaw, "Except that Michigan has produced both a Heisman trophy winner and a President of the United States."

"You're reaching for it, buster." James laughed. "You call a president who never even got elected vice-president, much less president, and only served half a term, something to brag about? Tell me, from where was the man who beat him in his only national election?"

"You're boasting about the Carter presidency?" George threw up his hands. "What else can you pull from the tail end of the corn shuck?"

"I'm sorry to interrupt the debate." Sunbeam approached them. "But I detect a large mortal presence out front."

Margarette peered out the window and turned to her Wilton Manor residents.

"You look white as a ghost." Jason stepped toward her. "I know, terrible analogy, bad joke." He opened the curtain, looked outside, and turned to the gathering. "Hey, all kidding aside. Margarette isn't wrong. This looks serious."

The Wilton Manor ghosts took their imperceptible form and floated through the exterior walls.

A tall, athletically slim man in designer slacks and a shirt rolled up to just below his elbows stood behind a cluster of microphones. Three TV cameras focused on him. He touched his copiously gelled and trained hair before speaking. "Good afternoon. I'm Trevor Brocton. Most of you know me from Brocton Copper Works. We have merged with Picardi Developments to form Brocton and Picardi Construction. Thanks to Charleston County's forward-thinking Planning Director, Mr. Malcolm Haisley, we were able to purchase this derelict eyesore and environmental and safety hazard. I shouldn't be praising Malcolm Haisley. His tough negotiations netted Charleston County an above-market price." Trevor paused for the gathering's polite laughter. "Some would argue that it should be restored. Enlightened people like myself and Mr. Haisley believe that the days of slavery should only be remembered in context as an evil institution. Rather than a monument to slavery and wealth inequality, Brocton and Picardi Construction are going to develop this in a way that will benefit the people of Charleston County. The Charleston County Planning Director has approved our plans to clear the land and construct 110 low-cost, two- and three-bedroom villas. Keep in mind that low cost does not necessarily mean low quality. We will not only maintain but exceed the quality standards that built Picardi Development's reputation. Now that Brocton Copper Works can directly supply much of the building materials, we will pass the savings on to the good people of Charleston County. Some think a man from California can't understand the Southern way. Well, I can assure you that I understand the American way. I know that Americans appreciate low prices and convenience. The new Wilton Manors is a hop, skip, and a jump to I-26 and State Highway 61. Moreover, Charleston County's schools, police and fire departments, and roads will benefit from the tax revenue the new Wilton Manors will bring. Anyone can say they understand the needs of Charleston County folk. Well, the new Wilton Manors will show that I know and care about y'all. I am therefore announcing that I am running as an Independent for the Governor of South Carolina. Thank you."

Margarette broke down in tears. Sunbeam put her arm around her and helped float her back through the wall and into the main drawing room. The ghostly residents gathered around the Lady of the House. In a long motion, Margarette wiped her eyes with a silk handkerchief. "This is a most unfortunate turn. How unfortunate, I can only dare say. If this house is demolished," Margarette paused to gain her composure, "we must disperse and find a new home."

Wilton Manor's ghostly residents groaned.

"Where can we go?" A woman dressed as a roaring twenties flapper asked.

"I wish I could tell you, Vanessa." Margarette tightened her mouth. "Unless your angel guide takes you somewhere else, you'll be on your own."

"Margarette," A World War I German soldier raised his hand. "You told us that if builders came in and renovated Wilton Manors, we could all stay."

"Klause, we can wash away mortals from our eyes and ears, and they won't see or hear us either. Those rules apply to construction workers and later swarms of tourists. The new life we've found would remain the same." Margarette sniffled. "Demolition ends it all."

Bobby stepped forward. "Margarette, why can't we do something about this Trevor Brocton guy?"

"We are ghosts, not demons. I sense that if your frustration were a wire, I could strum a sad tune on it. I dare say, we are powerless to engage in the affairs of mortal men and women."

"So, what the fuck are we?" Jason scowled. "Casper and the ghostly trio?" Jason turned to the gathering. "I say we do something, and we start with that arrogant prick," Jason pulled his face and rolled his eyes, "Captain Hair Gel."

Sunbeam grabbed Jason's arm and glowered at him.

"Hush now, Sunbeam." Margarette touched her hand. "Let's not further trouble our hearts. He may not have expressed his thoughts like the fine Christian gentleman we all know; nonetheless, he's feelin' what we're all feelin'."

"Margarette," Erica spoke, "Our Isolde Maria took Bobby and me to both my mother and my sister."

"Isolde Maria soars above the Angel Guides. She is a Heavenly Counselor. God created the Angels a level above humans, and a Heavenly Counselor above other Angels." Margarette extended her open hands. "That should answer y'all's questions on why her beauty, presence, and wisdom reflect Heaven itself. Even without our angel guides, we can take human form and talk to humans." Margarette nodded. "Just so long as y'all never encountered 'em in your mortal life. Only a Heavenly Counselor can take us to someone we once knew. With Isolde Maria's permission and her guidance, y'all can speak to Trevor Brocton. Even under her direction, we can't physically stop that scoundrel. Even she cannot allow us to reveal our identity as undead. We can only talk as if we were mortal humans. We ghosts may one day rise to the level of Angels. For now, we must live within the means of our power and abilities."

Jason adjusted his Green Beret before derisively singing the theme song to the cartoon, Caspar the Friendly Ghost. Sunbeam silenced him by elbowing his ribs. Margarette collapsed into a chair, looked around her manor house, and cried. James and George brought her a glass of lemonade.

Chapter 19

The Pussy Cat Lounge only had a smattering of customers. Cloretta had stripped down to a G-string and twirled around a pole. She didn't smile or make eye contact with the customers. "Let's give a big hand for Thais," a voice spoke over the intercom. None of the patrons clapped. The Master of Ceremonies put on another loud, electronic dance song while a heavily tattooed stripper came out in a red and black robe. She let it fall to her ankles as she grasped the pole in the center of the stage.

Cloretta walked over to a man wearing a flannel shirt and a John Deere ballcap. "Do you wanna tip my dance?"

"Yeah, why not?" He reached into his pocket and stuffed a one-dollar bill in her bra strap.

She approached the other customers likewise. Five of the six also gave her a dollar bill. Cloretta sat at the bar and dropped her head.

"What's wrong, honey?" A black dancer wearing a red, silky and lacy, low-cut halter top sat next to Cloretta.

"Everything, Armani, I am desperate, as in dire straits. My rent is due on Tuesday, and I'm four hundred bucks short. I came up short last month, too; this time, the landlord is serious about evicting me and my two boys. It's a shitty single-wide in a slummy trailer park with a broken air conditioner. At least it's a roof over our heads, if we're kicked out," Cloretta raised her head. "CPS will step in and kidnap my children. As it is, I'm struggling to buy them food."

"Yeah, things in this place ain't what they used to be." Aramani slid her hand down Cloretta's arm and held her hand. "A lot of the customers, and even most of us, think you're the hottest babe here. There's got to be a rich dude out there who would want you as his girlfriend, and, lucky you, you can double your chances." Armani put her hand on Cloretta's inner thigh and winked. "If I didn't have a man, I'd sure wanna be your girl."

"You got an NFL football player for a boyfriend. Why risk it by working here?"

"Risk it? He loves me working here." Armani cupped her hands under her breasts and jiggled. "He even paid for these."

"Why would he want you here? This place could be a circle of Dante's Inferno."

"He has three reasons." Armani kissed Cloretta on the lips.

After a brief touch of tongues, Cloretta pulled her head away. "Thank you," Cloretta placed her hands on her shoulders. "I'll admit that helped, and I wouldn't mind doing it again. But you know management frowns on it. As much as I hate this place, it's the only job I can find. Maybe I can work for minimum wage somewhere that don't do background checks, but that won't support my sons. Besides, my problems run deeper. You know I'd love to get out of here. Growing up, everyone told me I could be a model and actress. They said I could do it on my looks alone. But first, I had to get away from my piece-of-shit, molesting stepfather, and I thought that biker dude was my ticket to ride. After getting slapped around for three years of hell, he upped the ante and beat me badly enough for a hospital stay."

"At least they locked him up for it."

"Yeah, that and for the drugs they found on him during the arrest. What good did putting him away do me? He headed for only the Devil knows after he got out. I've never gotten a penny of support for our kids. Yeah, bad boys…"

"And speaking of bad boys, here comes one with money. I'll leave him for you." Aramani put a twenty-dollar bill in Cloretta's right bra strap. "I hope that gives him a prompt." She looked both ways and quickly French-kissed Cloretta.

The man walked closer, and Cloretta recognized him.

"So, we meet again."

"Get away from me, or I'll have the bouncer throw you out on your ass."

"I don't think so. I've tipped the bouncers more than this dump pays them. I see you're off to a good start. Will you object to me bettering it?" Trevor stuffed a hundred-dollar bill in her left bra strap.

Cloretta tore the note from her bra strap. *'Throw it in the bastard's face.'* But then, she paused. Cloretta shut her eyes and put the bill in her purse.

"Ha! Ha! Ha! I thought so. Your children can't eat your pride." He smirked at her. "CPS won't approve of them living in your car either. Ha! Ha! Ha! From the looks of your Hyundai, soon it won't even be a mobile home."

"What do you want?"

"It's not about what I want, it's about what you need." Trevor pulled out his wallet, removed a stack of hundred-dollar bills, and riffled them in her face like a seasoned Vegas dealer with a deck of cards.

"You, you…Bastard. You know I hate your guts."

"Ha! Ha! Ha! You can say all I want from you is already in my silver pill box."

Cloretta cocked her arm to slap him.

"Ah, ah, ah." He grabbed her wrist. "What will it be? Lose your children, possibly never seeing them again, or a harmless little romp in the hay with me?"

Cloretta wept.

"I have ten of these." He again riffled the hundred-dollar bills in her face. "Stop your blubbering, get in my new Ferrari, and they're yours."

Cloretta imagined the police taking her two and four-year-old boys. The young one wailed. The older one screamed while resisting his police abduction. *"Please, Mommy! Don't send me away! I'll be good! I promise I'll be good. I love you, Mommy! Don't send me away! I'll be good!'*
"Okay," Cloretta continued to weep. "Just a standard job. You must first promise no rough or freaky stuff."

Trevor covered his mouth. "I promise." He nodded his head toward the door. "My time is money." Trevor walked over to the manager and handed him a hundred-dollar bill. "Thais has an emergency with her youngest son. Her 1989 Hyundai won't get her there in time. I hope you don't mind my driving her in my Ferrari. I'll bring her right back." As he walked through the door, he stopped and gazed up and down at the bouncer. "I can see that your deltoids have gotten even bigger since the last time I saw you."

"You noticed," The bouncer beamed. "Thanks, future governor, I read a Ronnie Coleman article in *Muscle and Fitness*. He said to super-set lateral raises with overhead presses." The bouncer touched his fists, put them over his waist, and flared his shoulders. "It works like a bomb."

"Keep up the good work." Trevor handed the bouncer a hundred-dollar bill. "This should help keep you in vitamin pills and protein powder."

***

Cloretta scrunched against the door of Trevor's Ferrari and fidgeted with her keys. Trevor laid his hand on her thigh and slid it under her shorts. She knocked it away as if it were a cockroach.

"Oh no you don't, we're on the clock."

"Why do you do this? You know I hate your guts. I hope you don't think I'm impressed by you throwing around those Benjamins. I know you're rich. You can have any escort in Charleston for half what you're paying me."

"Shall I keep my money and take you to the trailer park so you can prepare your kids for CPS kidnapping them? Be sure to say a long goodbye. You know that they'll get lost in the foster care system. If you're lucky, they won't get placed in a home headed by a man like your stepfather. Ha! Ha! Ha!" He moved his eyes sideways and raised half the left side of his mouth. "Do you feel lucky?"

"I hate you! The more I know you, the more I hate you." Cloretta prodded. "You make my skin crawl. For starters, you didn't so much as bat an eyelash at the death of your parents. You know what else creeps me out even more?"

"Do you have to tell me? I'd rather you shut up and start earning your grand."

"Adele was your girlfriend. She loved you. Not only did you not care about her death, but it made you happy. That comment about saving sixty-five thousand dollars scared me. Now I think my suspicions are true. I was there the night the bouncers threw out Spike McClenahan. I saw you help him to his feet and talk to him in your car. A lot of drugs are goin' around in my trailer park. Spike is now the sole dealer. Word is you set up his turf and you supply him." She jabbed his ribs with her forefinger. "I don't know why you wanted Adele dead, but I think you hired McClenahan to kill her."

"Smart girl. Too bad you didn't choose police work instead of sex work. Ha! Ha! Ha!" Trevor's laugh turned even more sinister. "My parents…Ha! Ha! Ha! What's that new age saying? What goes around comes around? My dear old dad had his own son, my brother, bumped off just because he was gay. Do you know what Novichok is?"

Cloretta's teeth chattered while shaking her head.

"It's a nerve agent developed by the Soviets. Only someone with the connections and means of a Brocton can get it. Even slight contact causes convulsions, paralysis, and cardiac arrest. I applied Novichok to our chauffeur's steering wheel. You know the rest."

"You're a monster!" Tears streamed from Cloretta's eyes. "Not only did you kill your parents, but you also killed the chauffeur and a family of four."

"You forgot the trucker. But, it's like Donald Rumsfeld says, 'collateral damage'. Ha! Ha! Ha!"

Cloretta tried to open the door.

"Besides the stupidity of jumping out of a car going 80 miles per hour, you didn't think a car of this caliber would have central locking?"

"Let me out! Let me out! I don't want your money. Please? Let me out." Cloretta broke down.

"Why? Don't you want to know why I had your dear friend Adele killed? She was pregnant with my baby. I'm running for governor. Knocking up a common tramp like Adele would end my run before I even get to the starting gate. Yes. Clever girl. I hired Spike McClenahan to kill her for sixty-five thousand dollars. Too bad Erica was collateral damage. I really wanted to fuck her and add her cunt hairs to my collection. Jenny's boyfriend was on the hook for five grand if I could do it. Not that I need the money. It's a guy thing; you get paid to understand." Trevor drove down Edgecombe Drive. "Well, we're here." He drove up the dirt drive to Wanderer Motel's cabin twelve. "Last stop." Trevor leered at her in a frozen expression that looked like a waxwork in a horror museum. "And I mean exactly that. Last stop. You didn't think I would let you live, knowing what you know."

Cloretta screamed.

Trevor disembarked the car, walked around it, and opened the passenger door with a flick of a button on his remote key controller. He grabbed Cloretta's brown hair with his right hand. She flailed at him, only landing glancing blows. He twisted her hair and used it to pull her from the car. With his left hand, he grabbed her right wrist and wrenched her arm behind her back.

Pain bolted through her every nerve ending. She screamed in agony and fear.

He let go of her hair, opened the door, and pushed her inside. She landed on her stomach. He kicked the door shut and locked it behind him.

The stench of decaying bodies hit her first. She climbed onto her hands and knees and hurled. She screamed upon seeing Jenny and Florence's rotting, naked cadavers posed on the bed. Trevor again twisted her right arm behind her back. With his left arm, he clutched her chin and pulled her head upward. "You already know Jenny. You all thought she left for a new age retreat in Colorado to find herself. You would be amazed at what computer technology can do. The top computer expert in the South works for me. He programmed a computer to replicate her voice. I called everyone she knew using it. Florence, like you, got offed because of her big mouth. She let it leak that she fucked my father. I imagine she's too old for you." Trevor released Cloretta, lurched over, and tossed Florence's body off the bed.

With an adrenaline surge born of fear and survival, Cloretta slugged Trevor in the jaw. He fell backwards and landed on his buttocks. Cloretta grabbed a chair, cocked it behind her head, and threw it at him. Trevor covered his face with his arms to lessen the impact. Cloretta ran for the door. Locked. She fell on her knees and vainly twisted the knob. Trevor got up, lurched over, and again grabbed her hair and twisted. She screamed in both pain and fear. "I'm a forgiving man. I bet you don't believe me. Well, I know you found Jenny attractive. Who wouldn't? But she didn't swing both ways. Great news, Cloretta, or shall I call you by your whore name, Thais?" Trevor spewed saliva as he growled at her. "I have turned Jenny out for you." Trevor forced Cloretta's face into Jenny's crotch. "Lick it! Lick it! Bring it back to life." Trevor jammed his left knee on the small of her back and his right knee directly on her C7 cervical vertebra, at the base of her neck. He clutched her jaw with both hands. He jerked her head upward while driving his right knee into her neck, fracturing three of her cervical vertebrae and killing her instantly. He ripped off her blouse and pulled off her shorts. He disrobed and, while pushing Cloretta's face into Jenny's privates, he violated her from behind. After three minutes, Trevor moaned, "Ahh…My nectar of life."

After getting dressed, Trevor punched in a number on his cellphone. "Hey, Bernie, I got another job for you. I'll be over in an hour. I need you to download another voice." Trevor hung up the phone and picked up Florence's body from the floor, *'Not much more I can do for you, old lady,'* and stuffed her into the closet. "I'm afraid even I can't cleanse you of my father." He slammed the closet door and stepped toward the bed. "Well, Jenny, it looks like you'll need more of my nectar of life. At least I got you company in the meantime." Trevor placed Thais's body next to hers. He rested her head on Jenny's chest. "Ah, my dear Thais. Someday soon, you'll dance for me again. 'Till then, rest up. I'll be back." He kissed both Jenny and Thais on their cheeks before leaving the room and locking the door behind him.

'I know it's hard to be humble when you're Trevor Brocton and soon to be Governor Brocton. Don't let pride make you careless. A Ferrari at a roach motel like this stands out in spades. Ted Bundy drove an inconspicuous Volkswagen. Maybe I should do likewise.'

Chapter 20

Jason, Sunbeam, Erica, Bobby, and George sat together sipping bourbon. No one said a word. Margarette silently wept. James refilled her glass first. They raised their heads and looked at each other as a floral aroma filled the room. Next, they saw two pillars of spectacles. Tears of varying degrees clouded their vision, yet nobody mistook the particles for anything other than human forms. Isolde Maria took shape first. She wore a gown of gleaming gold silk; the V-cut bodice across her chest was diamond-encrusted. A white belt embellished with heart-cut rubies girded her waist. Her gown ended slightly below the knees. She wore white sandals with emeralds enhancing the straps. She had flung her wavy, indigo tresses behind her, allowing her gold and emerald earrings to shine. Her hair reached her buttocks. Another woman formed next to her. She was bloodied and bruised. Isolde Maria braced her shoulders and kissed her forehead. Her wounds vanished. All tattoos and piercings disappeared. She stood tall as the angel. The woman wore a white gown and the same white sandals as the angel, sans the gems. The woman accompanying Isolde Maria boasted rounded cheekbones and a distinct, albeit feminine jaw. Her slightly below shoulder-length brown hair curved forward at the ends. She now radiated beauty. "Greetings." Isolde Maria stepped forward. "I have a new guest for Wilton Manors." Isolde Maria placed her hand on the woman's shoulder. "Introducing Cloretta."

"Why, Miss Cloretta," Margarette stood. "How lovely to have you with us. I do hope to use my ghostly powers to make your time here as pleasant as possible." Margarette wiped away a tear. "But it pains me dearly to start your stay on a somber note. I fear your stay will be briefer than we all wish."

"Fear not, Margarette." Isolde Maria smiled. "Cloretta wishes to address all of you."

Cloretta first looked at the angel before speaking. "Bobby, Erica, Isolde Maria wants me to tell you everything. Bobby."

Bobby stood. He glanced at Erica before facing Cloretta. "Yes."

"Your fiancé was unfaithful, but it's not what you think."

"What do you mean?"

"She cheated on you with Trevor Brocton, the heir of Brocton enterprises and the one who wants to demolish your home."

"So, it wasn't Spike McClenahan." Bobby spread his palms. "But he murdered her and Erica with his car."

"Erica," Cloretta took a deep breath. "You deserve to know what happened. Yes. McClenahan killed you and your sister. But there's more to it. Trevor Brocton paid him sixty-five thousand dollars to do it. Trevor celebrated when Spike got himself killed in the act because he could keep his money."

"But why?" Bobby asked.

"You know that Brocton is running for governor." Cloretta closed her eyes and took a deep breath. "Adele was pregnant with his baby."

Bobby gasped. Erica dropped her jaw.

"I know that comes as a shock to you both." Cloretta pursed her lips and nodded. "He thought the scandal of impregnating a woman out of wedlock, and who he considered beneath his social class, would hurt his chances of getting elected governor. You and your sister are not the only ones. He murdered his parents by putting a Russian nerve poison on their chauffeur's steering wheel. He murdered and raped an older woman whom I don't know and…and…," Cloretta lowered her head. She looked up with teary eyes. "He murdered and raped Jenny Carter."

"Adele's best friend!" Erica fired her words like a gunshot.

"Yes."

"How does he get away with it?" Sunbeam put her glass of Bourbon on the table. "Wouldn't people miss her, and why won't the police investigate?"

"He had a computer whiz program her voice. Brocton called everyone using Jenny's computer-generated voice to say she was leaving for a new age retreat in the Rocky Mountains."

"What about you?" Jason asked.

"He…he…he…" Cloretta broke down and bawled. Isolde Maria embraced her. Cloretta held her strongly as a wrestler, putting an opponent in a bear hug. Bright light covered Cloretta and the Angel. After their hug, Cloretta stood next to the angel, holding her hand.

"Cloretta is completely healed of her physical trauma. I have healed much of her psychological and emotional trauma. My healing is limited partly by being a woman. She needs an honorable man to hold her close and complete the healing process." Isolde Maria smiled, "Bobby. I want you to dance with Cloretta. I will sing."

Cloretta walked Bobby to the center of the drawing room. Even wearing sandals, she stood only a half inch shorter than Bobby. Her white gown seemed to enhance the length and shape of her legs. She wrapped her arms around Bobby, put her chin on his shoulder, and rubbed her cheek against his cheek.

Isolde Maria sang in a mesmerizing tone and perfect pitch. "Heaven, I'm in Heaven. And my heart beats so that I can hardly speak, and I seem to find the happiness I seek. When we're out together dancing, cheek to cheek."

Cloretta and Bobby held each other closer and tighter as the angel sang to them. As they danced, Cloretta kissed his cheek.

Erica narrowed her eyes while watching them dance. Her jaw and lips locked. Her face remained fixed on them.

Sunbeam noticed Erica's distress. She poked Jason and nodded toward Bobby and Cloretta. Jason walked over and tapped Bobby on the shoulder. Bobby nodded to Jason and bowed. Jason and Cloretta embraced and swayed as the angel sang.

"Dance with me. I want my arms around you. Will carry me through to Heaven."

***

Isolde Maria called Bobby, Erica, Jason, Sunbeam, George, and James to another drawing room.

"Trevor Brocton is not fit to walk God's green earth. He's a monster from the depths of Hell." Margarette shook her fists. "Hanging is too good for him."

Isolde Maria stood behind Cloretta. She placed her hands on her shoulders. "Even as a Heavenly counselor, I am not permitted to physically smite him. Each of you is aware of your ghostly limitations." Isolde Maria smiled, "I can allow each of you to appear to him in your physical form and talk to him. I have a plan." She winked. "I want you to brace yourselves. We are dealing with what is called, in Bobby, Erica, and Cloretta's time, a serial killer. Cloretta is going to tell you some disturbing things about him and his tactics. You need to know everything if you're going to stop him."

The gathering pulled up closer to the Angel and Cloretta.

Chapter 21

Bobby marched into the Offices of Brocton Copper Works. The temp receptionist followed him. "You can't go in there without an appointment."

Trevor sat behind his desk. His eyes opened wider than silver dollars.

Bobby wore a fishing outfit. His long-sleeved shirt had vent panels and multiple pockets. A utility belt supported quick-dry cargo pants, and his wide-brimmed fishing hat had a neck buff. Large, mirrored sunglasses further hid his identity.

"Even with all that stuff you're wearing, I know it's you." Trevor pointed with a jittery finger. "But you're supposed to be dead."

"You wish, don't you? The explosion that allegedly killed me obliterated everything within a ten-meter radius. Our executive officer went on our mission. He blubbered for his mommy before running around like a chicken with its head cut off. Otherwise saying, he made a clusterfuck of the whole thing. The soldier who was killed, SGT Fuller, investigated the explosive device. Before I could help him, I went behind a barricade to take a piss. During the confusion after the explosion, I managed to sneak away. I wanted out of Iraq. Moreover, faking my death got my parents close to a million dollars in government benefits. If I'm found alive, not only will I get court-martialed, but my family will have to pay back the money. They've already blown through some of it. They would be in debt until they die."

"Why risk it by coming here?" Trevor's lips quavered. "What do you want from me?"

"I wanted to meet Jodie. You fucked my gal while I was away at war, and she got killed as a result. And I think you know that bringing the affair to light will make the public suspect that you're responsible."

Trevor stood. He took three deep breaths. He held up a cigarette box-sized electronic device. "I hope you're not threatening me. All I have to do is push this button, and security officers the size of NFL linemen will bolt through that door. After they practice their martial arts on you, they will turn what's left of you over to the police. Your gig will be up. You'll be cracking rocks in Leavenworth, and your parents will be more broke than the rocks."

"Ha! Ha! Ha!" Bobby folded his arms over his chest. "I know you won't do that." He tilted his head and skewed his face. "Mr. Governor."

"Okay, I get it. How much?" Trevor tensed his lips. "I'll make a one-time payment. Ask again, and I will arrange for you to join your slut ex-fiancé and her stuck-up sister.

Bobby reached for a silver cigarette box sitting on Trevor's desk, took out a cigarette, and lit it. "I am going to admit, your money tempts me. Let me say that you don't impress me in the least. You're correct about one thing. Adele was a slut. If a bad boy loser like Spike McClanahan can have her, why would you bedding her impress me? So, what do you say we place a bet? I win, and you give me what the government says my life is worth. Five hundred thousand dollars."

"A bet?" Trevor folded his hands behind his neck. "Even if I took your bait, how would you cover a bet like that? You said your family had already spent much of the life insurance premium."

"You're right. I don't have the means to cover a half-million-dollar bet. If I lose, I will give you something you want more than money. After all, half a million is chump change to a man of your wealth. You win, and I will drop to my knees and kiss your ass." Bobby opened his hands, "After I kiss your ass, I will go prostrate and verbally acknowledge that you're not just more man than me, but more of a man than anyone."

Trevor pushed the remote device closer, grinned, and put his thumb over the button. "I already know that I'm the ultimate male. Look at me, poor boy. Tall, handsome, and wealthy. Do I need to add powerful? There's no way on Earth that you can prove you're more of a man than me."

"Not so fast, Mr. Governor. My partner knows I'm here. Have me arrested or worse, killed, and she calls the press. The scandal not only ends your chances of getting elected, but it will also hurt Brocton Enterprises."

"Partner?" Trevor put the device on his desk. "Let's hear about this bet."

"We have something in common, Trevor. We both fucked Adele, and we both wanted more- to have her sister, Erica." Bobby puffed a smoke ring at Trevor. "I have something in common with Erica. My so-called remains were obliterated in an explosion. Erica's body was presumably incinerated in the car fire. Guess what? The passenger in Adele's car was a new stripper from North Dakota that no one missed. Erica let the police think she was killed, so her invalid mother could collect her life insurance premium. Her mother is gone, but Erica is not. We're business partners. Right now, that's all it is, but, like you, I want a whole lot more."

"Oh, I think I get it. The first one of us to bed her wins."

"You got it." Bobby extended his hand. "Do we have a bet?"

"Before I shake on it, we need to establish some rules. You're already working with her. You and she may be cooking up a plot to scam me." Trevor smirked and nodded. "I'm not stupid, despite how your jealous mind may have corrupted your thinking. I have a way to prove the winner. The first to get one of Erica's cunt hairs wins." Trevor folded his arms. "You won't get away with a fake. Not too many women have her shade of auburn hair, and a lab could easily determine if you dyed it," Trevor prodded, "and law enforcement and the insurance company will do a DNA test to prove she faked her death. Next, she will drop a dime on you in exchange for leniency," He prodded. "So, don't try anything."

"Why would I want to cheat?" Bobby grinned. "More than your money, I want to beat you fair and square. You seduced my fiancé. I'm going to prove that I'm more of a man than you and that you never would have bedded Adele if I weren't away. I want to go head-to-head with you for Erica. I'm going to shut you up once." Bobby smirked.

Bobby and Trevor shook hands.

"Erica is waiting for me at Horrible Hank's Tavern." Bobby stood. "Why don't you show up a few minutes after me, sit with her, and take your first shot. It's the last thing I do to help you. Nevertheless, I can't be satisfied with winning unless we have a level playing field."

***

Bobby sat with Erica at a table in the corner of Horrible Hank's Tavern. She wore a scarf over her hair and large, black plastic sunglasses with round lenses.

Five minutes later, Trevor walked in. He had changed into beige Brioni slacks, a gray Brunello Cucinelli sport shirt, and brown Salvatore Ferragamo loafers. He had retrained his hair with copious Oribe's hair gel. He strolled over to the table. "I was suspicious at first glance. But I knew your sister in every intimate way possible. I got your vibe right away. How are you, Erica?"

261

"Ha! Ha! Ha! Clever, aren't you, Sherlock?" Erica scowled and pointed at Bobby. "I knew it! I told you not to, but you did anyway. You tried to shake him down for money, and you ended up spilling the beans." She sneered at Bobby. "There are reasons why Mr. Brocton's a multi-millionaire, and you must pretend to be dead for a few hundred thousand. One reason is that Mr. Brocton is a whole hell-of-a-lot smarter than you."

Bobby bit his lip.

James, wearing dirty jeans, a red flannel shirt, and a baseball cap identifying him as a Vietnam War veteran, walked over to the table. "Even with all the fishing attire you're wearing, a warrior knows another warrior. You sure look like Bobby Sand, the part-time Citadel student killed in Iraq."

"I thank you for your service," Bobby extended his hand to James. "I'm Bobby Sand's brother. I thank you for recognizing his sacrifice for the country we all love."

"Well, if you're his brother, you must be twins. You sure look like Sergeant Sand."

"We're what they call Irish twins. We were born less than a year apart."

"Well, I honor you for being a Gold Star Family member. I'll tell the bartender that your next beer is on me." James walked away.

Bobby stood. "I gotta get outta here. That old man recognized me. I'd better leave while he still thinks I'm my brother."

Bobby marched out the door.

After two minutes, Erica stood. "Oh, Shit!" She ran out the door. Erica re-entered Horrible Hank's wearing a frown, trudged back to Trevor's table, and plopped into her seat. "There goes my ride. Now I'm stranded in this God forsaken out in the middle of nowhere honky-tonk. I don't own a cellphone, and I don't even have change for the payphone. I don't know the number of a cab, assuming a cab driver will even come all the way out to this dump. Moreover, I can't afford the fare, and the driver may figure out where I am staying." Erica stood. "Maybe the bartender will call a cab. I should have enough to make it to the Lee Street Walmart. The driver won't suspect anything." She stood and started toward the bar.

Trevor grabbed her arm. "Relax, enjoy your beer. It's all on me. Sit. Let's talk. Fear not. Your secret is good with me. After all," he beamed at her, "Do I look like a snitch?"

"Of course not, Mr. Brocton." Erica sat.

"Why the formality? Call me Trevor."

"I'm not used to being with a man of your stature, influence, and power." Erica beamed. "And that's right now, when you're governor, your power will be unassailable." Erica held Trevor's hand. "You will be governor. The Republican nominee is a frumpy woman, and the Democrat is a nerdy little man. You're young, tall, handsome, and dynamic. Moreover, you're smart. What more can I say other than South Carolina is ready for an Independent like you."

Trevor beamed. He squeezed her hand tighter and moved his head towards her.

"Oh, no." She pulled her head back and held up her hand. "Not yet, anyway. Let's make one thing clear. I'm not Adele. I am not remotely promiscuous. You must prove a whole lot more before I consider you worthy of my affections. You thought the Beauchamps were beneath the Broctons. That attitude gets you nowhere with me. Bobby is a nice boy, yes. He's all about hunting, fishing, and NASCAR. He drinks Budweiser and eats barbecue. I'm a whole lot more sophisticated, and the man who earns my affections had better prove likewise."

"Look at how I'm dressed. I would say that my clothes alone would cost Bobby a month of his pay," Trevor sniggered, "if he had a job. When you went outside to chase Bobby, I'm sure you saw my Ferrari 36- Modena. How many houses in Bayhaven would it take to equal the price of my ride alone? And that's just one of several. I also own a Porsche Carrera GT and a Lamborghini Gallardo." Trevor reached out and took Erica's hand. Erica squeezed it in return. "So, why wait an hour for a dirty taxicab that you can't afford? What do you say I take you someplace special in my Ferrari? You want sophisticated? Instead of Budweiser and Jim Beam, we can sip Valdespino sherry and top it off with Dom Pérignon champagne. Let's ditch this low-life honkytonk. How about I take you to the Wentworth Mansion?"

Erica chuckled. "I thought you were smart enough to distinguish sophistication from snobbery. You disappoint me. I thought you wanted a real woman, not some debutante cutout. I like danger and adventure. It's more than your money that attracts me. You turn me on because you're dangerous. I love danger. It makes me hot. The Wentworth Mansion poses no threat. I want a thrill. Take me to something out of a horror movie. How about a motel like from the movie, *Psycho?*"

"I've got just the place." He put his hand behind Erica's neck, pulled her in, and kissed her lips. His tongue hit a dental block.

"You're hot and make me moist. But you're not yet irresistible. You still have more to prove before you can have me." Erica pulled her head back. "So, just where did you have in mind for our dangerous misadventure?"

"Have you heard of the Wanderer's Inn?"

"Ha! Ha! Ha! You're forgetting that my sister and her best friend worked as waitresses at the Pussy Cat Lounge. The Wanderer's Inn is notorious. I am impressed, nonetheless. That's exactly the misadventure I'm in the mood for." Erica arched her eyebrows and half smiled. "Did I just tell you that I'm in the mood? How indiscreet of me."

"Are you in the mood for a ride in a Ferrari to the Wanderer's Inn?" Trevor stood, held Erica's hand, and pulled her to her feet. She smiled at him and air kissed.

As Erica walked out of the bar hand in hand with Trevor, she put her free hand behind her and flashed James a thumbs-up. Five minutes later, James used the payphone to make a phone call.

***

Trevor pulled his Ferrari up to Cabin 12 of the Wanderer's Inn. Croaking frogs and buzzing dragonflies ushered in the gloaming. A mosquito landed on Erica's arm. Trevor swatted it, drawing a blood smear. A tall, attractive woman wearing short, shorts and a tight T-shirt cut above her naval stepped out of the cabin.

"You didn't tell me you already had a playmate." Erica spread her palms. "What's going on here?"

"Thais." Trevor jabbed his finger at her. "Get out of here."

"But your nectar of life brought me back. Please. I want more."

"You're breaking my mood." Erica faced Trevor. She narrowed her eyes. "Why do you have to be rude to her? And what's this 'nectar of life'? Why just her? I want some." Erica walked over to her. "Thais? I heard that name from my sister and Jenny Carter. Do you know them?"

"Yes. We worked together."

"So, you're *the* Thais. They both said you're the hottest dancer at the Pussy Cat Lounge."

"Thank you." Cloretta smiled. "But I think you're hotter than me."

"Why don't we all go inside?" Erica took both of Trevor's hands and faced him. "This may prove a greater adventure than I dreamed."

After they went inside the Cabin, Trevor closed the door behind him and locked it. George had hidden behind the Motel office. After spotting them, he made a phone call from the payphone.

'I knew this was coming, but the sight of Cloretta's remains and the stench'... "I am at a loss for words." Erica stood between Trevor and Cloretta. "I have never slept with a man on the first date, and," Erica smiled at Cloretta, "I have always been curious, but never have I acted upon it."

Cloretta licked her lips. "There's a first time for everything." She smiled and fluttered her eyes at Erica.

"Oh my God! I can't believe I'm going to do this." Erica hugged Cloretta and French-kissed her. After five seconds, Erica turned and faced Trevor. "I can see by the bulge that we turned you on."

"Like flipping the switch of a nuclear power plant." Trevor beamed.

"I promise that's the first time I'd ever done that. I don't know what to think, much less say. She's gorgeous, but you too, Trevor. I also meant it when I said that I've never slept with a man on the first date. For me to take that step, I first want to ensure that you're skilled enough for me to justify compromising my morals. Trevor, I want to watch you make love to Thais. If you can please her, and I know you will, you can have all of me." Erica winked. "That includes a contribution to your silver pill box."

Cloretta switched into her Thais mode and slowly, seductively disrobed. Trevor tore off his clothes. Cloretta lay on top of her corpse. Trevor mounted her and hungrily smeared her face with kisses while thrusting his hips atop her pubic bone. Cloretta disappeared, leaving her dead body behind. Trevor continued to violate the cadaver.

Four police cars with flashing lights bolted into the motel driveway. George ran up to them. "Cabin 12! They're in Cabin 12!" He pointed. "I heard a gunshot and a scream!"

The police officers, guns drawn, kicked open the door. "Police! Don't move!"

Trevor, stark naked, stood, his erection pointing at the cops. He first made eye contact with a policewoman, "It's not what you think." He spread his arms. "It's not what you think."

"Freeze! Don't move!" A large, square-jawed policeman who looked like something from a Marine Corps recruiting poster moved in and handcuffed Trevor.

A black police officer read him his Miranda rights. He nodded to the other officers. Two of them dragged Trevor from the cabin, stuffed him into the back of a patrol car, and drove away. He was still naked. The remaining law enforcement officers secured the scene. Cloretta and Erica were long gone. George also vanished.

Epilogue

Bright, white light flooded Wilton Manor's main drawing room. Despite the glow's intensity, it caused no glare. Isolde Maria stood before them. Her oceanic blue eyes seemed to have an exotic but ever-so-slight tilt on the edges. The plumage of her wings' purity reflected pearlescent lights. Her long, flowing indigo hair did likewise but with a darker hue. Light also cloaked Wilton Manor's main staircase, with a brighter glow of the spectrum's every color at the top of the stairs.

"You have all fulfilled your missions as ghosts." Isolde Maria raised her arms in a gesture of embrace. "You stopped a monster and prevented even more future horror." She beamed. "And you did it all within your limitations. All of you have heard the news that Trevor Brocton confessed to murdering six other women in California, all his crimes in South Carolina, including his parents, and he exposed his father for having his brother killed." The angel placed her hands on Margarette's shoulders. "Margarette. The National Park Service has designated Wilton Manners as a National Historic Landmark. Wilton Manors is safe. You may now accompany me to Heaven at the top of the stairs."

Margarette bowed her head to the angel. "Isolde Maria, I am so grateful for all you've done, and only a Heavenly Angel could offer an invitation as divine as this. But I dare say, my fellow and future ghosts need me. May I stay just a little longer, if you please? I know Heaven is grander, but Heaven lives in my heart when I care for my fellow ghosts."

"Margarette," Isolde Maria beamed. "You please me in every way. Of course, I'm delighted to let you stay. Sergeant Fuller has also chosen to stay. He says his obligations to the soldiers of the War of Independence and his duty to his country come before leaving for Heaven. Margarette, I bless you." Isolde Maria kissed her forehead. "Your name will be sung among the Angels of Heaven." Isolde Maria chuckled. "But the Brocton name is now disgraced unto the pit of Hell. The name Brocton is now synonymous with murder, rape, and necrophilia. The family is also hated for executing one of their own just for being gay. Yet Trevor Brocton did manage to use family money to pay lawyers to help him escape the death penalty."

George laughed. "A lot of good it did him. After what the other inmates did to him in the shower, he saved the State of South Carolina the trouble. He hanged himself like Judas. As far as I'm concerned, it was still too good for him."

Isolde Maria looked at him with a straight face. "Hanging himself only begins his real troubles. As for you." Isolde Maria beamed. "Someone wants to see you."

Spectacles appeared beside Isolde Maria. It formed into a woman wearing a gold silk gown. The gown hugged her hourglass figure, and its sheen accentuated her coal-black skin. Her brown eyes and short curly brown hair made her high cheeks and full lips even more balanced and symmetrical. She extended her hand to George.

"Aurellia!" George beamed. "You look even more beautiful than the last time I saw you!"

"I come for you, George." Aurellia extended her hand. "Will you take my hand and follow me to the top of the stairs?"

George took her hand. They both ascended to the light at the top of the stairs.

A muscular black man wearing a leopard-skin vest and a lion-tooth necklace appeared to them. "James. Even though you fought on the wrong side of the war, you're a man of courage, bravery, and honor. Let me take you to the top of the stairs."

"Well, Joshua Magumba, I fought on the right side. States rights, unjust tariffs, and taxation without representation still have meaning." James laughed. "But I'm tired of arguing about it. It ended damn near a century and a half ago. Let's go to the top of the stairs." Joshua and James ascended to the top of the stairs.

Margarette openly wept.

"Don't cry, Margarette." Isolde Maria hugged her and patted her back. "I know it's sad to say goodbye. It's not permanent. You can be with your friends again whenever you choose."

"Of course, I will miss them." Margarette cried and returned the angel's embrace. "I am happy for them, and I am forever grateful to you for helping us save Wilton Manor."

"Bobby, Erica, you experienced only a preview of the joy and bliss of Heaven." Isolde Maria stepped forward and placed a hand on each of their shoulders. "When you were on the Isle of Anafi. You both experienced love freed from mortal flesh. You two experienced love from the depths of your souls and a blending of your spirits. How much greater is God's love? He created trillions and trillions of stars and galaxies. God's love is as infinite as the Universe he created, and Heaven is even grander. The power of his love has no limits or boundaries. God's love compared to a mortal's love is like contrasting a supernova with a firecracker. You only experienced a hint of how much God loves you. If you choose to follow me to the top of the stairs, know that you will be as I am. An angel. As angels, we can't be married or given into marriage; we will all be as brothers and sisters, married to God the Father, Son, and Holy Ghost. Are you prepared for the final steps of your journey?"

Erica and Bobby gazed into each other's eyes. They turned and nodded to Isolde Maria. She went first. Bobby and Erica followed her to the light at the top of the stairs.